DOCTOR WHO

DREAMS OF EMPIRE

The Doctor Who 50th Anniversary Collection

Ten Little Aliens
Stephen Cole

Dreams of Empire
Justin Richards

Last of the Gaderene
Mark Gatiss

Festival of Death
Jonathan Morris

Fear of the Dark
Trevor Baxendale

Players
Terrance Dicks

Remembrance of the Daleks
Ben Aaronovitch

EarthWorld
Jacqueline Rayner

Only Human
Gareth Roberts

Beautiful Chaos
Gary Russell

The Silent Stars Go By
Dan Abnett

DOCTOR WHO

DREAMS OF EMPIRE

JUSTIN RICHARDS

BOOKS

1 3 5 7 9 10 8 6 4 2

First published in 1998 by BBC Worldwide Ltd.
This edition published in 2013 by BBC Books, an imprint of Ebury Publishing.
A Random House Group Company

Doctor Who is a BBC Wales production for BBC One.
Executive producers: Steven Moffat and Caroline Skinner

The Random House Group Limited Reg. No. 954009
Addresses for companies within the Random House Group can be found at
www.randomhouse.co.uk

A CIP catalogue record for this book is available from the British Library.

ISBN 978 1 849 90524 4

MIX
Paper from
responsible sources
FSC
www.fsc.org
FSC® C016897

The Random House Group Limited supports The Forest Stewardship
Council® (FSC®), the leading international forest-certification organisation.
Our books carrying the FSC label are printed on FSC®-certified paper. FSC is
the only forest-certification scheme supported by the leading environmental
organisations, including Greenpeace. Our paper procurement policy can be
found at www.randomhouse.co.uk/environment

Editorial director: Albert DePetrillo
Editorial manager: Nicholas Payne
Series consultant: Justin Richards
Project editor: Steve Tribe
Cover design: Two Associates © Woodlands Books Ltd, 2012
Production: Alex Goddard

Printed and bound in Great Britain by CPI Group (UK) Ltd, Croydon, CR0 4YY

To buy books by your favourite authors and register for offers,
visit www.randomhouse.co.uk

INTRODUCTION

Back in the misty depths of time in the era that Earthlings call 1997, Editor and *Who*-Supremo Steve Cole asked me to write a Second Doctor novel, and I was happy to oblige. More than happy. The Second Doctor is one of my favourites – he's the Doctor of my formative young years, and as so much of his era no longer seems to exist he is, sadly, a misty memory himself…

Most of my novels sort of emerge from a fog of ideas, coalescing over time as I gather pieces, discard notions, fit it all together into the plan for a coherent narrative. That's certainly true of this book, but I do recall the starting point.

I was watching a television documentary about Julius Caesar. I have to say in tribute to the blurb writer that it was far more interesting in *Radio Times* than it was on the screen. But I stuck with it, trying to convince myself I wasn't wasting my time and wondering, as I often do with history: 'What if…?'

Which was when my much-missed friend and fellow author Craig Hinton rang. 'Are you watching this?' he asked. He didn't say what – he didn't need to as we were very much on the same wavelength. He knew that, of his friends, I'd be the one tuned in to Ancient Rome right now. 'Boring, isn't it?' he added. We didn't pause live television then, so we talked as we both watched.

I agreed that yes, it was rather boring, though that wasn't

really history's fault. 'But what do you suppose would have happened,' I asked, 'if Pompey had defeated Caesar?' What, I wondered, if Caesar had crossed the Rubicon to defeat. Or shied away from dipping his toe in the water at all.

We talked a bit how Rome could have stayed a Republic and what that might have meant. But in my head I was already pondering what they would have done with Julius Caesar if he hadn't died in battle – the popular war hero suddenly a traitor and would-be despot. They couldn't execute him. What prison could hold him when he had such a following?

The answer I thought would be some sort of guarded exile – like Napoleon sent to St Helena.

And that was the starting point for this novel. It gave me the situation – a republic torn apart by one man's (perhaps justified) Dreams of Empire. The best of friends who find themselves on opposite sides idealistically (and, possibly, for more personal reasons).

It gave me a canvas on which to start to paint the layers of the picture of the story.

There are other influences too, of course. The chess motif, my own fascination with the collision of history and technology, the image of the Man in the Iron Mask, and the notion that nothing is ever quite what it seems…

Binding it all together is the Doctor. And what a Doctor.

I've written novels depicting most of them – and written for all of them in one form or another. The Second Doctor may be the most difficult to depict in prose. Perhaps that's why he's always been a bit short-changed in the novels – backgrounded, or not quite getting his fair share of the bookshelf. (As an aside, I was delighted and excited when Stephen Baxter wanted to write for the Second Doctor – what a way to redress the balance!)

I think the reason the Second Doctor is so difficult to capture in prose is two-fold.

First, this is a Doctor who is at odds with his appearance more than any other. He seems to be a buffoon, it appears that he's out of his depth, when he saves the day it's possible it could all just have been a lucky accident. But there are moments, flashes, when we glimpse the strategic genius beneath. If the adventure was a game of chess (I thought) he'd win without really seeming to be involved at all. Only after laying down his king would his opponent begin to realise that maybe he'd been outplayed right from the very first move…

Getting that across without seeing Patrick Troughton's incredible performance is very difficult. Maybe it's impossible. But I did the best I could.

Of course, I cheated. There is one sequence where I deliberately showed the Doctor the other way round. We see the darker player behind the mask manipulating a captive into getting exactly what he wants. And only afterwards do we realise that perhaps, after all, it wasn't planned at all and it just happened that way and nothing was quite meant as it was interpreted. You'll know when you get there…

I said there are two reasons that Patrick Troughton's Doctor is so difficult to bring to life on the page. The other is almost the opposite. If the first is down to what we don't see; the second is all to do with what we do see. The Second Doctor's face is constantly animated, always expressive. His hands are rarely still. Even the way he walks into a room speaks volumes about his mood and his intent.

This is most obvious in the more humorous moments of 'business'. But it's there throughout. Yes, as a novelist I could describe it all – I could take the reader through every mannerism and quirk, every expression and movement.

The trouble is, that would take forever and slow everything down.

So I started with more, describing the details, upping the humour (sandwiches play a role here, as you will see). Then I gradually faded it out and let the story take over, allowed the characters to get on with their lives. My hope (possibly forlorn) was that in the reader's imagination it's all still going on – that they will fill in the blanks and actually *see* the amazing performance which I am convinced Patrick Troughton gives as the Doctor in *Dreams of Empire*.

I make it a rule not to choose favourites among my books. People often ask, and I always say that actually I have three favourites. One is the book I've just finished because I'm so pleased with it and, well, it's finished. The second is the book I'm working on right now because I'm having so much fun with it and enjoying the experience. And the third is the book I'm going to write next – I have so many ideas and I just can't wait to get started.

But if I *had* to choose a few favourites from my novels of the past, then I think *Dreams of Empire* would be among them.

Justin Richards
September 2012

For Alison, my White Queen,
and Julian and Christian – two slightly tarnished Knights

Opening

CHAPTER ONE
PLACING THE PIECES

All colour seemed bled from the walls, the floor, the ceiling. No detail, no identity, just a flickering halon bulb struggling to make itself seen in the darkness.

A strip of light fell across the grimy floor as a door creaked open. A dark shape was silhouetted against the brightness for a split second as it slipped inside, furtive as a ghost at daybreak. The door clicked shut behind the figure. The only noise was the dull fizz of the failing bulb, and the nervous breathing of the man.

A voice from the deepest darkness. 'You are late.'

A gasp.

'Did I startle you?' the voice continued.

'You could say that. I can hear my heart making more noise than that damn light. We should get it replaced.'

A dry laugh. 'I'm sure that can be arranged.'

'I meant the light.'

'No. It is better like this. Too dark for a clear spy-cam image, too deep under the Senate for reacher-mikes.'

'You're paranoid.'

The deeper shadow detached itself from the edge of the room, strayed towards the black shape of the new arrival. 'I'm alive, aren't I.'

'Let's make this quick. Now that Kesar has declared himself Consul General for life, we haven't much time. The other Consuls haven't objected. Not yet.'

'You're right. If he can pull this off, if he can get ratification from those spineless dolts above us, then he will be almost unassailable.'

'He will be Emperor in all but name. And be sure: that name will follow.' A deep breath, a hesitant question. 'Do you think we are too late already?'

'I said *almost* unassailable. I control two media networks. If you can sway Gethreed that would give us another. Three of the main four networks should be enough to challenge his credibility.'

'We must tread carefully, though. There could be war over this.'

The laughter echoed round the room, a stark contrast to the hushed whispers of the conversation. 'Of course there will be war. We're only discussing who will win.'

The door cracked open again. For a moment, the dusty light from the corridor outside fell in a jagged streak across the Senator's face. 'Talk to Gethreed. We'll meet again tomorrow. I'll tell you where and when.'

Darkness.

They met in the open the next day. A strong breeze gusted across the park, blowing their words away from the possibility of long-range microphones. They were not so bothered about cameras. Two prominent Senators walking together, discussing which way the political wind was blowing – what could be more natural in these troubled times?

And the times were troubled. Kesar was the elected Consul General, now maintaining his right to hold the position for life. The other Consuls were the insipid politician Gregor Jank and the General in Chief of the Armed Forces, Milton Trayx.

The problem facing the Senators who walked together in Victory Park that morning was that Trayx was a man of honour willing to leave the politics to politicians. He had been elected Consul on the strength of his military prowess, and knew the extent of his abilities. He was unswervingly loyal to only two things – the Republic and his friends. Trayx and Kesar had been the closest of friends since their schooldays.

'With Trayx on our side, we couldn't fail,' the junior Senator – Frehlich – agreed. 'But he would never side against Kesar.'

'I think you underestimate his loyalty to the Republic,' Senator Mathesohn replied. He drew a deep breath of the cold morning air and blew it out in a long steamy mist. 'Convince him that Kesar's ambitions are not in the interests of Haddron – of the people and the Republic –and he would come out against Kesar.' He cocked his head to one side as he admitted: 'Perhaps.'

'Neutrality I can believe. He would not want to be thought supportive of his friend above the needs of the Republic.'

'Indeed not,' Mathesohn murmured into the breeze. 'Not until the outcome is clear, anyway. Milton Trayx is an honourable man.'

'So the Republic may soon be an Empire.'

'Unless something happens that persuades Trayx that his friend's accession would be detrimental rather than beneficial. Convince him of that, and he would fight to his dying breath to keep Kesar from the imperial throne.'

They walked on in silence for a while, unconsciously keeping step. Their minds trod the same territory as they made their way back towards the Senate building, circling down from the big picture to the minutiae of plan details.

*

The white-tipped waves rolled and crashed on to the huge rocks. The thunderous sound of their impact could be heard clearly through the open doors from the balcony as Ruther poured drinks.

It was a civilised if somewhat low-key setting for such an important meeting. Dinner had passed amicably beneath a soothing blanket of small talk, and now they sat in the Seaview Room of Rutger's mansion and drank his wine. The real work – the straight talk and the debate – would start once Helana left. Rutger handed Helana Trayx a glass. She smiled up at him from the sofa. The smile was full of thanks. But it also told him that she knew it was time to leave the men together.

Rutger gave his two friends their glasses as Helana shifted her position. She rose gracefully from the sofa and crossed to where her husband sat.

'I think I'll sit outside while you talk,' she said. Her young voice was a soothing counterpoint to the crash of the waves outside. 'I love watching the sea.' She put her hand on Milton Trayx's shoulder and squeezed lightly.

Trayx took her hand, and kissed it. 'Don't wait up if you're tired,' he said.

'I'll be fine.' She smiled again at Rutger, and nodded towards Kesar as she crossed the room. She pulled the doors to the balcony closed behind her, cutting out the sound of the sea.

Rutger sat on the sofa where Helana had been. Normally it would have been elating to have his two closest friends to himself for a few hours of conversation, for memories and reminiscences. Gerhart Rutger, Hans Kesar and Milton Trayx had known each other since they were children, had been inseparable from the time they first met until the demands of adulthood split them apart. They had changed so much in what seemed such little time. Now Rutger had money, most of it inherited but some of it earned. Trayx was a Consul and General in Chief of the Armed Forces of Haddron. And Hans Kesar, senior Consul, had just declared himself Consul General in perpetuity – Emperor in all but name.

They drank in silence for a full minute. Usually they were easy in each other's company, and silences were signs of their closeness, not of awkwardness. But this silence was heavy with unspoken words.

Rutger looked from Trayx to Kesar. They made a good team, the three of them. Trayx was the voice of reason and the epitome of honour, a brilliant strategist. Kesar was impulsive and charismatic, fiercely intelligent. And Rutger – he bound them together. His analytical and diplomatic skills and his shrewd ability to compromise and negotiate could bring the two geniuses together in ways that more than doubled the effectiveness.

But not today. He could tell that already. Kesar's decision had been taken in a vacuum, without recourse to either of his closest friends. He had taken advantage of his popularity with the people to further his ambitions. If there was one irreconcilable difference between Kesar and Trayx, it was that Kesar's every action and thought were motivated by his own personal goals and ambitions. Milton Trayx, by contrast, saw the good of the Republic as the guiding principle for everything he did – his acceptance of the Consulate, his brilliant frontier campaigns, his work to give the outer colonies some limited autonomy so that they were less likely to rebel. Only in marriage did he seem uninfluenced by this guiding principle, taking Helana as his wife rather than cementing relationships with the political houses of Praxus Major, as had been widely predicted.

Trayx exhaled loudly, setting his wine down on the table beside him. 'Why did you do it, Hans?' he asked Kesar. 'What possessed you?'

'It seemed like a good idea.' Kesar sipped his wine. 'It still does. The Republic needs a strong pair of hands at the helm.'

'It has one. In fact, it has three.'

'Two,' Rutger corrected him. 'Even I would find it difficult to persuade anyone that Gregor Jank has a strong hand.'

Trayx met his gaze. 'I didn't mean Jank,' he said levelly.

Rutger raised his glass, nodding his acknowledgment of the compliment.

'The question remains,' Trayx said quietly.

'The Republic,' Kesar said smoothly, 'needs to *know* there is strong control.'

'You think it doesn't?'

Kesar's eyes gleamed as he leaned forward, setting down his glass. Rutger recognised the signals, the passion and determination behind the posture. 'I'll tell you what I think,' Kesar said, his voice hard-edged and low. 'I think that Haddron has gone soft. I think we've had it too good for too long. Without your military skills, we'd have been forced into retreat by the frontier worlds long ago, and would have ceded control of a dozen of them by now. I think the time has come for some consistent and constant leadership rather than the political dance we lead every few years as the Consuls change. And I think now is the time. Now, while I have you as a Consul, and while our popular support is riding the crest of a wave after your campaigns on the Rim. I think that if I don't do this when I should, someone else – someone less suitable – will have to take action when it's already too late.' Kesar leaned back into his chair, his fingers stroking the base of his wine glass as it stood on the table beside him. 'I think the Republic needs us now more than ever. Haddron needs *me*.'

Trayx stared at Kesar. His eyes were moist and his voice was quiet. 'I think it could tear the Republic apart.'

Kesar snorted. 'Only if we let it.' He stood up suddenly. 'I need your help, Milton. Without you, Haddron *will* be torn apart.' He looked across at Rutger, perhaps hoping for a reaction. Then he turned and left the room.

Rutger waited until the door into the dining room closed behind Kesar. 'He has a point,' he told Trayx.

Trayx said nothing for a while, twisting the stem of his wine glass and watching the light reflect through the cut facets of the crystal. 'Yes,' he said at last. 'He has a point.' He looked up at Rutger. 'But he got to the point *after* he made the decision.'

'Rationalisation rather than motive, you think?'

'Don't you?' Trayx lifted the glass, held it up to the light for a second, then drained it in a single swallow. 'It's all a game to him. Chess on a grand scale. The question is, what do we do now – you and I?'

'Either way,' Rutger said slowly, 'the Republic could be split. Whatever we do, whether we give our support to Kesar, or remain silent for the moment, Haddron could be plunged into civil war.'

'And what,' Trayx asked quietly, his voice barely even a whisper, 'what if we side against him?'

'Then there will be civil war within days. You know that several of the legions would join Kesar rather than us – the Seventh, for example, and the Fifth. Thousands, if not millions, of our own people would die before we return to a semblance of the political stability we currently enjoy. Or rather, enjoyed.' Rutger got slowly to his feet and took Trayx's empty glass. He refilled and returned it. 'We have to do whatever we can to keep the Republic together. Unless

Hans somehow loses a large part of his popular support, he can probably pull this off without bloodshed. No one would dare move against him without a good excuse or cause.'

'Probably.'

Rutger slumped back into the sofa. 'Even doing nothing makes a statement,' he said. 'We have to decide what statement we should make.'

The waves that broke their backs against the massive rocks below the balcony were a stark contrast to the smooth calm of the moonlit sea further out. Helana stood at the balcony rail, looking out over the distant ripples and depths.

She did not turn when she heard the footsteps behind her. 'Hello, my darling.'

His hands were firm against her shoulders as he squeezed. She sighed and nestled in close, feeling the warmth of his breath as he whispered softly to her.

'They're still talking in there.'

'What will they decide?' she asked.

Hans Kesar shrugged. 'You tell me,' he said. 'He's your husband.'

'He will do what he believes to be right.'

'Even if it means siding against his friend?'

She turned to face him, put her finger to his lips. 'You know he will. And nothing I can say to him will alter that.' She moved her finger across his lips, caressed his cheek.

'I wasn't going to ask.'

'Good.' She turned back towards the sea. 'You'd better get back to them.' A wave crashed on to the rock below, showering her with soft bubbles of foam and spray. 'I hope it won't come to war,' she murmured distantly as the door to the dining room slid shut behind her.

*

'But I don't believe we can be seen to move either way,' Trayx was saying. 'If we declare our support for Kesar now, we are open to accusations of siding with him out of friendship rather than conviction. Better to wait, to be seen to deliberate.'

'And suggest that even Kesar's closest friends do not agree with his actions?' Rutger asked.

Trayx walked over to the doors out on to the balcony, peering out through the glass. He could just make out the silhouette of his wife as she stood looking out over the water. 'Appearances,' he said. 'Everything we do is tempered by appearances.' He turned back to face Rutger. 'We must do what we believe to be best for the Republic, and appearances be damned.'

'And what *is* best?'

Trayx shrugged. 'For the moment, I don't know. The next few days will tell. I know you don't approve of doing nothing, but I think we must wait.'

Rutger joined him by the doors, put his hand on his friend's shoulder. 'I don't disapprove of doing nothing,' he said. 'Provided we actually decide that it is best to do nothing, rather than allow ourselves to be trapped into inactivity through indecision, that's fine.' He smiled. 'And I agree: for now it is best to wait, and throw our weight behind the right choice for Haddron – when we know what that is.'

Trayx nodded slowly. Suddenly he felt incredibly tired. He poured himself more wine and sighed. 'If it comes to the choice of betraying my friend or the Republic,' he said softly, 'God give me the courage to betray my friend.'

The door from the dining room opened and Hans Kesar came in. He looked at his two friends, then burst out laughing. 'If you could see yourselves,' he said. 'If you could see how grim you both look.' He joined Trayx by the wine, pouring himself a generous measure. 'Maybe we shouldn't celebrate political events,' he said evenly, 'or even discuss them. But we should at least be grateful that circumstances have brought the three of us together again.' He raised his glass to them. 'It has been too long, my friends, far too long. May we meet again soon.' He took a long sip of wine, then smacked his lips together appreciatively.

Helana Trayx watched the sea hurl itself against the intractable rock on which Rutger's mansion was built. Inside she could hear the muffled conversation and laughter of the three men. Above her, the moon shone brightly down at the sea, oblivious to the dark clouds that were gathering near by.

The debate was crucial, a turning point. Trayx's mind was still in turmoil as he approached the Senate Room. He was so preoccupied that he barely noticed the figure that emerged from a side corridor and walked beside him.

'Consul, do you have a moment?'

Trayx stopped, momentarily startled, and turned towards the man. It was Senator Frehlich. Trayx knew him well, a sycophantic weasel who would face which ever way he thought the wind was currently blowing. 'The debate starts in a few minutes,' Trayx said levelly. 'I think it is important we be there. Don't you?'

'Indeed. Indeed yes.' Frehlich was rubbing his hands together nervously, looking round all the time. 'But if you can spare just a moment or two before that, I think it would be time well spent.'

'Oh?'

'This way.' Frehlich gestured towards the nearest conference room. 'It really is important, Consul.'

Trayx considered. A few moments of his time would not hurt. And it was possible that Frehlich really did have an important point to make. Normally, Trayx resisted the lobbying and political posturing that was endemic at the Senate. But these were not normal times. He pushed the door open and went into the conference room.

'Consul, I'm so very pleased you could spare us a few moments.' The gaunt figure of Senator Mathesohn rose to his feet and shook Trayx's hand. He waved Trayx to a chair on the other side of the round table. 'I know your time is precious. But we live through dangerous days.'

Trayx sat, arms folded. He would listen for a few minutes only to whatever Mathesohn had to say. Frehlich sat midway between Mathesohn and Trayx, a move intended to draw the two closer together.

'Well?'

Mathesohn appeared to consider for a second, staring down at his hands clasped on the table before him. Then he looked up, his eyes meeting Trayx's. 'We have had our differences, Consul. We have disagreed on...' He waved a hand in the air as if searching with it for an example.

'On everything,' Trayx said bluntly.

'On several matters, shall we say.' Mathesohn smiled. Just for a second, then the humour was wiped away and he leaned forward. 'But things are happening around us that we neither of us can ignore. We must put the past behind us, Consul. For the good of the Republic, we must make difficult decisions. We must put aside our differences, our personal animosity.'

'Just as we must not allow our judgement to be clouded by personal friendship?' Trayx suggested.

Mathesohn froze in position. Frehlich glanced at him, worried.

13

'So that's what this is about.' Trayx sighed and stood up.

'Wait.' There was a hint of desperation in Frehlich's voice. Trayx hesitated.

'Consul, I would not have spoken to you if I were not convinced that it was important.' Mathesohn's voice was more level, his tone reasonable. 'There are others whose opinions I could better spend my time trying to sway. But I –' he glanced at Frehlich – 'we need your advice.'

Trayx frowned. 'Advice? Go on.'

'There are difficult decisions to be made, Consul. Desperate decisions. And we cannot make those decisions in the usual way, tempered by political and factional considerations.' He leaned forward again, his eyebrows knitted tight in sincerity. 'This is the Republic we're talking about. We are beyond politics, beyond friendships now. And you, Consul, you more than anyone have your finger on the pulse of the Republic. You are outside the factional nonsense and personal rancour.'

'You want me to tell you what to do? How to vote?' Trayx could not believe that Mathesohn would accept that.

'No. That is a decision we must each make for ourselves. But I want to know, outside the debate and posture of the Senate Room, I want to know how you see things, how you interpret events. And I want to be sure you are yourself properly prepared for the debate.'

Trayx felt the blood freeze in his face. 'What do you mean?' His voice was quiet, tense. 'What do you know?'

Mathesohn's surprise was complete. Perhaps too complete. 'You haven't heard, Consul?' He shook his head in apparent amazement. 'A good job we spoke. Otherwise, his arrogance and incompetence would have appeared even more extreme. You know that Kesar has refused to attend this morning? I see that you do.' He shook his head.

'But not even to inform the General in Chief of this latest development.'

Trayx sat down again. His head felt heavy. In that moment he knew what would happen, how the debate would go. And he knew how he must vote.

Frehlich and Mathesohn were both leaning across the table at him as Trayx stared back at them, seeing not the Senators but the face of his friend as if across a chessboard. Mathesohn's words echoed slightly in the enclosed space of the room. 'The Fifth Legion, Consul. He has lost the Fifth Legion.'

The debate was noisy and ill-disciplined. The Senate Speaker shouted for calm and decorum but to no avail. The Sergeant at Arms shifted nervously on more than one occasion, afraid he would be asked to remove the more rowdy Senators.

There were only two people who could command complete silence while they were on their feet in the Senate. One was Kesar, by the sheer force of his personality and his charisma. It cost him dear that he was not there in person that day. In person he might have countered the growing swell of opposition.

The turning point was Consul Trayx's speech. He rarely spoke in the Senate. When he did it was short and to the point. And it was always worth hearing. There was complete silence as he spoke, without notes, for an unprecedented seventeen minutes. He called for calm; he called for unity; he called for reason. He urged each and every Senator to weigh the matter on its own merits, devoid of partisan lines and factional politics. He blinked a nascent tear from his eye as he moved the motion for the impeachment of Consul General Hans Kesar.

*

It surprised no one that Kesar ignored the Senate vote. He rallied his considerable forces and established a command centre on one of the moons of Geflon. First blood went to Kesar, with a resounding victory against the Senate forces at Yerlich. His main advantage was surprise. Trayx had refused to attack the Geflon sector until all the diplomatic possibilities had been exhausted. Kesar had no such scruples, and ordered his troops forward just hours before he was due to accept a diplomatic mission from Haddron to debate the issues.

The advantage that Kesar gained at Yerlich enabled him to hold out against the Senate forces for another year. But in the end, despite broadly equal numbers of Haddrons and mechanised forces on each side, Kesar stood no chance against the strategic genius of his friend. Trayx's superior skills and strategies flowed through the VETAC command network, giving them superiority at every point in the decisive battle of Trophinamon.

Kesar's forces were surrounded, his command net penetrated and undermined. When his personal VETAC bodyguards succumbed to a subversion routine, Kesar realised the end had come. Together with his most senior general, he surrendered to the same VETAC commander who just minutes before had been programmed to prize the Consul General's life above everything else.

Trayx met Kesar in the middle of the smoking battlefield. Since Kesar was still technically Consul General of Haddron, Trayx saluted him.

They walked side by side through the devastation, Trayx's VETAC guards following at a discrete distance.

'Fifteen thousand dead today,' Trayx said. 'To say nothing of the VETAC units that have been lost.' Kesar said nothing, so Trayx went on. 'A total of nearly a million dead in the war.'

'It was your decision.'

'No,' Trayx said quietly. 'No, I won't have that. It's proof that I made the right decision.'

'We could have had it all, my friend.'

'Yes, we could. But it would not have been worth it.'

'Was this?' Kesar waved his arm over the ruins of Trophinamon.

'If it stops the madness, then yes. And it was madness. You never had a chance.' Trayx stopped, gripped his friend's shoulder. 'Why did you even try? You could have stepped down, and kept your honour intact.'

Kesar shook the hand from his shoulder. 'Honour – that's what it comes down to with you, isn't it? Honour and the Republic. What about friendship? What about dreams?'

'What about morals, about what is *right*?' Trayx countered angrily.

'We subjugate a thousand worlds in an obscure sector in the name of the Republic – is that *right*?' Kesar shook his head. 'It is all madness, you know. All of it. There's no such thing as honour, no such thing as right. There is only you and me amid the ruins, arguing over the might-have-beens.' He kicked at the shattered remains of a VETAC trooper. 'And now the dream is over.' He looked up at Trayx, his mouth curled into a half-smile and his eyes full of tears.

Trayx stared into Kesar's eyes, saw the dream fade. Then he pulled his friend to him and they embraced, each feeling the other's sobs through the heavy armour. After a while they separated. Each took a step back, and saluted the other.

'I'll see you at the trial,' Trayx said. Then he turned and walked away, into the dying smoke of the battle.

The trial of Hans Kesar lasted less than a week. Despite

the huge popular support he still enjoyed, the verdict was never in question. Kesar's defence had been that the Haddron Republic needed him – it needed his strength of character, it needed his charismatic popularity, it needed his understanding of the big picture if it was to survive. The irony that the Republic was in more serious danger of splitting apart because of Kesar's actions and the massively destructive civil war he had instigated was not lost on the prosecutor.

Kesar stood straight and proud together with his surviving officers to hear the sentence. The dilemma now facing the victorious forces was that to have Kesar executed would be to make a martyr of him – either immediately or in the near future as times got worse. Kesar smiled as he heard what fate had in store for him – he could identify the combination of Trayx's strategic thinking and Rutger's feeling for acceptable compromise in the sentence. And he also recognised and appreciated the compassion of his friends.

The forensic analysis that followed the explosion showed that a quantity of Zenon VII had been mixed with the combustible material. It was this that fuelled the intense heat of the fireball as well as giving it the distinctive orange colour. But it was the sound that Trayx remembered.

Kesar was led out first, flanked on either side by a detail of VETAC troopers. The remains of his headquarters staff and field personnel followed a short way behind. As Kesar reached the final bend of the corridor, as he turned the corner so that the doorway that led out of the Senate Building was within sight, the wall caught fire.

The explosive compound had been painted thickly on to both corridor walls. A radio frequency pulse triggered the blast, passing a current through tiny filaments etched into the paint. The sound was like a gunshot rattling and ricocheting down the passageway as the filaments ignited the compound. The walls blistered with the heat and then exploded outward in a startling display of orange light.

The VETACs either side of Kesar were engulfed by the fire, their armour dripping off their burning bodies as they collapsed in flames. But their bodies shielded Kesar from the worst effects of the blast. He lay face down as the fireball rolled over him and burst out through the outer doorway. The corridor was angled such that almost all of the blast was channelled away from the others and towards the outside.

Trayx was at Kesar's side in a moment, pushing his way through the screaming, shouting people who struggled and fought in the confused corridor. Rutger was close behind him as Trayx knelt beside the body. He reached down, feeling the heat from Kesar's scorched uniform. The hair was blackened and shrivelled on the back of Kesar's head as Trayx slowly turned the body over.

Rutger drew in his breath sharply as the blistered, ruined face rolled into view.

Trayx clasped the charred form to his chest, rocking backwards and forwards as he cradled his friend in his arms. Rutger slowly sank to his knees beside them. Their sobs echoed along the blackened corridor.

CHAPTER TWO
THE GAME OF DEATH

The pieces were of frosted glass, slightly rough to the touch. The board was a slab of white marble, the black squares hewn from onyx and crafted flawlessly into the surface. The older man watched his opponent closely. His thin fingers stroked a short white beard. The light from the lanterns around the walls made the cracks and lines of his face seem deeper than they really were. Cruger was a man whose features were old before their time, though he was still fit and healthy. His mind was every bit as sharp and calculating as it had ever been as he watched his opponent slowly move a piece across the board.

Cruger considered. 'A good move, my Lord. Very good.' He stretched out and moved a bishop. 'But not good enough.' His lips parted in a thin smile as he sat back on the hard wooden chair.

The light from the lanterns glimmered into the dark recesses in the bare stone walls and spilled across the flagstones. Heavy tapestries seemed almost to absorb the illumination, and the simple wooden furniture was thrown into stark relief.

The figure opposite Cruger leaned forward to consider the game's development. He reached out a gauntleted hand towards the board, then hesitated and clenched his fist. The glove's flexibility belied its appearance. The metal was intricately jointed to match the bone structure beneath. The man's face was a blank mask of the same bronzed metallic material. Dark, recessed screens took the place of the eyes, and the nose was a stylised bulge in the centre of the burnished face. Grilles either side of the head allowed sound through to the ears, enhancing it on the way. Beside them small wing nuts held the front of the mask screwed to the backplate. The mouth was a tight mesh with riveted steel lips holding it in place.

The man in the mask reached out again, his glove closing over a rook. He moved the rook forward, past the bishop. The bearded man's queen was removed from the board, and the rook took its place.

The voice was filtered through the grille-mouth, an electronic rasp that amplified the words but drained them of intonation and inflection. 'Once again you look to the battle front while leaving your king undefended, my friend.' The gloved hand placed the taken queen carefully by the side of the board. 'Check.'

'And once again, my Lord, you pull victory from the jaws of defeat.' Cruger shook his head as he examined the positions on the board. 'If only real life were as straightforward as a game of chess.'

A discordant splutter erupted from the grille in the man's metal face.

Cruger gently laid his king on its side. 'I'm glad that I can still offer some amusement to alleviate the tedious hours, my Lord.'

The mask turned slowly to face him. 'The ancients called it the Game of Death.'

Floating somewhere between the now and the then, between the here and the there, the TARDIS swirled through the eddies and waves of the space-time vortex. Hordes of angry chronons hurled themselves at the battered police-box shell of the craft; temporal paradoxes tried to lure it through the more vicious parts of the maelstrom. But despite its inconsequential appearance, the TARDIS continued on its course, unwavering and unimpressed.

Regardless of the chaos outside, the interior of the TARDIS was calm and quiet. The almost clinical pallor of the decor was a soothing accompaniment to the gentle rise and fall of the central column of the hexagonal console which formed the centrepiece of the main control room. And round the edges of the console, a quite different storm was brewing.

'Why can't we go somewhere nice for a change, Doctor?'

The Doctor was staring at one of the control panels, a half-eaten sandwich clasped in one hand. 'Mmm,' he said in a tone that suggested he was not really listening. 'Yes, Victoria, I'm sure.' The sandwich sagged. It was drying at the edges.

'I mean somewhere *safe*.' Victoria folded her arms. She was still not entirely comfortable in what she considered an almost indecently short cotton summer dress. Even the sleeves were shorter than she would have liked. But it was comfortable, and it was practical.

Jamie, like Victoria, could see that the Doctor was paying more attention to the TARDIS than he was to the conversation. 'Och, come on, Victoria,' he said. 'You know he doesn't decide where we end up. It's a complete mystery to him as well as us.' He edged closer to her. 'But at least you've got me to protect you from whatever he wishes on us.'

Victoria giggled despite herself, not managing to stifle the reaction in time. 'Oh, I'm sorry Jamie,' she spluttered. 'But strength and good intentions aren't always the answer to everything.'

'Yes, well, tell that to Toberman,' Jamie said sulkily. 'Or Kemel.'

Victoria looked down at the floor, shuffling her feet uncomfortably. 'I think that proves my point,' she said quietly.

But not so quietly that Jamie did not hear. 'Oh yes?'

She looked straight at him. 'Yes. They were both strong, and they both meant well.'

'And they both died saving us.'

'But strength and good intentions aren't any good without intelligence and common sense.'

Jamie drew himself up to his full height. 'Are you saying I'm stupid?'

'Of course not, Jamie. Not really.' She looked away. 'I'm just saying that being strong is no use if you're... dead.' She hesitated over the final word, as if embarrassed by it.

Jamie seemed unsure what to make of this. So, as ever, he turned to the Doctor. 'What do you say, Doctor?'

The Doctor continued to stare at the panel. Then suddenly, he was a blur of motion as he pulled his crumpled handkerchief from the top pocket of his equally crumpled jacket and flicked it across the top of the console. Crumbs flew from the panel, and the Doctor nodded in approval. Then he used the hanky to polish a readout and blow his nose loudly. Finally, he wrapped the remains of the sandwich inside the hanky and stuffed it back into his pocket.

'What do I say?' His face seemed to sag round the laughter lines as he frowned at the question. 'It's either tom-ar-to or tom-ai-to.' His eyebrows furrowed in further thought. 'Or is it potato? I can never remember which.'

'He's not listening,' Victoria said. 'As usual.'

'Now that's not fair, Victoria,' the Doctor immediately responded. 'I may be a little preoccupied, but I'm never too busy to listen.' He looked across at his friends, his face suddenly set like drying putty. 'Now then, what were you asking me about, Jamie?'

'About strength and common sense.'

'Ah yes. Well. Yes.' The Doctor leaned forward and peered at a dial. He tapped it, as one would a barometer, then shrugged. 'Both admirable qualities, and ones which I'm sure we shall need in abundance when we arrive.'

'When we arrive where?'

His tone was suddenly light again. 'Wherever we're going, of course.' He beamed at the inherent logic and elegance of this conclusion. Seeing no reaction from either of his companions, the Doctor coughed and turned his attention back to the TARDIS console. 'Now I think it will be a little while before we land, and I for one could do with something to eat. I wonder, Victoria,' he went on with a sudden brilliant smile, 'if you could possibly rustle us up some sandwiches?'

Victoria's expression betrayed her lack of enthusiasm. 'All right.'

'Splendid.' The Doctor clapped his hands together in satisfaction. His smile somehow morphed into a slightly sour expression as if he were chewing a marble. 'Now if I can just calibrate this meter properly, Jamie, you could tell me what you two have been muttering about.'

The chessboard was set again for a new game. Cruger was gone, the lamplight flickering on the artificial cheek of the man left sitting silent and still. The pale light picked out slight imperfections in the curves of his face, shied away from small pockmarks of tarnished metal.

Cruger's voice appeared as if from the air, filtered by the communication system. 'You wish to start another game, my Lord?'

'Perhaps.' The electronically enhanced voice betrayed a hint of tiredness. 'But it is late. Not against the clock, Cruger.'

'Of course not, my Lord. I would suggest just a few moves tonight. We can finish at your leisure.'

'Very well.'

As if in answer, another chessboard appeared. It swam into pixelated existence in the air, hovering in the corner of the room. 'Your turn with the white pieces, my Lord,' Cruger's disembodied voice said.

The Lord walked stiffly towards the virtual board, the servos that moved his left leg hissing slightly. He paused in front of the board. Then he took hold of a knight and jumped it forward.

In his own room, Cruger watched as the knight moved apparently of its own volition. He nodded slowly as he contemplated his own move. Once again, the game was afoot.

Outside Cruger's room, the stone-lined corridor rang to the solid tread of the guard as he checked the doors.

There was a heavy knock at the Lord's door as he watched Cruger's move. Without looking up from the board, he called, 'Enter.'

The duralinium-core wooden door swung slowly open. In the dim light that spilled from the corridor outside, two figures could be seen. One was male, one female, each dressed in battle armour. The man carried a field blaster in a holster built into the armour.

'Is it time already?' He turned to face the soldiers.

'It is, my Lord.'

He nodded to the man. 'Then I wish you good night,

Darkling. And you, Haden,' he continued, turning to the female guard. 'May your watch be uneventful.'

'Thank you, my Lord.' The figures stepped back, and the door swung shut again. After a moment, the deadbolts shot home, sealing the room.

The lone figure returned his attention to the game. It was late, and he was tired. He was tired of the game, tired of the room, tired of everything. Just a little longer, and then perhaps it would at last be over. He moved a pawn automatically, not really thinking through the move. At once he knew it was a mistake, and his mind was suddenly alert again as he began to work through the possibilities, to build strategies for recovering the situation and turning it to his advantage. If he could make the sacrifice he had offered into a poison pawn – a trap, a lure...

Beneath the heavy, uncomfortable mask, he smiled as Cruger responded with the predictability of a machine. He glanced up at a point in the stonework where he knew one of the cameras was concealed, watching his every move. Literally. Perhaps, after all, he would finish the game tonight.

Darkling and Haden continued their patrol, locking the doors as they passed. Occasionally a voice called out to them, and they responded with a cheery 'Good night', or a ribald comment.

At last they reached the edge of the Secure Area, a huge pair of heavy doors. A short walk brought them into the Banqueting Hall. The light was better here, largely because there were more lanterns. A long table ran down the centre of the room. Various displays of traditional weapons lay at intervals along it. In the alcoves and at the doorways stood heavy, metal-armoured figures, so still and stiff that one could tell at a glance that nothing living inhabited the heavy suits. A gallery ran high along one wall, a huge fireplace beneath it, in which the embers of a half-forgotten fire glimmered in the half-light. Blast shields and laser swords hung on the walls. The ceiling was a vaulted monument to the architect's skill with structural gravitic manipulation.

But the two soldiers saw none of the splendour or the glory as they made their way through. They had seen it all too many times now. Satisfied that everything was quiet and as it should be, they continued their patrol.

One whole wall of the room was covered with screens, their images constantly in motion. Cameras tracked back and forth across their appointed domains. The screens flickered and changed from camera to camera, from viewpoint to viewpoint, from room to corridor to stairway.

On one of the screens, Darkling held open a door for Haden. Haden paused on the threshold, said something which was not amplified by the speakers in the side of the screen, though it was captured perfectly together with Darkling's laughter on the digital recording. On another screen, Haden entered a sparsely furnished room. The door slammed closed behind her.

Outside, Darkling locked the door. Then the image changed to show a view of the Banqueting Hall. The still figures stood like sentries round the edge of the room. The dying light of the fire burned on the instrument panels set into the chest of the nearest figure.

A shadow moved darkly across one of the screens, the camera seeming to shy away from it, panning across to the opposite side of the corridor. The shadow continued on its way, the hint of a cloak swirling behind it as it walked. Deep in an anteroom on one of the lower levels of the fortress, another cloaked figure stepped from the shadows. Its face was hidden beneath the cowl. The concealed camera in the room tracked the movement carefully, adjusted for the dim light. The image became slightly more focused, the edges of the shapes slightly sharper.

Then the shadowy figure from the corridor entered the room. In a blur of darkness, the figure stepped in front of the camera and raised a gloved hand. The device in the hand gleamed as a facet caught the light from a distant lamp. Then the image snowed over with a blizzard of static and white noise.

The screens continued their endless vigil, throwing images across the wall, picking out every nuance of life within the monitored part of the fortress, recording every whispered monitored conversation both within the Secure Area and beyond. Except one.

The Doctor seemed bent almost double as he scurried round the console. His coat tails hung improbably close to the TARDIS floor as he adjusted controls and tapped meters. Eventually he stopped, and looked up as Victoria returned with a plate of sandwiches.

'Ah. Thank you, Victoria. You're very kind.' The Doctor helped himself to a sandwich with each hand, and returned to the console. He reached out for a small lever, seemed to realise he was holding a sandwich in the same hand, and tried to take it with the other hand. That one was also full of sandwich, so he jammed it into his mouth.

Jamie helped himself to a sandwich, and thanked Victoria. She put the plate down on the heavy wooden chair beside the inner TARDIS door.

'Are you not eating, Victoria?' the Doctor asked. As he started speaking, his mouth opened enough for the sandwich to fall out. He caught it with his free hand, looked at it in apparent surprise, then smiled and took a large bite.

'I'm not hungry, actually.'

The Doctor frowned as he considered this statement. He finished one sandwich and took a bite from the other. 'Nor am I,' he admitted after a while, and put down the remains of the sandwich on the console. He clapped his hands together, rubbing them so hard it seemed that fire might spontaneously erupt from the palms. 'Now what was it we were talking about?'

'Common sense,' Jamie mumbled through a shower of crumbs.

'Oh yes. That was it. Well –' the Doctor's face took on a heavy frown – 'the thing is to cultivate a good balance of both common sense and physical acumen.'

'Acu-what?'

'He means,' Victoria said, 'that you need both. Common sense and physical strength. Intelligence and good intentions.'

'Oh. Aye.' Jamie nodded in knowing agreement. 'That's what I thought.'

'Take me, for example,' the Doctor continued. 'As your role model in our adventures, I make a point of displaying a perfect combination of all these attributes and talents.'

Neither Jamie nor Victoria spoke.

The Doctor looked from one to the other. Then he coughed, and returned his attention to the console. His frown seemed to have deepened, but perhaps it was merely a trick of the light. He reached out for a dial, and gave it a twist. The dial did not move, and he let go of it and inspected his fingers. 'Yes,' he said as he whipped out his hanky again, 'a perfect combination of tremendous strength and superior intelligence fuelled by keen observational and deductive skills...' He gripped the dial through the handkerchief, ignoring the half-eaten sandwich that fell out of it. His face tensed with the effort.

Jamie and Victoria exchanged glances. Still neither of them commented.

The Doctor gave up the unequal fight with the control after a few more moments. He stuffed the remains of the curled-up sandwich into a jacket pocket, and dabbed at his brow with the hanky. Then he returned it to his top pocket. 'I wonder, Jamie, if you could perhaps give me a hand with this?'

Jamie took up position next to the Doctor and gripped the dial.

'Good. Now twist it a quarter turn anticlockwise, would you?'

Jamie turned the dial easily.

'Thank you, Jamie.'

'That's all right.'

The Doctor continued to stare at the dial. 'Anticlockwise would have been nice, but I'm sure that will do.'

'Physical strength,' Jamie muttered to Victoria as he joined her on the other side of the console.

'Phew, I'm really quite worn out by all this excitement,' the Doctor announced. He shook his head, beamed, and backed away from the console, feeling behind him for the arm of the chair by the door.

'Keen observational skills,' Victoria said to Jamie.

He nodded. 'Aye.'

'What are you two worrying about now?' the Doctor asked from the chair. 'We shall be arriving soon, and I don't want any arguments while we're exploring.'

'No, Doctor.'

'Best behaviour.'

'Yes, Doctor.'

The Doctor shifted position slightly on the chair. 'That's better. Good.' He exhaled loudly. 'I don't remember this chair having a cushion on it,' he remarked at last.

'It doesn't, Doctor,' Jamie told him.

'Oh?'

'No, Doctor,' Victoria said. 'You're sitting on the sandwiches.'

The game was already won, the man in the mask knew as he made another move. But Cruger seemed determined to fight to the end. Typical of the general. He had displayed an uncharacteristic lack of long-term thinking in the early stages of the game, and now he was expertly drawing the match out as long as possible. But the end was inevitable. It was just a matter of time, patience, and concentration.

The Lord leaned forward, watching closely as Cruger's bishop sliced across the board. 'Excellent, Cruger, excellent,' the Lord breathed. His metallic voice scraped on the stone walls, but elicited no reply from his unseen opponent. The Lord could imagine Cruger hunched over the same virtual board in his own quarters, desperately looking for a way to turn the game to his advantage. Cruger hated to lose, which was why he so resented the long boredom of his current life. It was also why the man in the mask let him win. Occasionally.

But not tonight.

'You have it?' The cloaked figure turned from the wall where the camera was hidden and checked the small device he had held up to it.

'Are we alone?' the other figure hissed. The dark outline of an archway was barely visible behind the figure.

'We are now. Even assuming that camera still works.'

'Thank goodness.' The man shrugged off the heavy hood of his cloak. In the dim light he was revealed to be a man in his middle years. His hair was short and dark, a moustache drooping slightly over his top lip. His eyes were deep set and his cheeks slightly hollow. 'I hate all this skulking about, all this hugger-mugger activity. The sooner I can get away from here, the better.'

'Then the sooner you provide me with the components I need, the sooner I can free you.' The other figure made no effort to remove its hood, keeping to the shadows. 'Now, do you have it?'

'Yes, I've got it. It wasn't easy, but I got it.'

The hooded figure held out a gloved hand.

'Oh no. It's not that simple.' The man's lips curled into a smile that nudged his moustache out of alignment and revealed yellowing teeth. 'Promises of freedom are all very well. But I'm free already – that's how I can get this stuff for you. It's not the Secure Area, the locks and bolts and surveillance systems that are keeping me on this cold rock.'

'It's your commission.'

'Too right.'

'You want to buy yourself out?'

The man drew a small transparent box from within the cloak. Nestled inside, held within foam packaging, was a tiny electronic component. He held it up for the other figure to see. 'You said it. This is my ticket to freedom. This is my pass out of the military, out of tedious guard duties and senseless patrols and back to civilisation.' He grinned. 'If you want it, and I know that you do, then you'll have to pay for it.'

The gloved hand withdrew, back inside the cloak. 'And where do you think I can get the money to pay you?'

'Oh you'll think of something. You've got contacts, so have I. Set up a deal back home, and I'll hear of it. When I get the credit chit, you get the phase regulator.' He tossed the plastic box into the air and caught it again. 'But not until.'

The cloaked figure neither moved nor spoke for a while.

'Oh come on,' the man said at last. 'I know what this means to you. I got you the other stuff, and I reckon I deserve a bit more than promises you may not be able to make good.' He cocked his head slightly to one side. 'Someone provides, someone has to pay. I provide, you pay. Simple as that.'

'Someone has to pay,' the other figure murmured. 'Yes, perhaps it is a simple matter of recompense.'

'And I'll hang on to this, until I get paid. Do we have a deal?'

The cloaked figure stepped forward. The gloved hand extended, palm open. 'We have a deal.'

The man smiled. 'Good.' The relief was evident in his voice as he reached out and gripped the gloved hand. 'Good. I knew you'd see sense.'

They shook hands firmly. Then the man with the moustache tried to let go. But the other's grip was tight, holding him firm. As he frowned, tried to pull free, the gloved hand snapped backward, dragging him suddenly close to the cloaked figure.

The man's mouth dropped open in surprise, a low guttural sound erupting from his throat. It was followed a moment later by a stream of blood.

The cloaked figure withdrew the laser dagger from the dead man's stomach and let the body fall to the ground. The whole of the front torso was sliced open, spilling its steaming contents on to the stone cold floor. A gloved hand reached down and sought through the man's pockets until it found what it was looking for – a small electronic component nestling inside a foam harness within a transparent plastic box.

'Someone always has to pay,' the cloaked figure hissed. Then it turned and walked away.

In the observation room, the screen of static slowly cleared. An image emerged from within the swirl of interference. It showed an enhanced image of a stone-lined room. The room was empty apart from the body lying on the floor.

The expert system that monitored each camera's output data and scanned the audio frequencies for key words and phrases registered the change. It cleared a flag that indicated that another camera had malfunctioned. It inspected the image, and compared it to the last stored image from the same camera at exactly the same angle. The system isolated the changes from one image to another, and ran a query on the resultant image content. When the system found a reasonable match, it invoked its artificial-intelligence programs to determine appropriate action.

Three-tenths of a second after the image from the camera had cleared, the alarm sounded in the duty guards' quarters.

Darkling was almost back at the barrack section when the communicator signalled. It was set directly into the breastplate of his light combat armour. When the emergency signal came, it was a low-level pulse of electricity through his nervous system – enough to nudge the adrenaline up a little and get his attention. It obviated the need for an audible bleep or a flash of light that might betray his position to an enemy.

It certainly got his attention, and Darkling pressed the receive button on his wrist, and listened to the voice that spoke through the tiny speaker set into his helmet. Then he swore, and started running. Before long, he could hear the sound of more running feet as the rest of the duty patrol converged on the same area.

The damp cellerage reverberated to the harsh, grinding, almost metallic sound. The flickering lamplight was augmented by flashes of white brilliance that strobed in time to the grating sound. Then, with a sudden thump of sound, the noise and the light both ceased abruptly.

In one dimly lit corner, a large blue box now stood where moments earlier had been bare flagstones and shadow.

Jamie was first out of the TARDIS. He paused in the doorway and sniffed at the damp air, then blew it out again in a steamy cloud. A moment later, he pitched forward as the Doctor pushed his way past, Victoria close on his heels.

'Och, Doctor.'

'Sorry, Jamie, but if you will stand in the doorway...'

'It's not that, Doctor.' Jamie peered through the dim light, struggling to make out the details of the stone walls. 'It's this place.'

The Doctor looked round, arms outstretched and palms open. 'It's certainly got character.'

'It's dark and damp.'

'It's freezing cold, too,' Victoria added, hugging herself. 'Oh, Doctor, can't we go somewhere else?'

But the Doctor was already halfway to an archway on the other side of the room. 'Just a quick look round, I think.' He paused in mid-step, and started jumping up and down.

'Now what's he doing?' Jamie wondered.

'Oh come on, Jamie. Walking will keep us warm, at least.'

They caught up with the Doctor just as he stopped leaping into the air. Instead he licked his finger and held it up above his head. 'That's strange.'

'What is?'

'There's a draught.'

Jamie sighed. 'Doctor, we're in a castle, by the look of it. Castles are always draughty. And cold and damp.'

'That depends on where they are, Jamie.' The Doctor beamed at him through the gloom. 'You need air round them to get a draught.' He turned and made for the archway again. 'Provided they're properly looked after, of course.'

'I'll tell you somebody who needs properly looking after,' Jamie muttered. Victoria took his arm and led him after the Doctor.

The Doctor was waiting in the archway. He seemed almost frozen in position, not reacting when his two friends joined him.

'What is it, Doctor?' Victoria asked. 'Where are we, do you think?'

The Doctor said nothing, and both Jamie and Victoria tried to see over his shoulder into the area beyond.

'Trouble?' Jamie hazarded.

'There's always trouble, Jamie.' The Doctor's voice was low, calm and serious. 'And I'm afraid we always seem to find it.' He walked purposefully across the room, hands thrust deep into his coat pockets.

Jamie and Victoria followed. Jamie's eyes were adjusting to the dim light now, and he could see the Doctor crouching beside something on the ground.

'I think perhaps you should take Victoria back to the TARDIS, Jamie.' The Doctor did not look up from the dark shape he was examining.

The light glistened on the wet floor, and Jamie realised that the shape was a body. A body that had shed a lot of blood. As he turned to shield Victoria from the sight, to lead her away, Jamie saw more shapes. But these were upright –

figures, grouped in the arched doorway behind them.

Not a word was said. The soldiers grabbed both Jamie and Victoria and roughly pushed them against the nearest wall, patting them down. Behind him, Jamie was aware of the Doctor being similarly searched for weapons. Jamie heard a slight intake of breath as the soldier that was searching him reached his lower leg. When he stood up, the man was holding Jamie's dirk. The narrow blade caught the light as he held it up for the others to see.

Then Jamie felt his legs kicked from under him, and he crashed to the floor. He threw his hands out to break his fall. They slipped on the damp floor, and he had to scrabble to keep from pitching face down into the flagstones. He slowly pulled himself to his feet again, aware of the Doctor and Victoria standing beside him, their hands on their heads; aware of the soldiers standing facing them with guns drawn and aimed while two of their fellows examined the ruptured body in the middle of the room; aware of the congealing blood smeared across the palms of his hands.

CHAPTER THREE
QUIET MOVES

Darkling handed the knife over to Captain Logall, and turned back to face the intruders. The younger man stared back at him defiantly. The older man, the scruffy one, seemed nonplussed. The young woman was shivering with the cold and perhaps fear. Darkling wondered briefly if he should apologise for the fact that the conditioners in the lower areas had long since packed up.

As he looked at the woman, as he admired the way her hair framed her face, how her lip quivered ever so slightly, how she met his gaze, he failed to notice the young man's movements. He bent over as if to adjust the sock where the knife had been concealed.

'Look out!' Logall's cry was just too late.

The young man's head caught Darkling hard in the stomach, throwing him backward as he doubled up in pain. He collapsed into Logall and two of the other soldiers.

Logall lunged forward, stumbling as he tried to negotiate Darkling's retching form. From the ground, Darkling's vision misted with tears as he tried desperately to catch his breath. He saw the two men run for the nearest door. The older man's coat tails streamed out behind him as he ran. The woman made to follow, but Logall caught her by the shoulder and dragged her back. He hurled her across the room towards Gregor, who grabbed her, holding her arms pinioned behind her back as she shouted and struggled.

Milles and Sanjak were already after the men, armour clanking as they ran. So much for the noise suppression.

'Sorry, sir.' Darkling dragged himself to his feet, reaching out for the wall for support.

Logall just glared at him. Then he punched the communicator on his wrist.

The woman was shouting at them, her voice high-pitched with nervous excitement, echoing off the stonework. 'Let me go, you can't keep me here. We haven't done anything. Who are you people?'

Logall grimaced, hand to his ear as he tried to listen for the connect signal. He waved at Gregor. 'Shut her up, can't you?'

Gregor clamped his hand over the woman's mouth. The noise subsided slightly, but she could still be heard in muffled gasps and exhortations. Gregor dragged her backwards through the archway into the next area, the sound of her struggles and gasps growing fainter as he went.

'Thank you.' Logall returned his attention to the communicator. 'Logall here. Three intruders in the lower area. We have apprehended one female. Two male intruders still at large, we are in pursuit.' He looked over towards the body lying in the middle of the room. One of the soldiers was standing beside it, his face drawn and grim.

'It's Remas, sir.'

Logall nodded. 'Remas is dead,' he said into the communicator. 'Get a forensic expert here.' His listened for a moment, then snapped, 'Well, whoever we *have* got then. A medic, first-aider, whoever.'

Another pause. Darkling was getting his breath back now, doing his best to stand to attention.

'You all right?' Logall mouthed at Darkling. He nodded.

'Description of the two intruders still at large,' Logall said: 'one is a young male wearing a skirt. The other is older and shorter.' He started to lower his wrist, then changed his mind, and added, 'And he's got a sandwich stuck to his bottom.'

The Doctor and Jamie had stopped running. They were making their way cautiously up a narrow winding staircase.

'What about Victoria?' Jamie hissed. 'We can't just leave her there.'

The Doctor held his hand up. He half turned on the stair. 'We'll soon meet up again when they catch us, Jamie.'

'If we're going to get caught any way, why not just go back? We can tell them we didn't kill that man. We weren't even there.'

'I'm sure they'll work that out for themselves, Jamie. But while they're not shooting at us, we have a chance to look around a bit. Find out where we are.'

'What good will that do?' Jamie asked as they continued up the stairs.

'It's always best to argue from a position of knowledge,' the Doctor said as they emerged into a long hallway. 'Though that doesn't stop some people, I admit.' The walls were lined with paintings and hung with heavy swords and shields. Lamps flickered nervously along its length. Serveral doors led off the hallway at irregular intervals. 'Now the important thing is to keep absolutely quiet and avoid being caught for as long as possible.' The Doctor stopped, index finger to his lips as he considered. 'Yes,' he whispered at last, pointing to a nearby door, 'this way, I think.'

It was a cupboard, full of cleaning materials. Several brushes and mops fell out and clattered noisily to the floor as the Doctor opened the door.

'Or perhaps not,' he admitted. They bundled the things back into the cupboard and set off along the corridor.

The air was noticeably warmer as they climbed the stairway. Victoria had lapsed into silence, realising that her protests were serving only to aggravate her captors. She was led up the stairs, and along a hallway. The castle seemed to be a strange mixture of old and new. The stonework and the decor for the most part suggested a medieval setting. But the sophisticated armour the soldiers wore, and the mix of manual and electronic weaponry that hung on the walls, indicated a far more advanced society.

Eventually, they stopped in front of a heavy wooden door. The guard captain – Logall – stepped forward and rapped on it.

'Enter.' The voice was surprisingly clear, and it took Victoria a moment to realise that it came not from behind the door, but through a small speaker set into the wall beside it. The door clicked open, and swung slowly back on its hinges. Logall ushered Victoria into the room, removing his helmet as he followed her in.

The room was unlike any of the castle she had seen so far. For one thing, it was brightly lit. Also, the floor was carpeted in a deep, dark blue. The walls were hung not with weaponry and images of war, but with huge portraits. The furniture seemed closer to the nineteenth-century splendour that Victoria was used to in her own home and at Maxtible's house near Canterbury than the simple wooden chairs she had passed in alcoves along several of the corridors.

The far end of the room was taken up with a huge desk made of dark wood – mahogany, perhaps. The man seated behind it rose as they entered, and came round to meet them in the centre of the room. He was tall and heavily built. His face was as craggy as the oldest of the stone walls they had passed. His eyes were deep set, but gleamed with interest and intelligence. He was dressed in a heavy robe of scarlet and blue.

Victoria looked up at the man, hoping she seemed less nervous than she felt. He regarded her in return, a hand pulling at his thick jaw.

'Thank you, Logall.' The man's voice was deep and rich. 'When you find the other two, bring them to me, will you?'

'Yes, sir. Sorry to disturb you so late, sir.'

'No matter.' The man turned and went back to the desk. 'I have to wait up for our visitors any way. Though I must confess I was expecting a short respite before their arrival.'

'Yes, sir.'

The man sat down again, pushing a folder to one side and linking his hands on the blotter. 'You may go,' he said to Logall. 'I don't think I am in any immediate danger, but leave one of your men just in case.'

'Sir.' Logall turned to one of the soldiers waiting in the doorway. 'Darkling, you're volunteered.'

The soldier stepped forward, taking up position beside the door as it closed behind his comrades. Victoria saw that he had also removed his helmet, and held it in the crook of his left arm. His right hand rested on the butt of the handgun at his side. He was tall, and young – not much older than herself, probably. His hair was short and fair, and his eyes were a deep green.

The man at the desk spoke, and Victoria turned back to face him. 'Now then,' he said, not unkindly, 'I think you have a little explaining to do.'

'Where am I?' Victoria asked.

'You don't know?' He leaned back in his chair.

'No. I don't. And who are you?'

The man's fingers drummed a quick beat on the desk. 'You know, I think you really don't know. And that means you have even more explaining to do.' He watched her for a while, swinging slightly from side to side in the chair. 'All right,' he said at last. 'I am Mithrael, Warden of Santespri.'

'What's Santespri?'

Mithrael frowned. 'This is.'

'You mean this castle?'

'You know,' Mithrael said, 'this could be both intriguing and amusing. If it were not for the circumstances.'

'You mean that you're expecting visitors?' Victoria asked, remembering his earlier words to Logall.

The change in Mithrael was immediate and pronounced. His face darkened and he leaned forward across the desk, his hands gripped tightly together. 'I mean that a man is dead.'

The door that the Doctor had eventually hazarded this time led into a large square room. Heavy tapestries hung on the walls to the sides of the door, faded and threadbare with age. There were several chairs arranged round a wooden table in the centre of the room. Much of the wall facing the door was taken up with a huge window. The surround was finely finished pale stone, the mullions of a similar material and design. Either side hung dusty velvet curtains. They had once been a deep red.

'Ah, now we're getting somewhere.' The Doctor closed the door behind them and made his way over to the window, rubbing his hands together in satisfaction.

Jamie followed. 'It's night time,' he said pointing to the window. Through it only a dark sky was visible. Tiny points of light glittered against the glass.

'I don't think so, Jamie.'

'Oh come on, Doctor, it's pitch black out there. You can see the stars.'

The Doctor was now standing at one end of the window, peering through it at an angle. 'That's not all you can see, Jamie. Come over here.'

Jamie joined the Doctor, craning his neck to see where the Doctor was pointing. 'Will you look at that!' he breathed.

Through the upper edge of the window, as the glass thickened slightly and distorted the view, he could see the rim of a planet. It was ringed, the graduated halos of colour seemingly suspended above the sphere. Its surface was a medley of reds and oranges with occasional dots of amber and lime green. And it was huge. They could see only one curved edge, the rings cutting out deeper into space, but the surface detail was clearly visible as the colours blended and melded.

'And look down there.' The Doctor pointed lower in the window.

Jamie turned to look. They were indeed in a castle, or a fortress. He could see the outer wall stretching round beneath them topped with fortified battlements. Several soldiers stood guard along its length, dressed in similar armour to the ones who had apprehended them in the lower part of the fortress. At the base of the wall, jutting out so that it was just visible to the Doctor and Jamie, was an outcropping of dark, jagged rock. It projected into the blackness, shadow against shadow. Jamie stared at it, trying to fit the scene into an acceptable interpretation of the world they were on.

'We're in space,' he said eventually. 'This castle is floating in space.'

'Very good Jamie.' The Doctor patted him on the shoulder. 'I think it's built into an asteroid.'

'But how can they breathe?' Jamie asked, pointing to the soldiers on the walkway below.

'Oh that's easy, just a simple osmotic field to keep the air from filtering out while allowing the light to get in. I imagine it keeps out stray meteors and energy bolts too. Anything travelling too fast like that, or too slow like the molecules that make up the air, will be blocked.'

'Oh,' said Jamie, trying to sound as if he understood and should have thought of this himself. 'Aye.' He examined the vista again, taking in the immensity of the view.

'There'll be some seepage I expect, but nothing too drastic,' the Doctor went on. 'Molecules that get too excited and break through.'

A tiny point of light caught Jamie's eye. He was sure it hadn't been there just now. As he watched, the light moved slowly across the window, growing bigger all the time. 'What's that?'

The Doctor followed Jamie's line of sight. 'I don't know, Jamie.'

The light continued its progress. After a few moments, they could see that it was not a light, but a metallic object that reflected the luminance of the stars.

The Doctor laughed and clapped his hands together. 'It's a ship, Jamie. A spaceship. They have visitors.'

The small patrol ship manoeuvred for docking. It spun slowly on its axis, seeming to stand on the flames that erupted from its base. With a grace that defied its size, it lowered itself towards the docking pad on the East Tower. The osmotic shield round the tower flared slightly as it absorbed and distributed the power from the engines.

As the ship passed through the shield and met the air, the noise of the motors cracked across the fortress like a sonic boom. The immediate eruption of sound slowly decreased as the output from the engines was reduced.

The landing gear swung free of its housing and clicked into place beneath the craft as it dropped slowly. The heavy vehicle bounced slightly on the hydraulic legs as they absorbed the weight on impact. Smoke and steam swirled round the top of the tower, for a while obscuring the view of the ship. Then the engines shut down and the dispersers in the docking pad began to draw the fumes and smoke away.

Through the clearing mist, a figure appeared. His purple cloak streamed out behind him as he marched purposefully across the turret and towards the entrance to the fortress. He was tall, walking with an air of determination and authority. His face was thin and weathered, his eyes constantly moving as they took in every detail. The Haddron insignia of a stylised striking bird of prey was emblazoned in red and gold across the breastplate of his armour.

Behind the man two other figures slowly appeared through the thinning mist. One was an equally tall man in tight-fitting battle armour, his handsome and symmetrical features set in an expression of indifference. The other was a woman, her long blonde hair blowing free in the draught from the dispersers and her thin white gown blowing tight against the contours of her body as she walked.

The main access door opened before the figures reached it. Warden Mithrael stepped out into the night and bowed low as the man in the cloak reached him. Mithrael straightened up, and saluted stiffly – right fist across his left breast. 'Welcome to Santespri, Consul.'

'Thank you.' Milton Trayx, General in Chief of the Haddron Armed Forces, waited for his wife and his aide-de-camp to reach the doorway. He let Helana pass through first. 'Is he here?' he asked Mithrael as they entered the fortress.

Mithrael's reply was almost lost in the sound of the door shutting behind them. 'I believe he is, my Lord.'

The soldier stood impassive and still by the door. Victoria remembered the captain addressing him as Darkling.

'Are you going to keep me here all night?' she asked as forcefully as she dared. It seemed like hours since Mithrael had left. Now Victoria was alone in the office. Alone apart from the unspeaking guard. 'Well?'

He turned to look at her – the most movement he had made since taking up his position. 'It's almost morning,' he said.

'Nonsense. It's still dark outside.'

Darkling frowned. 'It's always dark outside.'

'And I don't suppose you're going to tell me where we are either.'

He turned away again, his face set back into its impassive stare.

Victoria watched him for a while. When he still did not move, she went over to Mithrael's desk and sat down in the chair behind it. That got a reaction.

'Hey, you can't do that. Get up at once.'

'I'm tired,' she snapped at him. 'I've been kept standing for hours. It's all right for you, you're used to it. I'm not.' She leaned back, hoping it was obvious from her posture that she was not about to get up.

Darkling hesitated by the door. He seemed unable to decide whether to ignore her, or to come over and lift her forcibly out of the chair. Victoria hoped he would settle on the former.

He was still dithering when the door swung open.

'About time, too,' Victoria called out.

But the figure that entered was not Mithrael. It was a

tall, middle-aged man. His face was worn, but he moved as if he were still physically fit. A purple cloak hung from his shoulders, beneath which he was wearing the same sort of armour as the rest of the soldiers. But across his chest was painted what looked like a fierce eagle mercilessly bearing down on its prey.

At the sight of the man, Darkling snapped even more uprightly to attention. 'Sir!' he shouted, crashing his right fist across his chest.

'As you were,' the man murmured. Darkling did not relax, and the man paid him no further heed. He walked quickly into the middle of the room, his expression unreadable as he looked at Victoria. Behind him, first Mithrael and then another soldier entered the room. They hung back, apparently in deference.

'Are you comfortable there?' The man's voice was firm and deep, but with a slightly ragged edge to it.

'Yes,' Victoria said, aware of the nerves in her own voice. 'Quite comfortable, thank you.'

'Good. Then answering a few simple questions shouldn't be too much of an indisposition.'

'What questions?' Victoria asked in alarm.

'Well, for a start, you can tell me if anyone has offered you anything to eat or drink.'

'No. No they haven't,' Victoria said in relief. 'Thank you.'

The man turned to the soldier who had followed him in. 'See to it, Prion. And have some wine sent in for us. I need to quench the dust of the journey from my throat.'

The man, Prion, saluted as Darkling had. 'Sir.' Then he turned and marched stiffly from the room.

'What about the other intruders, my Lord?' Mithrael hissed. 'I told you, there are still two male fugitives at large. Either of them could be the –'

The man cut him off. 'You worry too much, Warden. If they're as aggressive and desperate as this young lady then I don't think we have much to fear.' He settled himself into a chair, angling it so as to be able to observe Victoria closely. 'And you know as well as I, Mithrael, that we can pick them up whenever we choose to.' He turned abruptly towards the warden. 'Why haven't you?'

'Sir, I – I was waiting for you. I thought you might wish to let them run, to observe…'

The man shook his head. 'I think not. They have run enough. You say there has been one death already. That should tell us almost everything we need to know. Some level of interrogation will no doubt provide us with any information we still lack. If that becomes necessary.' He brushed a hand across his knee, as if dusting the shining armour. 'But I doubt they are the ones. When I've had my wine, then we can look at the data.' He turned back to Victoria. 'For now, we can perhaps find out all there is of interest to know from our guest here.'

Victoria summoned her courage and said, 'I have a question.'

'Go on,' the man replied with the ghost of a smile.

'Who are you?' she asked. And as Mithrael gasped in astonishment and apprehension, the man threw back his head and laughed.

'Look at the size of this place, Doctor.' Jamie was standing in the arched doorway at the end of the corridor. The Doctor joined him, and through the open doors they surveyed the large room in front of them.

'Yes, it is impressive, isn't it?' the Doctor agreed. 'Some sort of great hall, I imagine.'

'The laird's room, most likely,' Jamie said.

The room was lit by two huge chandeliers that hung from the high, stone, vaulted ceiling. The flickering electric lights that made up the chandeliers were reflected in the polished floor. The floor itself was a chequerboard of deep-red and brilliant-white marble. Blue veins threaded their intricate way through the stone, as if holding the whole construction together.

A long wooden table ran down the middle of the room. Heavy chairs stood to attention either side of the table. A huge fireplace was set into the right-hand wall, and above it a gallery ran the length of the room, seen through wide arched windows in the stone wall. Below the gallery, beside the fireplace, similar windows gave out on to the spacescape beyond the castle.

The walls were hung with ancient weaponry – swords, a mace, shields and crossbows. Interspersed with the old were more modern artefacts of war – laser rapiers, blasters and energy dispersers.

Jamie took several seconds to assimilate all this. Then he saw the figures standing round the edge of the room, and took a step backwards. 'Doctor,' he hissed urgently.

'Jamie!' The Doctor's answering cry was urgent and full of fear and anguish.

Jamie spun round. 'What is it?'

The Doctor exhaled slowly and closed his eyes. 'You trod on my foot.'

'Sorry. But do you see –'

'The figures, yes Jamie.' The Doctor pushed past him into the room. With no sign of fear or apprehension he walked up to the nearest of the figures. It was standing on a raised plinth within an alcove, and Jamie could see as he approached that it was wearing armour. The visor was down, a heavy blast screen covering the eyes. The torso was bristling with attached weaponry and electronics. A patchwork of tiny indicator lights were set into the chest, and a small circular ring was set into a recess on one side of the breastplate. The forearm had the points of knives protruding from below the wrist. The hands were massive gauntlets with sharp studs in place of knuckles and fingers that ended in cruel points. Behind the wrist Jamie could see the dark opening of a small nozzle, like the barrel of a gun. The whole suit was studded with rivets and bolts, and teemed with electronic attachments and readout screens.

'It's all right, Jamie.' The Doctor reached out tentatively and tapped at the figure's chest. It made a metallic ping. 'I think it's just an empty suit.'

'It's like the armour those soldiers were wearing,' Jamie said. 'Only more...'

'Sophisticated, yes.'

Jamie nodded. 'And big. Huge.' The whole massive suit towered over the two of them. It looked incredibly heavy, and Jamie could not imagine wearing it for any appreciable length of time. The large, polished metal boots would soon fill up with sweat.

But before he could comment, the room rang with the sound of other heavy boots on the stone floor of the corridor outside. Jamie turned at once, grabbing the Doctor's shoulder instinctively just as the Doctor grabbed his. Several guards were running along the corridor towards them. They held long rifle-like weapons across their chests as they ran.

The Doctor's arms flew up in the air as the soldiers approached. 'Run, Jamie,' he shouted as he spun on his heel. But he spun too far and too fast on the shiny marble floor. His feet skidded from under him and he lost his balance, sitting down heavily at Jamie's feet.

'Run,' the Doctor shouted again, looking up plaintively at Jamie and waving his hands excitedly.

'I'm not leaving you,' Jamie told him, grabbing one of the Doctor's flailing hands and yanking him to his feet.

The Doctor was already running, legs whirling in space, when his feet landed on the floor. He ran with his head down, his coat tails streaming out behind him and his hands lost in the long sleeves of his shapeless jacket. Jamie was about to follow, when he paused and turned back to the massive figure standing in the alcove beside him. He glanced at the rapidly approaching soldiers, then at the distance to the heavy wooden table in the middle of the room. Not ideal, but worth a try.

'You keep going, Doctor,' he shouted. 'I'll catch you up.' Jamie grabbed the suit of armour by the arm and heaved on it. It was every bit as heavy as it looked. Probably more so. Jamie pulled again, casting another glance at the soldiers as they entered the room at a run.

Movement. He could just feel the suit beginning to sway on its massive feet. Jamie heaved again, straining every muscle in his powerful body in his attempt to topple the giant figure. It swayed slightly forward on its toes, and Jamie relaxed a little, let it sway back so it rocked on its heels. Just as it righted itself once more, Jamie pulled again, keeping the armour moving forward. He felt the weight shift as it passed its centre of gravity, and looked up in satisfaction as the enormous metal figure started to fall.

Towards him. Jamie was immediately underneath the suit – directly in its path as it slowly pitched over. With a cry he leapt out of the way, turned and started to run.

Behind him the suit crashed to the floor. It remained intact despite the horrendous impact, the sound echoing round the room. The first soldier slammed into the side of the fallen figure, too late to stop or avoid it, cartwheeling over the top of the metal suit. The others started to scramble over the obstruction, but they had been slowed down considerably.

The Doctor was already through the adjoining room and out of sight as Jamie reached the door. He paused for a moment and looked back in satisfaction at the confusion as the soldiers tried to pull each other clear of the armour. Several were running round the other side of the table. Jamie smiled and turned to follow the Doctor.

The dark-grey barrel of a weapon was under his nose as he turned, just too close to focus on properly. He could smell the gun oil as he slowly raised his hands and put them behind his head. The figure behind the gun nodded back down the banqueting hall towards where the soldiers Jamie had obstructed were now approaching once again.

'This way, I think,' the guard said.

The Doctor made his careful way through what seemed to be the living area of the fortress. The floor was carpeted, and as far as he could tell there were bedrooms and staterooms on this floor. The whole air of the place became more splendid and opulent – more château than castle. The walls were no longer bare beneath the displays of armaments and paintings, but panelled in dark wood or hung with large tapestries.

But after a while, he found that the carpet disappeared, and the decor reverted to something more akin to the medieval, Spartan appearance of the lower level where they had landed. He arrived at a pair of massive wooden doors. They were open, and a keypad was set into the wall nearby, which the Doctor guessed controlled the locking mechanism. Beyond this point, the doors to the rooms became heavier, with conspicuous locks and large bolts.

The Doctor tentatively tried one of the doors, but it refused to open. He listened at the keyhole, and could hear sounds of movement from inside. So he put his eye to the small hole and peered through. The room beyond was dark, and he could see nothing but shadows.

He moved on to the next door, and was about to repeat the process there, when the flickering half-light suddenly flared up into brilliant luminance. The Doctor stifled a cry and leapt for the nearest cover, which seemed to be an alcove. In fact, there was a door in it, and as the Doctor jumped in front of it, the door began to swing open.

The Doctor's head cracked painfully against the stone wall as he was knocked back by the door. He managed to stay upright and hidden behind the door as it opened to its full extent. Through the crack between door and wall he watched as a line of guards marched through. They split into two groups, one going each way along the corridor. The Doctor listened to the sounds of the guards' progress – heavy boots on stone, and the rattling and chinking of keys.

Swinging the door slowly back, the Doctor emerged from his concealment and edged his way to the corridor. He looked carefully round the corner. At the far end of the corridor, a guard was unlocking the last of the doors. The Doctor strained to hear what the man said as he swung the door open. But he could not make out the exchange of comments. After a moment, the guard laughed and then continued down the corridor, disappearing round the corner.

Weighing up his options the Doctor looked both ways along the corridor, then returned to the door the guards had emerged from. Beyond it was a sort of hallway with several more doors leading off it. There was an archway that seemed to lead back towards the main doors and the better-furnished areas beyond, and another that gave into another, darker passageway. There was also one more heavy wooden door. It looked similar to the doors the guards had been unlocking in the corridor, except that it was braced with heavy strips of rusty metal.

The door was ajar, and as the Doctor watched it was pushed open. He stepped back into the shadows, or what shadows were left now that the lights were fully on, as two men emerged from the room. The first man was a guard dressed in the same lightweight battle armour as all the others. The second man wore a long faded robe. His face was heavily lined and the Doctor guessed he looked older than he really was. He wore a short white beard that was perfectly trimmed.

As the Doctor watched, the guard locked the door behind them.

'Afraid that I might break in?' the robed man asked.

'Procedure, sir,' the guard replied. 'Everything here follows procedure – you know that better than I.'

'Indeed.' The man sounded bored and resigned. 'So, let us proceed ourselves.'

When they were almost out of sight down the passageway, the Doctor followed. They passed several doors and alcoves and another corridor that intersected at right angles. Eventually, the two figures stopped outside another heavy, metal-bound door. The guard unlocked it.

The Doctor edged closer, curious, as the guard then knocked on the door, and waited a while before opening it. He stood deferentially aside, and allowed the bearded man to enter. The Doctor could just see the man stop on the threshold, and bow. Then the guard shut the door behind him, and locked it again.

After the guard had gone, the Doctor stepped out of his alcove and crossed to the door. He listened, but could hear almost nothing through its thick frame. He peered through the keyhole, but there was something obstructing his view on the other side. Or perhaps the keyhole did not penetrate the whole way through the door. That would certainly make the lock more difficult to pick from the inside.

The Doctor clasped his hands, pressing the ups of his fingers together as he thought. After a moment, he pulled a cylindrical metal device from his inside pocket – his new sonic screwdriver. He made several adjustments to the control settings, then held it close to the keyhole. Nothing happened, and he frowned. He held the sonic screwdriver up to the light, banged it on his palm as if knocking out a recalcitrant pipe, then tried again. Still nothing.

With a sigh, the Doctor adjusted the setting. Perhaps he had still not quite got all the gremlins out. When he tried again, he could just hear the sonic pulses as they worked on the barrel mechanism of the lock, but he knew they would be out of the range of hearing of almost any other humanoid species. He smiled in satisfaction. As he suspected, there was a strong sonic signal on the same frequency as he had first tried – probably a subspace emission of some sort. It had interfered with the screwdriver's function. But a slight adjustment to the frequency and everything was hunky dory.

Sure enough, after a few moments there was a metallic scraping sound, and the lock turned over. The Doctor smiled to himself, pocketed the sonic screwdriver, and pushed the door open.

There were two figures seated in the room in front of him. They were either side of a low table in the far corner. One was the man with the white beard he had seen enter. The other had his back to the Doctor.

The man with the beard was already leaping to his feet. 'What the deuce – how did you –' He stepped forward, eyes glittering with menace. 'I'm sorry, my Lord,' he said to the seated figure. 'There is a disturbance.'

The Doctor took a step into the room. 'A disturbance? Oh, I do beg your pardon,' he said, 'I don't wish to intrude.'

'You do intrude,' the man snapped back.

'So I do,' the Doctor said with a grin. He scampered over to the table. 'But I love a good game of chess.' He examined the board in front of him. 'White to win in eight moves,' he murmured. 'Very good. Very good indeed.'

Then he looked at the figure still seated at the table, and the smile froze on his face.

'You play chess?' the figure asked. Its face was a burnished mask of shining metal, apparently riveted to the head. The eyes were recessed screens of dark plastic, the nose a slight bulge in the metal 'face'. The mouth was a mesh-covered slit, from which its voice emerged as a metallic scrape, as if the turning lock had learned to speak.

'Yes,' the Doctor said as he took in the sight. He coughed to mask his awkwardness. 'Yes, a little.'

'More than a little, I think.' The masked man turned slightly. 'Perhaps we shall have a new player join us in our humble surroundings, Cruger.'

The bearded man sat down again. 'Perhaps, my Lord,' he said quietly. He looked at the Doctor, his eyes narrowing as he asked, 'Mate in eight moves, you say?'

The Doctor shrugged. 'It's possible in seven. But I think eight, yes.'

'Tell me one thing,' the artificial voice rasped close to the Doctor's ear.

He turned to see that the man in the mask had risen and was standing beside him. 'If I can.'

The impassive face was inches from his own, reflecting the Doctor's features back at him as if in a distorting glass. 'Why did you kill Remas?'

CHAPTER FOUR
KNIGHT'S TOUR

Trayx barely paused to knock on the door. He threw it open even before he heard the call of 'Enter' from inside. He knew it was rude and would be seen – by Cruger at least – as an act of arrogance. But he also knew that, despite what his instincts told him, speed might be vital.

He saw as soon as the door swung open that he need not have worried. Close by Trayx's arm, Prion stepped forward. The ADC was raising his right arm, but Trayx lifted his finger. The slight gesture was enough, and Prion's hand dropped back to his side.

All three of the people in the room were seated round a chessboard. Cruger's features were set in a study of concentration as he moved a single piece across the board. The feelings of the man opposite him were as ever obscured by his mask. Between them sat the Doctor. The index finger of his right hand was pressed up into the soft part of his cheek, the pressure sending ripples right across the side of his face as he watched Cruger's hand on the board.

'Only Milton Trayx knocks in that peculiarly dramatic manner.' The masked man did not turn as he spoke, but continued to study the board.

'I apologise for the intrusion, my Lord.' Trayx crossed the room and stared down at the activity on the board. Cruger moved the chess piece – a knight – again. The Doctor was nodding enthusiastically.

'You have come,' the masked man said, 'for the Doctor, I presume.'

'Indeed, my Lord. But it appears there is no urgency.'

Now the man did look up, and as ever Trayx was unsettled by the non-stare with which he was fixed. 'None at all. He is proving an interesting conversationalist and has a shrewd grasp of chess.' The mask angled slightly, catching the light from a nearby lamp within the plastic shield over one eye so that it seemed to twinkle with amusement. 'He might even be a match for you, General.'

'We must have a game.' Trayx kept his voice level. 'Perhaps even a tournament if we have sufficient takers.'

The masked laugh was a rasp of static from the grille-mouth. 'I don't think the result would surprise any of us, except perhaps the Doctor. I play you only to remind myself of my new-found humility, Trayx. And Cruger has long since given up playing you at all.'

Trayx glanced at Cruger. He was tempted to suggest that Cruger's problem was his total lack of humility. But he doubted the man was listening, or that the comment would achieve anything.

'I think the problem,' the Doctor said suddenly without looking up, 'stems from that seventh move.'

Cruger's hand hesitated on the knight. His eyes were darting to and fro across the board, searching for the next move. Then he gave a grunt of displeasure and let go of the piece so forcefully that it toppled over.

'How do you know my name?' the Doctor asked, looking up at Trayx at last. His eyes were a piercing green. Or was it blue?

Trayx blinked, startled by the intelligence peeping from within the eyes, by the force of the stare. 'From your friends,' he said, and nodded to Mithrael, who was standing in the doorway.

The Doctor leapt to his feet as soon as Mithrael stood aside to let Jamie and Victoria enter the room. He rushed over to his companions, shaking each suddenly and vigorously by the hand. 'There you are. I'm so pleased. How are you both?'

'We're fine,' Jamie said sullenly.

'They asked us lots of questions, Doctor,' Victoria added.

The Doctor whirled round, staring at Trayx once again. 'We didn't kill that man, you know.'

'I know. And we only asked them questions. I had to be sure you were not –' Trayx broke off, considered his words. 'That you were guests and not intruders here.'

'Guests?' The Doctor was suddenly smiling, rubbing his hands together. 'How kind. You know, I'm famished.'

Trayx smiled despite himself. 'Yes, so am I.' He turned to Prion. 'I don't care what time of day they think it is here, I want some dinner.' He turned to Mithrael. 'With your permission, warden.' He did not wait for a response. 'Our guests will join us.'

Prion nodded, and departed without a word.

'Oh good.' The Doctor was back at the chessboard now. 'Have you eaten?' he asked the two seated figures.

Cruger grunted, saying nothing. The man in the mask answered, 'I don't think the invitation extends to us, Doctor.'

'Sadly not,' Trayx said quickly. 'Though we shall talk. About many things.' He clapped his hand on the masked man's shoulder so hard that the clunk of his glove on the metal beneath the man's cloak echoed round the room. 'We shall talk of battles lost and won, of chess and fine wine.'

'And, perhaps, of why you are here.'

Trayx sighed. 'Yes. Of that too.' He turned to find the young man, Jamie, standing beside him, peering down at the board.

'What are you doing, Doctor?' he asked. His voice was accented, Trayx noticed. Perhaps he was from one of the outlying colonies.

'Oh just a simple chess problem, Jamie.'

'Simple?' Cruger shook his head.

'Chess?' asked Jamie.

'Jamie!' The Doctor was suddenly beside the young man, arm round his shoulder in sympathy. 'You don't know what chess is?' He beckoned to the woman. 'Victoria, explain to Jamie about chess, will you?'

'Of course, Doctor,' the young woman said. 'But I don't think I know this version. There's only one piece.'

The Doctor looked back at the board, empty apart from the single fallen knight.

'Nor I, Doctor,' Trayx admitted. 'You mentioned a puzzle.'

'Yes, indeed.' The Doctor allowed Trayx to steer him towards the door. 'It's called the Knight's Tour.'

'I've not heard of it.'

They were out in the corridor now. Behind him, Trayx could hear Victoria trying to explain the rules and concepts of chess to the boy. It did not sound as if he was a quick learner.

'Well,' the Doctor went on, 'the idea is to move the knight from its starting place on the board to every other square in turn. The order does not matter, but you must cover every square once and once only using moves that are valid for the knight.'

Trayx nodded. 'Sixty-four different squares in sixty-four moves.' No, that wasn't right. 'Sixty-three moves,' he corrected himself, 'since the knight starts on its own square. I must ask Prion how many solutions there are.'

'There are three,' the Doctor said. 'But there is a variation in which the knight's last move, its sixty-fourth move, must return it to the square from which it started.'

Trayx stopped, beckoning Mithrael to join them. 'My guess is that there is but one solution to that problem. And I think you must know the answer.'

'What are problems for, if not to be solved?'

Trayx smiled. 'To confound your enemies,' he said. Then he turned to Mithrael. 'See that the Doctor and his companions are given rooms.' He saw the beginnings of a smile on Mithrael's lips, and added, 'In the guest quarters, not the Secure Area.' The smile died. 'They will join us for dinner in an hour.'

'Thank you.' There was an undercurrent of genuine gratitude in the Doctor's voice.

'We'll talk more at dinner, Doctor,' Trayx said. 'I think that we each owe the other several explanations.'

There were three rooms, in a triangular arrangement with interconnecting doors. While they were in the better-furnished area of the castle, the walls were bare stone and the flagstone floors mitigated only by thin rugs thrown across them. Each room had a door that gave out into a corridor that ran round the suite, as well as an internal door to a small *en suite* bathroom. With the interconnecting doors open, it was possible to position oneself in one of the rooms and see into both the others.

Jamie was slumped on the hard bed in his room. Victoria sat at a heavy wooden desk in the corner of the same room. Each of them watched as the Doctor flitted between all three of the chambers. He prodded at areas of the wall, and he examined the floors. He ahhed at the tapestry that hung on the back of his door, and hmmed at the similar hanging in Victoria's room. In Jamie's room he got down on his hands and knees and peered under the bed. Then he went and stood in the doorway through to Victoria's room and looked all round, frowning the while.

Jamie and Victoria exchanged bewildered looks as the Doctor waved to attract their attention, then put his finger to his lips and hissed a violent 'shh' at them. Neither of them had said more than a few words since they had been shown into the rooms.

The Doctor was now rummaging through his pockets. He pulled out several handkerchiefs and dumped them in a dishevelled pile on the desk beside Victoria, patting them carefully before rushing to the door and pulling at the tapestry that hung on its back. It came free with the sound of breaking threads and a sprinkling of light dust. The Doctor ignored this, and scampered across the room with the heavy material. He held it up against the wall opposite the bed, and put his ear to the wall beside it as if listening. After a moment he moved the tapestry over slightly, listened again, and nodded with satisfaction.

'Jamie,' the Doctor whispered loudly.

Jamie propped himself up on his elbow, unsure whether he was supposed to answer out loud.

'Over here, quickly.' The Doctor was almost jumping up and down with impatience as Jamie pulled himself off the bed. 'Come on.' Only the heavy tapestry hampered his movements. He was trying to hold it against the wall, but was too short to reach up where he wanted it. Before Jamie reached him, the top of the embroidered canvas slipped away from the wall and fell over the Doctor's head. It sent up a cloud of dust, and from beneath came the muffled sounds of the Doctor sneezing frantically.

Jamie pulled the canvas from the Doctor and pushed it back up the wall again.

'Ah, thank you, Jamie,' the Doctor said in a relieved, low

voice. 'Now just keep it held exactly there, will you?' He did not wait for an answer, but ducked away beneath Jamie's arm.

'Hey,' Jamie called out as the Doctor retrieved his hankies from the desk.

'Don't worry, Jamie.' The Doctor sounded pleased with himself. That was always worrying, in Jamie's experience, and his next words did nothing to alleviate the feeling. 'Just hold it here for the moment until I think of a way of fixing it in position.'

Jamie waited as patiently as he could, doing his best to hold the heavy tapestry in place. He could feel the dust tickling his nose, wanted desperately to scratch it. Meanwhile the Doctor rushed round the room draping hankies over various parts of the furniture and floor. He tapped at points on the wall, and stuffed handkerchiefs into slight cracks in the stonework. Finally, he gestured for Victoria to stand up, dragged her chair across the room, then hefted it on to the bed.

Jamie and Victoria both watched in amazement as he climbed first on to the bed, then up on to the chair. The chair wobbled dangerously as the Doctor rocked back and forth in a desperate effort to keep his balance. It did not help that he was reaching high above his head with both hands, clutching the last hanky. The cloth was taut between his fists as he swayed precariously. Eventually, after several near disasters, he got his balance sorted. And jumped.

Jamie almost dropped the tapestry. But somehow the Doctor had managed to land back on the chair. As it toppled over, he jumped down on to the bed, then immediately bounced off and landed neatly at Victoria's feet. All three of them looked back at where the Doctor had executed his initial gymnastics. High above the bed, a white-spotted red handkerchief hung squarely over an arm of the chandelier.

The Doctor chuckled and rubbed his hands together. 'Well, at least they can't see us now,' he whispered. 'Help me get Jamie sorted out, would you Victoria? Then we can decide what to do about the microphones.'

Someone cleared their throat, wiping the smile from the Doctor's face. They all turned towards the sound, which came from the outer door to the room. Sure enough, the door was open. On the threshold stood Prion, Trayx's aide-de-camp.

Prion's voice was crisp and precise. It was devoid of accent, and there was but the barest hint of amusement as he spoke. 'I trust you have found everything you need?'

The Doctor's boyish grin was back, spread across his face in an instant. 'Oh yes, thank you. I think we've found absolutely everything.'

'Then when you are quite ready,' Prion went on, 'the General in Chief asks that you join him for breakfast.'

Jamie stepped forward. 'We don't take orders from anyone,' he said loudly, aware that the strength of his words was somewhat diluted by the sight of the tapestry sliding to the floor behind him.

Prion, however, seemed nonplussed. 'It is an invitation, not an order,' he said. 'You are free to accept or not, depending on your own inclination.'

'And on how hungry we are, no doubt,' the Doctor added.

'Indeed.'

'Oh.' Jamie nodded, trying to look as if he had gained a concession. 'Well, that's all right then.' He turned back to the tapestry.

Before Jamie could lift the tapestry again, Prion said, 'I wouldn't bother. That camera doesn't work.'

'Oh?' the Doctor asked with just a trace of eagerness.

'Nor do three of the others. Maintenance is a problem with concealed systems. We would have to rip the walls and floors apart to get at the fibre optics. And that's assuming we had access to sufficient spares and expertise.'

'Yes,' the Doctor agreed. 'I can see it would be a problem.' He coughed, as if to excuse changing the subject. 'You mentioned breakfast.'

'In the Banqueting Hall. As soon as you are ready.'

'Thank you. We'll be along in a moment.' The Doctor smiled. 'We just have a few things to discuss in private, if you don't mind.'

'Not at all.' Prion nodded to them, and stepped backwards out of the room and into the corridor. As he closed the door, almost as an afterthought, he said, 'Oh, and the microphones you mentioned haven't worked for months.'

'So where are we, Doctor?' Victoria asked as soon as the door was closed. 'What's going on here?'

'I'm not sure, Victoria. But there is something odd.'

'That's right, Doctor,' Jamie chipped in. 'First they try to arrest us for murder, then they let us go again.'

'Mmm. They do seem to have given us the run of the place,' the Doctor mused, tapping his chin with his index finger. 'Then there's the man in the metal mask. And the games of chess.'

'We must be in the future,' Victoria said. 'If these people are playing chess, they must be from Earth.'

The Doctor was already on his way to the door. 'Oh not necessarily,' he said as he opened it. 'Chess is rather odd in itself. It's the only game that seems to have originated in pretty much the same form in the majority of civilised cultures without any external influence. You find it from one end of the Spiral Nebula to the other side of the Geratic Divide.' He was off down the corridor now, Jamie and

Victoria hastening to keep up. 'Even on Earth, you'll find that the game of chess evolved independently in both China and India, and in almost exactly the same form.'

Victoria gave a short nervous laugh. 'How can that happen?'

The Doctor stopped dead in his tracks, and turned to face her. 'I really have no idea,' he said. 'I don't know everything. But I think it's time we got some answers to the more immediate concerns.'

'And how will we do that?' Jamie asked.

'Let's ask someone in authority, shall we?'

Despite the brighter light, the Banqueting Hall still seemed to have more shadows and dark corners than the geometry of the room should accommodate. Beside the heavy suits of armour round the edges of the room stood several armed guards, almost as impassive and still.

The long wooden table down its centre was laden with silver dishes and tureens. Five places were set, two of them already taken. In one sat Trayx, a large goblet of wine in front of him. Beside him was a young woman. She had long, straight blonde hair. Her skin was perfect and pale as alabaster, and she wore a thin white dress that seemed to cling to her body. Prion was also seated at the table, but he had no silverware or crockery in front of him.

Victoria followed the Doctor's example and took one of the free places. Jamie sat opposite her. Trayx and the woman were already eating.

'Forgive me,' Trayx said, half rising to his feet as Victoria and the others sat down. 'My wife and I have had a long journey. And I know wine seems a little extravagant at breakfast, but my body at least believes it to be the middle of the night.'

'Oh, please carry on,' the Doctor said happily. 'We know the problem of adjusting to the local time all too well.'

'Aye, we certainly do,' Jamie mumbled.

'Thank you,' Trayx acknowledged, raising his glass. 'Do help yourselves to whatever you want. And when you feel suitably settled, perhaps we can address the tedious necessity of introductions. For the moment, I think you know my aide-de-camp, Prion. This is my wife, Helana, and I, as you may already know, am Milton Trayx.'

Helana nodded to them. 'I am pleased to make your acquaintance,' she said. Her voice was soft and low, but had a hard edge of determination.

Jamie was already lifting lids and ladling hot food on to his plate. Victoria had no idea what most of the dishes were, though one looked suspiciously like scrambled eggs and another smelled rather like bacon. As she followed Jamie's example, the Doctor was making their own brief introductions.

'Travellers?' Trayx seemed amused.

'Yes,' the Doctor said, apparently delighted that he had grasped the concept so readily. 'We, er, travel.'

'And you really have no idea where you are?'

'No, as I say, our navigational equipment is a little faulty.'

'Completely useless, if you ask me,' Jamie said through a mouth full of yellow stuff.

'Now, Jamie,' the Doctor admonished. 'Have you tried the green things?' he added. 'They're really not that bad.'

Trayx sat back in his chair, watching the three travellers intently. 'You are on Santespri,' he said, and Victoria could see that he was watching for a reaction.

'And where, may I ask, is that?'

Helana gasped out loud, covering her mouth immediately as if embarrassed at the display of surprise. Prion, by

71

contrast, seemed unconcerned.

Trayx's own reaction was masked as he dabbed at his lips with a heavy napkin. 'Doctor, you have indeed travelled a long way if you do not know of Santespri.'

'We don't know anything,' Victoria said.

'Ah,' Trayx said, 'now there you do yourselves a disservice. You can detect things that even the guards around this table do not officially know of.' His raised finger stopped the Doctor's comment on his lips. 'But we'll talk more of that later.' He took another sip of his wine. 'Would I be correct in my supposition, then, that you have very little knowledge of the recent history and politics of the Republic?'

'Ah, that depends on which republic,' the Doctor told him.

'Haddron.'

'I thought Haddron was an empire.'

Trayx took a mouthful of food, allowing his wife to answer. 'There are some who call it an empire. And in all but name it is.'

'But while the distinction is subtle,' Trayx said, 'it is indeed important. In fact –' he leaned forward slightly – 'it is that distinction which is the *raison d'être* for Santespri.' He took a mouthful of food, and chewed it slowly. 'It is interesting,' he said after a while, 'that while you have heard of Haddron, you are not aware of the significance of this fortress. Tell me, where exactly were you headed when your craft crash-landed on the asteroid? How did you get through the exclusion zone without being detected on our scanners? And where have you come from?'

The Doctor glanced at both Victoria and Jamie before answering. 'It's a long story,' he said. He drew his words out so that even this short sentence seemed to go on longer than necessary or desirable. 'And we have been rather out of touch recently. Frozen out.'

'Aye,' Jamie agreed. 'Why don't you tell us about this place? Why's it so important?'

'Yes,' Victoria added, 'please tell us.'

Trayx laughed. 'There are certain security questions I should like answered before too long. But I can see I shall get scant answers to my questions until your own peculiar curiosity is satisfied. Well, so be it.' He nodded to his aide-de-camp. 'Prion, perhaps you could explain briefly where we are and why we are here. At least then I can be getting on with my breakfast.'

'Briefly, sir?' Prion asked.

Trayx sighed. 'Always so literal. About two minutes.'

Prion nodded and turned towards the Doctor and his friends. 'Haddron, as you now know, is a republic,' he said. 'It is governed by a Senate which is presided over by three elected Consuls. The senior of these is the Consul General.'

'What's that got to do with this place?' Jamie interrupted.

'Shh, Jamie,' Victoria said with a frown. 'Let him tell us.'

'Nearly two years ago, Consul General Hans Kesar declared himself Consul General in perpetuity. In effect he wished to make it a lifetime post. He garnered a lot of popular support. Of the other two Consuls, one was politically weak and unlikely to pose a threat to his aspirations, while the other was Kesar's closest friend since childhood.'

'So,' the Doctor said quietly, 'Kesar tried to set himself up as Emperor and only the Senate could stop him.'

'So it seemed. But while he was also popular with the army, Kesar had not reckoned on the fierce loyalty to Haddron of the second Consul. When the crucial Senate debate took place, Consul Milton Trayx, Commander in Chief of the Haddron Armed Forces, spoke out against his former friend. The vote was a landslide against Kesar.'

The Doctor turned sharply, and looked at Trayx. Jamie and Victoria both followed his gaze. But Trayx seemed not to notice as he pushed his fork into a chunk of meat. It was Helana who met Victoria's stare. She gave the slightest of nods, then looked down at her own plate.

Prion continued, oblivious to this. 'While Kesar was popular with the military, he could not command the sort of loyalty that Consul Trayx could. The armed forces were unequally split in Consul Trayx's favour, though Kesar's troops were already prepared. There was a year of bloody civil war before the Republican forces triumphed. Kesar was defeated and captured. He was tried for crimes against the Republic and inevitably was found guilty.'

'Thank you, Prion.' Trayx pushed his empty plate away from him and dabbed his lips with his napkin. 'You can probably guess some of the rest, Doctor. Kesar could not be executed. He still commanded a tremendous following among the people as well as some of the military. Making him a martyr would simply open the door to another potential emperor and start the cycle again.'

'Exile?' the Doctor asked.

'Yes. Exile. Kesar was stripped of his title of Consul General, although technically he had another year of office left. He was exiled to a distant outpost, a frontier fortress long since within the outer boundaries of Haddron space, but nonetheless remote and forbidding. He was sent here, to Santespri.'

'Then,' the Doctor said slowly, 'the man in the mask...'

'Is Hans Kesar. Yes. And his chess partner is his former General in Chief, Axell Cruger.'

'That old man?' Victoria asked, astonished.

'That old man,' Trayx said loudly, his voice suddenly edged with uncharacteristic emotion, 'was once known

74

as the Blade of the Devil. He was the most ruthless officer under my command. Ruthless and costly. He would sacrifice the long-term advantage for a quick victory, commit men needlessly to a hopeless situation to save face in the short term.'

'A tactician rather than a strategist,' the Doctor mused. 'I guessed that much from his chess.'

Trayx poured himself more wine from a pitcher on the table in front of him. 'That is a generous description, Doctor,' he said. 'But it matters not now that he is here. Kesar and his retinue are treated well. His troops even share some of the guard duties. Patrols are organised during the day so that Kesar's men work with my own.'

'Is that not dangerous?' Jamie asked.

'They are Haddron soldiers. They deserve to keep their dignity, whatever their loyalties may have been. They are locked into their quarters within a secure area at night, as are Kesar and Cruger. In that way they are reminded of the error of their ways, of their crimes against the Republic.'

'You're not just thinking of them, though, are you?' said the Doctor.

'No, Doctor. That is very perceptive of you.' Trayx sipped his wine. No one spoke. 'There is a fine balance,' he went on at last, 'between victory and defeat. But for the grace of the gods, it could be us who are the captives and Kesar and Cruger our jailers.'

'You should always treat others as you would want them to treat you,' Victoria said. 'My father taught me that.'

'A fine maxim.' Trayx was staring off into space. 'And that grace goes double for me,' he added quietly. 'If I had chosen to join Kesar, who knows what victories and defeats might have followed?'

The Doctor studied Trayx's impassive features for

a moment. 'Oh I think that it's you who do yourself a disservice now,' he said. 'What do you think, Prion, as an impartial observer of this conversation?'

Prion's answer was immediate, and confident. 'Whichever side had Milton Trayx as commander in chief of its forces would have won.'

Jamie gave a short laugh. 'I would say that depended on the odds.'

Prion turned slowly to face Jamie. 'Then,' he said levelly, 'you are privy to information that I am not.'

'Yes, well be that as it may,' the Doctor said quickly, 'there is one other question I should like to ask.'

'Yes.' Victoria guessed that this was the same question she herself had. 'Why does he wear that mask? Is it a part of the punishment?'

Trayx did not answer immediately. Instead he stood up. Helana reached out her hand to him as he walked slowly past her chair. He took it, caressed it for a moment, then let it go as he went over to the fireplace. He carefully set down his wine on the wide mantel shelf, and turned back to face the table. He was standing close to one of the flickering lights, and Victoria could see that Trayx's eyes were moist.

'After his trial,' Trayx said, 'Kesar was taken away to await deportation.' Somewhere beneath Trayx's words was a well of suppressed emotion. 'He was in the corridor, on his way out under guard when –' He broke off, pausing for a moment before he continued. 'It was a bomb, something laced with a huge amount of Zenon VII. It caught us in the confined space, but Kesar and his guards took the brunt of it.'

'Zenon VII,' the Doctor said quietly, 'is a powerful incendiary. It burns hotter than molten lava.'

'The guards were killed outright,' Trayx was saying. 'None of them stood a chance. But somehow Kesar held on to life.

Despite the burns.' Trayx took a deep breath. 'The flesh was stripped from his face. His vocal cords melted, the heat was so intense.' He turned back to face the fire, head leaning forward so that it rested on his arm on the mantel.

'So, he was lucky to survive,' Jamie said.

'No.' Trayx's voice was mumbled through his sleeve. 'I do not think so.' He turned back to them, his face and voice as composed as ever. 'You will recall what I said about making a martyr of him. It is we who are lucky.'

There was silence for a while. Then the Doctor stood up. 'Thank you for the meal, Consul,' he said. Trayx waved a hand in acknowledgment. 'Now perhaps Prion could show my friends back to their rooms? They are rather tired after our ordeals.'

Trayx nodded to Prion.

'What about you, Doctor?' Jamie asked. 'Are you not joining us?'

The Doctor bustled Jamie and Victoria in the direction of the main door. 'I'll be with you soon,' he said. 'I just want to try some of that excellent wine. That is,' he added, raising his voice, 'if Consul Trayx doesn't mind the company?'

'I am always glad of intelligent company, Doctor,' Trayx said. 'And I think there are several matters we have yet to discuss.'

'Yes indeed,' the Doctor said with a laugh. 'Now run along, you two and we'll sort out all the boring stuff.'

'Well, if you're sure, Doctor,' said Victoria.

'Quite sure, thank you, Victoria.'

Behind them, Helana was also on her feet. 'I shall leave you to your important matters,' she told her husband. She had to stand on tiptoe in order to kiss him gently on the cheek. Then she turned and swept out of the room. Several of the guards, stoically impassive during the breakfast conversations, leaned forward slightly to watch her as she passed.

Victoria and Jamie were still in the other doorway. 'Come on,' Jamie said quietly. 'It's clear he wants us out of the way.'

Victoria nodded. She turned to look at Prion, standing patiently beside them. His face seemed somehow too balanced, his eyes piercing blue and his complexion pale and smooth. 'Perhaps you can tell us about this castle,' she said to him. 'The decor and the architecture are fascinating.'

'Aye,' came Jamie's sarcastic murmur as he followed them out of the Banqueting Hall. 'Fascinating.'

Somewhere in the velvet blackness of the ninth sector, a tiny light gleamed alone in the dark. The vague light of a distant star system shone faintly on the gunmetal fuselage of the craft as it continued on its preset course.

Within the craft, readings were constantly checked against flight tables and navigation charts. Weapons systems constantly ran integrity checks, as untiring and ceaselessly patient as the ship's occupants.

On the main screen, the Commander watched through cold unblinking vision inputs as a small luminous blip showed the ship's position along its planned flight path. The path itself was an arcing line of brilliant white, cutting across solar systems and making minor concessions for a black hole in its mechanistically efficient track towards its target.

As soon as the Doctor asked about the surveillance system, Trayx had motioned him to silence and dismissed the guards.

'So,' the Doctor said when they were alone in the hall, 'not everyone knows that they are observed and monitored the whole time.'

Trayx smiled thinly. 'If only that were the case, Doctor.' He drained his wine and set the goblet down on the table. 'The reality is far from the promise of the systems when they were installed. Just as the reason for it is now but a slight excuse.'

'Yes, I gather you're having some problems.'

'The system's on its last legs. Nearly half of the cameras have packed up, and the microphones would have us believe that most rooms in this fortress are filled with hiss and static.' He shook his head. 'In truth, we rarely use the surveillance systems now. It never really worked anyway. Only the Warden, myself and a few others officially know of it, though everyone else has guessed by now. And even with the expert systems that filter the input so that we only need to see and hear certain portions of life within these walls, there is too much data for us to assimilate.'

'And what,' the Doctor asked, 'is that data for?'

'The intention was to keep Kesar and his men under surveillance in case they planned to escape, to send for help or try to foster support among the garrison.'

'And I take it you never expected they would.'

Trayx shook his head. 'An overcautious approach forced on us by a paranoid oversight committee of the Senate,' he said. 'But Consul Mathesohn and his cronies are terrified that Kesar will escape and rally his forces against them.'

'You don't share his concern?' the Doctor asked.

Trayx laughed, a short humourless burst of sound.

'But now,' the Doctor went on, 'there has been a murder. Was that captured on your surveillance system?' He stepped up to Trayx, looked up at the tall man. 'Is that why you are so convinced that we are not to blame?'

Trayx looked down at the Doctor. He seemed to consider

for a moment. Then he said, 'I don't know who you are, Doctor. I don't know where you come from. I don't know your name even. And I confess that I am expecting a stranger to appear here. That is why I have come. But I do not think that you are he.'

'No?'

Trayx shook his head. 'No. But despite your improbable appearance and your incredible story of how you arrived,' he said, 'for some reason I trust you.'

The Doctor laughed, his face becoming one huge grin as his mouth stretched and his eyebrows rose. 'Oh, thank you.'

'Come with me,' Trayx said, suddenly turning on his heel and striding towards the door.

'With you? Where to?'

He paused in the doorway. 'To watch a murder,' he said.

*

Jamie was bored. He wandered listlessly round the room, only half listening to what Prion was telling Victoria about Kesar and Trayx and their background history. He felt he should be doing something, although he was not sure what. But there was a murder to solve and probably several other mysteries that the Doctor had identified lurking below the surface.

And now the Doctor was off somewhere with Trayx, and he was left with Victoria and Prion – who seemed set to lecture them on Haddron history for the next hour or more.

'Whereas Trayx joined the military,' Prion was saying, 'Kesar stood for public office and built his career along political lines. He was governor of a minor colony, but won a reputation for political acumen and perspicacity. Trayx meanwhile commanded the Second Legion at Tolokabad, and that was enough to secure his promotion to general.'

'Tolokabad was a battle?' Victoria asked.

'A great battle,' Prion replied as if reading from a book. 'Lieutenant Milton Trayx took command of the legion and had his colonel arrested for dishonouring Haddron when he tried to retreat. Tolokabad was a frontier post. It came under siege from the Mezzanyre Hordes. The legion was outnumbered five to one and it was obvious that the post would fall.'

'So what happened?' Jamie asked, interested despite himself. Battles and wars were something he could understand in this world of paradoxes and contradictions.

'Trayx attacked the Hordes' lead ship with the last of his frigates. The death of their leader in this attack left the Hordes in disarray. Trayx kept his forces focused and disciplined despite the odds. The enemy was routed and the hold of the Mezzanyre in the quadrant was broken for ever.' There was no hint of pride or satisfaction in Prion's voice as he spoke, and Jamie could imagine the similarly disciplined troops under Trayx marching forward against their terrified enemy. 'Trayx was promoted to general immediately. Within three years he was General in Chief. His election as Consul was a formality.'

The Observation Room was a distinct contrast to the medieval splendour of the rest of the fortress. The whole area was jammed full of technology. One wall was lined from floor to ceiling with monitor screens showing flickering images of life within the fortress. Digital recording devices stretched along another wall, while the computer that hosted the expert monitoring system stood, as plain as it was efficient, in a corner. Cables that had once been fixed in place had broken free of their brackets and trailed in snakes down the walls and across the floor, looping in and out of the functional furniture.

The Doctor watched as Trayx and Warden Mithrael adjusted various controls.

Mithrael tapped one of the monitors. 'I'll relay the recording to this one.'

Trayx and the Doctor both watched intently as the image on the screen changed from an empty corridor into a darkened room. As they watched, a cloaked figure stepped from the shadows, its face hidden beneath the cowl of the heavy cloak it wore. The camera tracked the movement carefully, the picture sharpening and brightening as the systems adjusted for the dim light. For the briefest moment, as the figure turned slightly, his face became visible. The picture froze, the features of the man smeared across the screen.

'I've programmed it to hold at that point,' Mithrael said quietly. 'As you can see, it's Remas.'

'The dead man?'

'Yes, Doctor.'

'Go on,' Trayx said, and Mithrael punched a key on the console in front of him.

The figure completed its turn, face once more obscured. Then another shadowy figure entered from the corridor. The figure's movements were rapid and controlled. The man – if it was a man beneath the dark cloak – stepped in front of the camera and raised his hand. A small metal object in the gloved hand gleamed for a moment in the flickering light. Then the image abruptly exploded into a storm of static and white noise.

The Doctor tapped his chin thoughtfully. 'I assume you know who was in this fortress at the time.'

'We're not sure exactly when you arrived,' Trayx said, 'but otherwise, yes.'

'And how do you know that's not one of us?'

Mithrael laughed. 'You'd have to be walking with bricks strapped to your shoes for one thing.'

'And for another,' Trayx said, 'we have studied your reactions and comments when you found the body.'

'Playing for the camera?' the Doctor suggested.

'I don't think so. You might be up to that, but the boy and the young woman…' Trayx shook his head. 'I think not.'

'So the question is,' the Doctor said, 'who remains unaccounted for at that time?'

'And the answer,' Trayx said, 'is that nobody is unaccounted for.'

The Doctor was somehow seated where Mithrael had been a moment earlier, examining the controls and playing back the recording once more. 'I thought you said only about half the cameras are working.'

'That's true,' Mithrael answered. 'But we can eliminate those in direct sight, and the expert system can track the positions of others by where they leave surveillance and where and when they re-enter it.'

'Plus it was at night,' Trayx said. 'All Kesar's men are locked within the Secure Area at night. Given the cameras that do still function, we know which corridors the murderer must have traversed to arrive at the scene unnoticed.'

'And you can eliminate everyone who could get to those corridors?'

'Everyone.'

'By direct sight?'

'Yes,' Mithrael said.

'No,' Trayx corrected him. 'Not quite. But good enough. Show him.'

Mithrael leaned over the Doctor's shoulder and operated a control. 'This isn't all of them, but here are a couple of examples of the way the system has eliminated some of those out of direct line of sight.'

The image on the screen switched to a high-angle view of a kitchen area. There was nobody in sight, but the noise of pans crashing together could be heard above the sound of someone whistling.

'The galley chef,' Mithrael explained, 'preparing breakfast. He is out of vision for ten minutes around the time of the murder. But he can be heard the whole while.'

'And,' Trayx said, 'the only exits from that area necessitate his crossing the camera's line of sight.'

'Which he did not do.'

Mithrael leaned forward again. 'There are several similar examples,' he said. 'Some of the sleeping areas and all the personal washrooms are not monitored, but typically have only one door, which is covered.'

The screen changed again. This time it showed the masked figure of Kesar, standing beside a chessboard. The board floated in the air before him, shimmering slightly even on the camera image, so that it was obvious that it did not really exist in a physical sense.

'The camera in Cruger's study is not operational,' Mithrael explained. 'But from his console there he is playing chess against Kesar. They do this most nights.'

The Doctor examined the image on the screen. 'And does Kesar always win?' he asked. 'It looks like he has the upper hand.'

'He usually wins,' Trayx said.

'In this case,' Mithrael said as he switched off the image, 'Cruger refused to submit. He played on well after it was obvious he would lose.'

'He is stubborn and proud,' Trayx said.

'That may be,' the Doctor said quietly. 'But you're still left with the problem that someone here is a murderer.' He stood up and stretched. 'Have you considered the motive?'

'This murder is something of a mystery,' Trayx admitted. 'But I believe the ultimate goal of our killer is to assassinate Hans Kesar.'

CHAPTER FIVE
PREPARED VARIATION

The images from the screens sent shadows skitting across the Doctor's face as he turned towards Milton Trayx. 'Is that why you're here?' he asked quietly.

Trayx nodded. 'As I have already said, Doctor, I cannot allow Kesar to die.'

'But you have reason to believe that there are others who do not share your concerns.'

Trayx pulled up one of the chairs and sat down. 'There have already been three attempts on Kesar's life since he was sent here.'

Mithrael coughed politely. 'Four, sir.'

Trayx shrugged. 'Whatever. They daren't kill him outright. Or at least, not until now.'

'So what has changed?'

'Perhaps nothing but their bravado and confidence. But there are rumours that supporters of Kesar are once again trying to build a power base. There is growing dissent at home, an increasing concern that Haddron is faltering, is ailing and sick. Economically, that's not far from the truth. The civil war cost us more dearly than the men and munitions that were expended, cut deeper than the personal losses. Economically, we are on the verge of collapse. Many people now see Hans Kesar as the only person with the ambition, the drive and the personality to lead us through the crisis.'

'So Kesar is rallying his supporters again?' The Doctor nodded – it seemed likely.

'Not Kesar,' Trayx said quietly. 'He knows it is over. But some of his allies…'

'And his enemies are more afraid of this growing support than they are of creating a martyr.'

Trayx nodded. 'I'm afraid that we may end up with both, the one fuelling the other.'

'Until now,' Mithrael said, 'their attempts on Kesar's life have been surreptitious. An apparent accident here, a possible mishap there. En route to this fortress, the cruiser bringing Kesar was almost hit by an asteroid. The asteroid had signs of fusion burns on the obverse side.'

'As if someone had blasted it out of its previous position and sent it into the path of the ship,' Trayx finished. 'More imaginative, though rather less subtle, was when they fused a layer of amphesite into the optical discs of a history gazette Kesar receives each month.'

The Doctor frowned. 'Nasty,' he said, wrinkling his nose at the thought. Amphesite was a mild poison. In small doses it was undetectable, but prolonged exposure to it as it evaporated from between the layers of the disc would bring on first mild paralysis, and then brain damage and death.

'But now they are getting desperate,' Trayx continued. 'I too have my sources of information. And while I don't yet have enough proof to impeach Mathesohn and the others I suspect –' He broke off, the shadow of a smile on his lips. 'I don't suspect, Doctor. I know. But I don't yet have proof. And my sources tell me that these latest rumours have driven them to take extreme measures.'

'They've sent an assassin,' the Doctor said.

Trayx nodded. 'So I am told. Whether he was here already

or has somehow been shipped in, I don't know. But the death of Remas, at such a time...'

'It's no coincidence,' the Doctor agreed. He cleared his throat and steepled his fingers, resting his elbows on the arms of the chair. 'And what makes you so sure that my friends and I are not the assassins?' As he started to speak, one of his elbows slipped off the armrest, pulling his interlocked hands down as well. He finished speaking while hunched awkwardly to one side, as if hoping they wouldn't notice.

Mithrael looked at Trayx, and he nodded. The Warden reached round the Doctor, who was trying to disentangle his fingers, sit upright, and turn to see what Mithrael was up to all at the same time. The Warden touched a control and the main screen shimmered into life once more.

The image on the screen was of the suite of rooms allocated to the Doctor and his companions. Jamie was lying on a bed, Victoria sitting at a desk nearby. The Doctor was wandering seemingly aimlessly through the rooms. Several other screens were now showing other aspects of the same scene.

'Ah,' the Doctor mused as he watched himself brandish a handful of handkerchiefs.

They watched as the Doctor tore down the tapestry and held it over a patch of wall. As the Doctor scampered round the room with his hankies, other screens blanked out, until only the main view – a high shot of the room – remained. It gave a good view of the Doctor's acrobatics from the chair on the bed as he tried to pitch a handkerchief over the camera concealed in the chandelier.

'What are you implying?' the Doctor asked when his antics finally ended with the last camera blanking out.

'No disrespect, Doctor,' Trayx said, failing to conceal his

smile, 'but I know the people I am up against. Their assassin will be a consummate professional.'

'Oh?'

'And we know he has a device which induces an apparent fault in the surveillance system.'

'Ah,' the Doctor latched on to this. 'You're saying that I wouldn't be stupid enough to have held it up in front of the camera for everyone to see.'

'I'm saying you would have used that in your own rooms, perhaps selectively to establish a safe zone, rather than indulge in these rather obvious manoeuvres.'

'Oh, well,' the Doctor said glumly, 'I suppose that's all right then. I thought for a moment there that you were implying we weren't terribly professional.'

Trayx coughed. 'Nonsense, Doctor. I can already see that you are at the very least a gifted amateur.'

The Doctor turned suddenly, his eyes meeting Trayx's with an intensity that made the General in Chief blink. There was a remarkable depth to the Doctor's gaze that somehow had been absent just moments earlier. His voice too had acquired an edge as he said quietly, 'No, I am not a gifted amateur, as you put it. Rather I am an absolute professional in fields that your people do not yet even count among the professions.' Then just as suddenly the depth and the seriousness were gone. The Doctor's eyes seemed to mist over, and his mouth turned down slightly. 'But I think you had made your mind up before my shenanigans with the cameras, hadn't you?'

'I must confess, my instincts told me when I spoke with the girl, Victoria, that you were unlikely to cause us undue trouble.' Trayx stood up. 'And you have already passed up a near perfect opportunity to kill Kesar when you were alone with him and Cruger.'

'So I take it we really are your guests, then.'

Trayx smiled, motioning Mithrael to open the door. 'Let me give you a short tour of Santespri, Doctor,' he said.

The Doctor leapt to his feet. 'Oh yes,' he said enthusiastically, 'I shall enjoy that.' He rubbed his hands together in anticipation as he followed Trayx from the Observation Room.

It seemed to Jamie as if they were some sort of exhibit. Several guards had looked in on them in the last hour, and soon after Prion had left them in peace Cruger had appeared in the doorway. He dismissed his guard, as if the man were there for Cruger's own benefit rather than as his captor, and introduced himself.

But if Cruger was more interested in Jamie and Victoria than in himself, he hid it well. After a few polite questions about who they were and where they were from, he appeared to grow bored with their predicament and want to talk about his own.

'Of course,' Cruger was saying, 'if it weren't for Senator Mathesohn's surreptitious manipulation of events there would have been no war.' He leaned forward slightly, his eyes narrowing, and Jamie guessed he was looking for some response from either himself or Victoria. Jamie stifled a yawn.

'You know Mathesohn, of course,' Cruger went on, still looking intently from one of them to the other.

'No,' Jamie said.

'I'm afraid we don't know anything about your world,' Victoria said. 'We're travellers, as we told you.'

Cruger leaned back, smiling. 'Of course,' he said quietly. 'So you said.' He smiled. 'Travellers who appear from nowhere, and will no doubt evaporate like the Fifth Legion when your business here is done.'

Again Jamie sensed an undercurrent, that Cruger was fishing for some reaction. And Jamie was getting bored and fed up with it. 'Look,' he said loudly, 'we've no business here. We arrived by accident, and we'll soon be on our way. That's all there is to it.'

Cruger's hands were spread wide, his face a mask of apology. 'I'm so sorry,' he said in apparent surprise. 'I meant no ill.'

'That's all right, General,' Victoria said. But Jamie could tell from the slightly high pitch of her voice that she was annoyed with the man too.

'Please, call me Cruger. I can't say I care for it more than the respectful use of my proper title, but everyone here calls me Cruger. It is a way of defusing the otherwise embarrassing fact that I outrank my captors.'

'Except for Trayx,' Jamie pointed out.

'Ah, but like you he is merely visiting,' Cruger said. Suddenly he was animated, jabbing his finger at Jamie. 'Nobody outranks Trayx. That is another of the embarrassments of this whole affair.'

'Oh?' Victoria asked.

'Oh yes, Miss Waterfield. While Hans Kesar languishes in his incarceration here, Milton Trayx is Emperor in all but name.' He laughed, though there was precious little humour in the sound. 'So the great Republican takes the place of the mighty Emperor.'

'Not so mighty,' Jamie pointed out. 'He lost the war.'

Cruger shrugged. 'Battle is but one of the games of state. I'll tell you this.' He was stabbing the air again. 'If Kesar had won the war, as he should have done, he could have held Haddron together. We should have a strong Empire, forged out of blood, sweat and tears. But instead? We have a weak Republican who cannot dare to assume the authority that needs to be exerted. We have Mathesohn and his allies desperate for another civil war to rend our territories apart and reopen barely sealed wounds. The coalition is inadequate to the task, too disjointed to wield the power needed to bring the people, the empire – yes I call it that – together again.' The emotion was straining at Cruger's face as he spoke, the passion spat out with his words. 'We all know there is only one man who can save Haddron now. That's what Trayx refuses to accept, that's what Mathesohn is scared almost to death of admitting. And that is the supreme irony. When we need him most, Kesar is left to rot in this forsaken place.'

Jamie looked at Victoria, unsure quite what to say to this. From Victoria's expression, she was none the wiser. But before either of them could say anything, Cruger stood up and walked to the door.

'But what is all this to you?' he asked, his tone as sarcastic as the sneer that he now wore. 'You are travellers who know nothing of our problems, and who care even less.' Then he turned, and was gone. The sound of his boots rang on the stone floor of the corridor, receding into the distance. It was joined by the noise of the guard's heavy footsteps, running to catch up with his prisoner.

The sight of a myriad stars unobscured by the atmosphere of a planet was not a new one to the Doctor. But even so, he found himself gazing up in awe as Trayx led him across the walkway between two of the high towers on the rim of the fortress. Behind them, the ragged rock of the asteroid was a dark cliff that melded with the blackness of space. But the sight forward, over the battlements, was as spectacular as anything the Doctor had seen. This was not a view through the thick glass of a small porthole in some rusting space station. Here they were out among the stars themselves, able to see the intricate colours on the edge of each dot of light, to discern the gradations in the rings around the nearby planet, to appreciate the silent emptiness of the void together with the majestic glory of the light that shone through the heavens above and before them.

'It's quite a view,' Trayx said quietly as the Doctor paused to look out over the ramparts. 'I never tire of it.'

'Do you often visit this place?' the Doctor asked.

'Not often enough. There is far too much to be done at home.'

'Magnificent,' the Doctor murmured. 'Magnificent.' He pointed to a distant speck of light. 'Is that Praxis Minima? I seem to recognise the red shift at its anterior.'

'You are interested in the stars and their courses?' Trayx was beside the Doctor now, leaning over the battlements with him. Below them, on a lower walkway, two guards exchanged words, beyond their earshot and oblivious to their commander on the upper level.

'I have some small expertise in the matter,' the Doctor admitted, 'and an interest, yes.'

Trayx clapped him on the shoulder so hard that his chest was pushed against the stone of the rampart. He winced, trying not to cough too obviously.

'Then I have something to show you, Doctor,' Trayx was saying. 'Something I think will appeal to your intellect as well as your sense of wonder.'

On the lower walkway, Darkling whispered to Haden. He knew there were microphones and cameras. Even if he had not been told, he could have guessed. What he did not know was whether the surveillance system could see and hear him at the moment. So he whispered, as if that would make any material difference.

'Which of the stars shall I bring you?' he asked her quietly.

Haden's laugh was as muted. She knew why he was whispering. She might have been on Santespri for only a few weeks, but already Darkling had told her almost everything he knew about the place. He had been assigned to show her around when she was transferred from the Frastis Penal Centre to replace another of Kesar's guards who had died in a loading-bay accident. There was a tortuous logic to having a Republican show round a new Imperial prisoner. The notion was that there would be little love lost between soldiers from opposing sides.

In fact, there was a camaraderie between the two garrisons that belied the function of the fortress. With the war over, there was little thought for recrimination among the military. They dealt with what *was*, not what might have been. And Darkling had taken immediately to the new young woman as he showed her around Santespri. Since that day they had both angled for duties together.

Darkling looked at her again, letting his eyes wander over her round, open face. He stared at her short hair, parted on the side as she pulled off her helmet, adjusted the chin strap and then replaced it. They were both wearing combat fatigues rather than full battle armour. The heavy blast-plating could be strapped over the fatigues in under three minutes should it prove necessary. There was a certain protocol to wearing full armour within the fortress, but out on the battlements there was an unwritten and largely unspoken agreement that the duty patrol could dispense with the armour. It was one way of getting volunteers for the most tedious and least necessary watch.

Darkling watched as Haden continued her own beat to the far end of the battlements, his eyes lingering on her perfect pacing and slight swagger. He watched the way her trousers bent smoothly with her leg as it flexed; how the fabric curved round her hips and her thighs.

Haden swung round at the far end, facing Darkling again. She smiled as he turned to resume his own patrol. And in that moment he was again struck with the familiarity of her face. Again he felt that he had seen her somewhere before. But where?

They had both been at Tembraka, he knew that. They had spoken about it several times, about the battle, about the noise, about the strategies of their commanders. They had been on opposite sides, of course, but that merely lent an edge to their reminiscences.

Each had their memories of the battle tainted. Darkling because he had been on the losing side. That time. Haden, he knew, remembered the battle not for the victory of Kesar's troops, but because of her own loss. Her brother had died at Tembraka.

The Stardial Chamber always had an effect on Trayx. In truth, it was the one reason why Santespri had been maintained during the empty years when it had lain all but neglected, before the civil war. The fortress was now far from the frontier it had originally been built to defend, lying alone and strategically irrelevant well within the borders of Haddron space. But the Stardial Chamber had set it apart from a dozen other similar outposts, all of which were now forgotten ruins.

The Chamber occupied the whole of the top half of the largest of Santespri's three massive towers. The size of the room alone was impressive, as Trayx was reminded when he threw open the massive wooden doors and gestured for the Doctor to enter.

'Oh, thank you.' The Doctor bobbed his head in a parody

of a bow as he edged past Trayx and entered the chamber.

He stopped dead on the threshold, his gasp of awed astonishment easily audible.

The room was huge, but it was not just its size that held the Doctor in awe. The walls were a mass of tubes, rods and cables which laced together high above the floor, forming a tangle of web work. Above this web, the top of the tower appeared open to space. Starlight glanced off the intricate mechanisms, glinting through the thick glass that focused it on to the inlaid marble floor of the chamber.

'You're impressed.'

The Doctor turned. Or at least, his body made a slight effort to turn back towards Trayx. His attention remained firmly on the room he now stepped into. 'I am. Yes, indeed.' He was looking all around as he walked slowly towards the centre of the floor. He laughed out loud, clapping his hands together and seemingly about to dance a jig on the spot. 'Oh, my goodness gracious me.' He exhaled loudly and ran into the room. He threw his arms open wide, turning a full circle in the middle of the chamber, all the while staring up at the top of the tower high above him.

Trayx joined the Doctor at the centre of the room. 'It had a similar effect on me when I first saw it,' he admitted. 'And it was a ruin then. Now it's been restored... Well, you can see for yourself.'

'I can.' The Doctor was nodding his head rapidly. 'I do. It's magnificent.' He beamed at Trayx. 'Thank you for showing me this,' he said. His voice was quiet and sincere, his eyes smiling. 'I've rarely seen anything quite like it.'

Trayx frowned. 'Rarely?'

But the Doctor seemed oblivious to Trayx's concern. 'Oh yes, very rarely. Of course,' he confided in a hushed tone, 'the real trick would be to fit it all into a small, blue wooden box. But we can't have everything, can we?' He nodded again. 'Oh yes, this is very impressive indeed.' He coughed, the sound echoing slightly in the huge chamber. 'Er, what is it? Exactly?'

Trayx shook his head and laughed. 'You know, Doctor, I am never quite sure when you are being serious.'

'I have that problem myself,' the Doctor replied quietly.

Trayx looked about him, wondering where to begin his explanation. In a sense, the room was an observatory. In another sense, it was a clock. Though in truth it was neither of these. The walls were lined with the rods and cables that came together high over their heads to form a latticework structure that broke the space above into quadrants. And it *was* space, for the top of the tower appeared open to the sky above. Actually, a massive lens was fitted into the tower in place of its roof, focusing the light of the stars above and beyond into the latticework so that it formed a condensed map of the space outside Santespri. The result was a sort of double image, with the actual stars visible dimly behind the focused points of light that represented them against the lattice.

The lattice itself was harnessed to the drive system. The drive system was an arrangement of cog wheels and gears that sprawled across the huge curved expanse of the tower wall. Even as Trayx struggled to explain the underlying principles to the Doctor, a cog clicked round one notch and the arrangement of the latticework above them changed, reconfigured to catch up with the progress of the stars within it.

'You measure time with this?' the Doctor asked as he watched the interlaced beams and girders shuffle their positions and click into new ones.

Trayx nodded. 'It's possible, though nobody would ever

come to this room merely to check their watch.' He broke off as he realised that the Doctor had pulled a gold pocket watch from within his battered coat and was shaking it. A thick chain attached the watch to somewhere indiscernible within the coat, though Trayx noticed that as the Doctor moved the watch and pulled the chain tight, so one leg of his checked trousers twitched in apparent sympathy.

'I take it there are no hands as such,' the Doctor was saying. 'More like a sundial, I suppose.'

'Yes, indeed.' Trayx pointed to the markings on the floor, and the Doctor jumped a foot in the air as if he had only just noticed them.

The floor was lined with polished black marble. The focused lights of the stars was reflected again in the floor, the depth of the stone making it seem as if they were lamps embedded in the floor itself. Inlaid in the centre of the circular floor was a seven-pointed star. Lines of polished white stone radiated from the points of the star, cutting through the three concentric circles that also rippled out from the star, as if it had been dropped into the tower and the shockwave recorded for ever in differing colours of marble. Each ring was divided into sectors by short markings across it, spaced evenly around the circle. The inner circle was cobalt blue, then saffron yellow for the middle ring. The outermost circle was marked off along its edge with dagger-like markings. It was blood red against the jet black.

'The points of the star,' Trayx explained, 'point to the postulated seven corners of the universe. The rings are each marked off in sidereal time drawn from the relative movements of different stars within the Haddron Republic.'

The Doctor considered this, tapping his watch to his chin as he followed the middle ring right round its course. All the while he studied the markings and lights on the floor in front of him. When he got back to where he had started he turned to Trayx. 'So what time is it?' he asked.

Trayx shrugged. 'I have no idea,' he admitted. 'The time is marked for every major city under Haddron rule. At least, those under Haddron rule when this chamber was built. Several have since ceded. Several others have tried and as a result are no longer cities of the same stature.'

'The great empire not quite what it once was?'

'The *Republic* is in good health.'

The Doctor grunted as if he did not entirely believe this, then turned his attention back to the air above them. 'You use the power, of course,' he said suddenly, describing circles in the air with his finger. 'That's how this Stardial works, I take it.' Without waiting for an answer, he went on. 'And to be able to plot the time in every major city means that every major star within the Republic must be visible in the heavens from this point. Correct?'

'Yes, that's right. Santespri is angled so it looks back in towards Haddron. When the fortress was built we were on the outer rim of Haddron territory.'

'And the power?'

'Yes, I believe the light that is focused here from the stars outside is somehow harnessed to drive the mechanisms within this chamber.'

The Doctor stared at him, open-mouthed. 'But only within this chamber?' he asked. 'You don't use it for anything else?'

Trayx was at a loss to understand what the man meant. 'Such as?'

'Well, to provide essential power for the rest of the fortress. Heating, lighting, life support.' The Doctor was waving his hands as if he could shake the ideas into Trayx's head. 'Cooking the dinner,' he finished in an exasperated squawk.

'I imagine the mechanism of the dial itself takes most of the collected power.'

'Really?' The Doctor seemed disappointed with the answer. 'Well, it can't be very efficient then, can it? The potential energy locked up in the solar emissions must be enormous. To say nothing of the cosmic rays and radiant heat.'

'I'm sorry, Doctor,' Trayx said quietly. 'I know little of such matters. But I do know that this room is one of the most awe-inspiring sights I have ever seen.'

The Doctor was smiling again. His voice had returned to its softer, almost lazy tone. 'I think so too,' he said. 'It's a marvellous place.'

Darkling watched Haden turn again at the end of the walkway. Yet again he was struck by a distant familiarity.

And at that moment, caught in mid-step under the open starlit sky of Santespri, his heart almost bursting with admiration – or perhaps something more – Darkling felt the blood run to ice in his veins. He was back at Tembraka, the smoke of the battle embracing him as he strode forward through the mud and guts. Then suddenly, it was pulled away leaving a corridor between him and the enemy. The sides of the corridor were glowing smoke, the diffuse light illuminating the path he trod, and shining on the figure in front of him.

The figure was looking down at the ground, picking its way carefully over the shattered remains of the attack units and the torn bodies of the dead. The man's armour was scarred and dented. But the insignia on his shoulder was clearly visible as he looked up. As he saw Darkling. As he raised the fusion blaster.

Darkling's attention was on the man's face, his blackened

and bloodied face, as he relived the moment. One moment among many. One death out of a hundred. A thousand.

And he saw it. It was in the man's stance. It was in his expression as he turned to face Darkling. It was in the set of his jaw as he noticed his enemy. It was in the way he fought to bring the gun up in time.

It was in his eyes as Darkling fired first.

Then it was gone, blown away by the same breeze that rolled the smoke back into place. Blown away by the still-echoing blast that hurled the man backward into the smoke, and a corpse into the mud behind him.

Her brother.

He was sure. Well, he was almost sure.

It was possible.

And Haden was still smiling at him, frozen where he was, as she started back along the battlements towards him. In his mind's eye, the smoke of the battlefield rolled away from her as she walked.

Perhaps she mistook the moisture in his eyes, misread the way his jaw quivered, misunderstood the emotion welling within him. She caught his arm as she passed, pulled him after her into the shadow of the wall, pulled him towards her in the half-light of the stars.

Darkling shook his head as she pulled off her helmet. 'No,' he muttered. 'No, don't.'

She was still smiling. She cocked her head slightly to one side. 'If not now,' she said quietly, 'then when?' Her voice was husky and dry. She dropped her helmet, reaching for his, drawing it over his head.

He wanted to say something. To tell her. But he wasn't sure. It was a possibility, that was all. And did it change anything? What was done was done. They both knew that. They both had lives where only the moment counted, where death might wait quietly behind any doorway or in any smile. 'The cameras,' he muttered. 'We don't know if –'

She put her finger to his lips. 'Then make it look good,' she said as she removed her finger and pulled him towards her.

The Stardial Chamber held less fascination for Helana Trayx than it did for her husband. But she knew how it affected him, and was not at all surprised to find he had brought the Doctor here. She watched the two of them as they walked round the chamber, their enthusiasm obvious from their animated and intent manner. She said nothing until their tour of the outer circle brought the Doctor and Trayx back to the doorway where she waited.

'I thought I would find you in here,' she said quietly. She had not expected her husband to show any surprise at her quiet presence, but she was intrigued that the Doctor also seemed unmoved. She smiled at them both, and went on, 'My husband has a certain fascination with this place that I am afraid I do not share.'

'Fascination?' the Doctor mused. 'Yes, I can see that.' He cleared his throat. 'So what does fascinate you, Mrs Trayx?'

'Helana, please,' she offered, by way of avoiding the question. If the truth be told, she believed herself beyond fascination. Helana had been young and naive when her marriage to Milton Trayx was agreed. She was besotted with him – her very own heroic knight – but she could not truthfully say she had been in love. But the fact that he had loved her was never in doubt. Right from their first meeting, at one of her father's political soirées, Trayx had been madly and obviously in love with Helana. She had been present largely against her will to lend an air of social refinement to an evening that was unashamedly political. And since neither she nor Trayx had any interest in the polities, they had naturally graduated to the same still point in the room. She had been immediately entranced, and he had fallen in love for the first and probably the only time in his life.

Since the marriage was good for both families, there had been no objection to the match. In fact, the encouragement their courtship engendered ensured an early – perhaps too early – marriage. Already Helana was beginning to realise that her fascination with Trayx was as much because of his differences from the people she was used to as for his own attributes. Helana found she had an equal fixation with many of Trayx's friends and colleagues. In particular, her attraction to Trayx's best friend – to Hans Kesar – went beyond mere fascination.

But the war had ended the affair. When her husband and Kesar were friends and colleagues, meeting Kesar had been as straightforward as it was exhilarating. But with the advent of the war, two things changed. First her access to Kesar was suddenly impossible. And second, she realised that much of Kesar's appeal was his similarity to Milton Trayx, was the fact that in effect he offered her more of the same.

It came to her one evening. She was alone in her bedroom, sitting in front of her dressing table brushing her long blonde hair. Trayx was away, away at the war. Perhaps fighting at that moment. Perhaps dying at that moment. As she watched herself, she became slowly aware that she was paying more attention to the bedroom door reflected behind her. She was hoping it would open, was willing it to open. To open and admit Trayx. And she was crying.

Trayx was away, and she had no idea where. She knew only that he was in the gravest danger, that the future of the whole Republic was vested in her husband. She knew that more than anything she wanted him there with her, wanted his arms around her, wanted to feel his breath on her cheek and the back of her neck. With her lover and her husband thrown into sudden violent opposition, Helana Trayx was amazed and elated to discover the true depth of her love for her husband.

Coming to Santespri was in many ways the culmination of that realisation. Trayx had never before let her accompany him, but this time she had insisted. There were things she had to finish. And she wanted them finished. Apart from her desire to be with her husband as much as possible, never to let him leave her again if she could avoid it, she had another mission. A part of her life was over, and she needed to bring it to proper closure. And to do that she needed to see Hans Kesar again. Alone.

She became aware that both Trayx and the Doctor were still looking at her, still expecting an answer. She shrugged. 'I admit this place is impressive.'

The Doctor seemed to watch her intently for a moment. Then he was suddenly spinning on his heels and striding off into the middle of the huge chamber. 'Well, what fascinates me,' he said, his voice carrying across the room with a power that belied its gentle tone, 'is the way that star is moving.'

'All the stars move,' Trayx replied.

'Ah, but this one is moving out of alignment.'

'Are you sure?' Trayx was moving to join the Doctor now, and Helana found herself following him.

'Of course I'm sure,' the Doctor almost snapped back. He pointed to a space above them. 'It was over there, part of that cluster. Now it's moved.'

'Maybe it's not part of that cluster at all. The sky is three-dimensional of course. That star could be –' Trayx stopped as he saw the Doctor's expression.

'Thank you, I do know a little about stellar cartography.'

His face softened. 'No, no, no. The refraction of the light, the amount of bleed round the edges suggests that it is a small reflective surface somewhere between us and the cluster. It isn't a star at all.' He pointed to the current position of the tiny dot. 'It's moving fairly constantly. And it's getting bigger.' Then he dropped to his knees, a magnifying glass suddenly in his hand as he studied the marble floor. 'We should be able to see the path it's taking more clearly down here,' he said. 'Could you move over a bit, madam, you're blocking the light. Ah, yes. Thank you.'

To Helana's amazement, Trayx was also on his knees examining the floor. 'A ship?'

The Doctor nodded. 'A big ship. A very big ship.'

'Could be a cruiser.'

'And I would say that it's coming this way. Look.' The Doctor crawled across the floor. 'I first noticed it here.' The magnifying glass was gone now, bundled into a pocket. Instead the Doctor was holding a stick of chalk. He drew an X on the floor. 'It has moved in a uniform line to this position.' He crabbed across the floor, back towards where Trayx was still kneeling. The chalk described a perfectly straight line in the Doctor's wake.

'It's coming straight for us,' Trayx said quietly. 'It's not navigating using any intermediate points of reference, or its course would not be so true.'

'You're not expecting any visitors, I take it?' Trayx shook his head. 'Then perhaps you should switch off the sonic subspace frequency you're broadcasting,' the Doctor suggested. 'They're probably homing in on that.'

Trayx opened his mouth to answer. But no sound came out. Instead he turned towards the door. Warden Mithrael was striding across the room towards them. Behind him, the Doctor's young friends, Jamie and Victoria, were following

106

diffidently. 'My Lord,' Mithrael called out. 'My Lord, there is a problem.'

'I'll say there is,' Jamie shouted after him. 'Doctor he's accusing us of –'

'Now, now Jamie.' The Doctor waved him to sullen silence. 'Let's hear what the gentleman has to say.'

'Well?' Trayx demanded as Mithrael reached them.

'Sir, all external communications have shut down. Every frequency we try is being jammed. It's just subspace static.'

Trayx nodded grimly. 'That ship.'

'What ship?' Mithrael asked.

But Trayx did not answer him. 'Doctor,' he said quietly, 'we are not broadcasting any subspace signal.' He turned to Mithrael. 'At least, not as far as I'm aware.'

'We're not broadcasting anything,' Mithrael said. 'And we couldn't at the moment if we wanted to.'

'Well,' the Doctor replied quietly, 'someone is. I detected it soon after we arrived here.'

Jamie drew himself up and folded his arms. 'And you didn't think to tell us about it?'

'Well, I didn't think anyone would be terribly interested, Jamie.'

'I think you can take it that we are interested now,' Trayx said. 'From the speed it's moving, that ship will be here within a day. And it doesn't seem to me as if their intentions are friendly and honourable.'

Along with everyone else, Helana Trayx craned to see the tiny moving point of light high above them. Beside her, she was aware of the Doctor. He was also looking upward, his expression grim as granite, and his finger pushed into the cheek at the side of his mouth in a gesture that could be either apology or determination. She had a feeling it was the latter.

MIDDLE GAME

CHAPTER SIX
HANGING PIECES

Victoria could tell that Jamie was still upset that the Doctor had not told him about the mysterious signal he had detected. As far as Victoria was concerned, if the Doctor had not told them, then there was a good reason for it. Probably he really had thought it was just a normal emission from the fortress. But Jamie seemed more wary, less trusting of the Doctor. She put it down to his eagerness to be included and involved in everything.

So when the Doctor suggested that they were all a bit tired and should get some rest, Victoria readily agreed. Jamie eventually, grudgingly, also agreed to return to their rooms and try to sleep for a while.

'I think that's best,' the Doctor had said quietly. 'I've a feeling we'll need all our energy when that ship gets here.'

Jamie had brightened a little at this, probably sensing the chance for some action. Victoria, by contrast, had shivered and looked away.

Yet now that they were in their rooms, it was Jamie who was sleeping while Victoria lay awake and unable to relax. She could hear his snores from the adjoining room as she lay on her bed and stared at the vaulted ceiling high above her, counting the strands of cobweb that laced the arms of the chandelier.

The Doctor, of course, after insisting they all needed rest, had gone off with Trayx and Mithrael rather than deign to get any sleep himself. Well, Victoria decided, if he could manage without sleep at his age then so could she. She got off the bed, tiptoed to the door of Jamie's room and opened it a fraction. She winced as the hinge creaked and protested. Through the crack she could see that Jamie was lying on his side facing her. His mouth was open and his eyes were tight shut. His snores continued to echo off the stone walls.

Victoria pushed the door shut again. She was less concerned about making a noise as she left her room and set off down the corridor. Whatever lay ahead of them, it would be useful to be better acquainted with the layout of the fortress.

The whole place seemed deserted. Their footsteps rang on the flagged floor of the corridor as the Doctor followed Trayx and Mithrael back towards the Observation Room. They passed nobody, saw nobody, heard nobody.

'Isn't it the middle of the day as far as you're concerned?' the Doctor asked Mithrael. 'Where is everyone?'

Mithrael gave a short laugh. 'Santespri is a huge place,' he said, 'and there are actually very few people here. It is not unusual to remain alone as you traverse the corridors. The duty guards make their rounds, but it is really a token gesture, a way of maintaining discipline and morale through regularity and routine.'

'I think that may change,' Trayx said. 'If we come under attack, then the gesture will need to be taken in earnest.'

They had reached the Surveillance Suite now, its door concealed behind a heavy curtain in an alcove on a side corridor. Mithrael pulled the curtain aside and held it back while Trayx and the Doctor entered. The door sprang open at Trayx's touch, keyed to his bio-imprint and confirming his identity by the level of electrical field generated by his own body.

'Should we vary the composition of the patrols?' Mithrael asked as he closed the door behind them. His voice was slightly raised against the hum of the equipment. 'At present,' he explained to the Doctor, 'the guards work in pairs. One each from our own garrison and from Kesar's retinue. Again it maintains morale and it acts as a check and balance system. We should know if Kesar's people were planning anything, and they in turn can be confident that we are playing no games.'

'Apart from chess,' mused the Doctor.

'Apart from chess,' Trayx agreed. 'Though finding opponents is increasingly difficult. Perhaps you and I should play, Doctor.'

'Well, let's get this business settled first, shall we?'

'Indeed.' Trayx turned back to the Warden. 'No, Mithrael,' he said, 'keep the patrols as they are. But double the frequency. If the ship's mission is to assassinate Kesar, and I don't see what else it can be, then we are all on the same side. Better that Kesar's men understand that right from the start.'

'And,' the Doctor added, 'we shall need all the help we can get.' He seated himself in the main chair and started fiddling with the controls in front of him. 'Let's see if we can isolate this signal then, shall we?'

'And block it?'

'It's possible we can emit a cancelling wave, yes.' The Doctor tapped a meter set into the console and frowned as the needle failed to move. 'Have you considered the implications for your murderer?' he asked quietly.

'Meaning?'

'Meaning that if your expected assassins are on that ship, the murder may not be directly connected.'

'A coincidence, you think?' Mithrael asked.

'No, I don't think so. I'm not very big on coincidence.' The Doctor swung round in the chair, intending to face them. His expression was thoughtful, his elbows resting on the arms of the chair as he steepled his fingers under his chin. But he miscalculated, and the chair kept swinging round so he was facing the wall instead. 'Oh, excuse me,' he muttered, and swung himself back. He cleared his throat. 'The murder is definitely connected. But there are things we have not yet considered.'

'Such as?'

'Such as the fact that the murdered man knew his killer.'

'Oh?'

But Trayx, the Doctor realised, was following his line of thought. 'He was waiting for him. He watched while the killer disabled the camera.'

'Exactly. Now why would they be meeting? What could this man Remas have that the killer wanted.'

Information of some sort?'

'Possibly. Yes, possibly.' The Doctor considered. 'You say he worked in the loading bays?'

'Yes,' Mithrael said. 'He was responsible for tracking and recording the goods coming into Santespri. Kitchen supplies, replacement components, everything.'

'So maybe,' the Doctor suggested, 'he had acquired something that the killer wanted.'

'Such as?'

'Oh, I don't know.' The Doctor turned his attention back to the control console. 'A set of saucepans perhaps? Or maybe a high-frequency sonic subspace emitter.'

Trayx nodded. 'All too possible, I agree. So why kill the supplier?'

The Doctor shrugged. 'Didn't need him any more. A loose end. A falling out among crooks and villains.' Suddenly he banged his fist down on the panel. 'How should I know? Now I really need to concentrate on tracing this signal and neutralising it. Why don't you two go away and leave me in peace?'

Trayx smiled thinly, and gestured for Mithrael to lead the way out of the room. 'Very well, Doctor. We'll check back with you later.' He paused in the doorway. 'Good luck.'

The Doctor grunted noncommittally as the door closed.

From outside in the corridor he could hear Trayx's receding voice as he and Mithrael headed away: 'Get Logall. We'll meet in your office. I want to review the defence procedures and the patrol roster. And check how long we have until that ship gets here, assuming its course and speed remain constant.'

The Doctor sank deeper into the chair, swinging it slowly back and forth. He was not at all sure he could trace the signal using the equipment to hand, or that it would do any good now. But he could try. He pulled his recorder from his coat pocket and put it to his lips, his mind already deeply engaged on the problem. In front of him, the images on the screens flickered and changed as the computer switched the cameras and swapped round the pictures according to which its expert systems felt were important.

The Doctor was halfway through the second verse of the 'Skye Boat Song' when he noticed that one of the monitors was tracing Victoria's progress along a corridor. He put down his recorder.

The system had arranged the images on the screens so that the Banqueting Hall was the adjacent image. It seemed to have keyed itself to Victoria as an interesting movement to track – probably since she was a stranger. If she kept walking along the corridor, she would leave the right side of one monitor to reappear on the left of the next as she entered the hall.

But she did not.

Victoria continued down the corridor and into the hall. The Doctor watched her off the side of the screen showing the corridor, and waited for her to appear in the Banqueting Hall. She never got there. The image continued to show an empty room, the armour arranged like sentries around the walls, as if these silent soldiers were also waiting for Victoria's arrival.

The Doctor frowned, tapping his recorder on his chin.

Victoria paused on the threshold of the room, once again taking in its size and magnificence. The table had been cleared, and the room seemed empty. Along each side of the room, the empty armour stood impassive and impressive in alcoves and against the bare walls. At the far end of the room, three archways faced Victoria across the chessboard marble floor. The centre arch was a doorway, higher than the other two. The side arches were merely deep alcoves, a suit of armour displayed on a plinth in each. In the angles between the arches crossed swords were fixed in position, and above them a massive painting depicted a bloody battle in intricate and unpleasant detail. Victoria grimaced and looked away.

As she turned, she noticed a slight movement in one of the alcoves off to her left. For a moment she thought the suit of armour it framed had moved, had somehow taken on life and stepped down from the low dais. Then she realised that it was a man that was moving. He was dressed in dark combat fatigues rather than the full armour the soldiers wore when on duty. He was facing away from her as he stepped backwards down off the dais. He had been standing so close to the armour that Victoria had not been able to distinguish the two in the shadows of the alcove.

She was about to call out, but something about the man's furtive manner stopped her. Instead, Victoria moved further into the room, and concealed herself in the nearest alcove, watching as the man moved on to the next suit of armour.

He had a small device in his hand. She could not make out the detail, but he stepped up on the dais, close to the armour, pressing the device to the panel on the breastplate. Across the room, Victoria could hear a faint electronic warble. Then after a few seconds the sound stopped, and the man stepped down from the armour. He moved on to the next one.

But before he reached it, he paused, as if sensing he was not alone. He turned directly towards Victoria, staring across the room towards where she was pressing herself desperately back into the alcove. His face was worn and craggy, a long scar running the length of one cheek. His expression suggested that whatever he was doing, he was not keen to be found.

Even though she realised that the man could not see her, Victoria instinctively pushed back further into the shadows. It was a mistake. The back of her leg connected with the low dais on which the suit of armour was standing, and she felt herself toppling backward. She grabbed out for support, catching hold of a long lance that was grasped in the metal gauntlet above her. But it was not fixed in position, and pulled free in her hand. Victoria continued her fall, trying not to cry out even as she saw the lance falling forward out of the alcove.

It clattered to the floor, the sound resonating in the large room. The man with the scar turned back towards the alcove. And this time, as she struggled to her feet, Victoria knew that he had seen her.

*

The image was unchanged. The Doctor sat frozen before it, going through the possibilities. Had Victoria paused between the points of view of the cameras for some reason? It was possible, but if so then she had been there for an awfully long time. Another possibility was that there was another doorway that he could not see from the cameras. But the more he thought about that idea, the less the Doctor liked it. For one thing, the expert system was keyed to Victoria, and would have tracked her through that doorway. And if the cameras there were not working, then it would have picked her up as soon as it could. More to the point, the Doctor did not remember a doorway at that position, and he trusted his memory rather more than he trusted any computer.

So he sat and examined the images on the screens. His distrust of computers meant that he was not as inclined as most people to take for granted what he saw on the monitors. Still, he had a tool, so he might as well make use of it. The Banqueting Hall was obviously empty, the main camera covering both the doorways. But there was movement. Lamps flickered slightly, throwing shadows across walls and floor, illuminating and reflecting off the armour and the wall hangings.

The Doctor zoomed the image in close to one of the lamps. He could see that the flickering was not random, but followed a definite rhythm, a sequence. This in itself was not evidence of anything wrong. The lamp might be programmed to flicker in that way for effect – to simulate candlelight, for example.

So he zoomed closer. Then closer still. Eventually, almost at the maximum level, he found what he had been looking for. A mote of dust spiralled downward, catching the light as it fell past the lamp. It tumbled, end over end, caught against the backdrop of a painting as it fell. The Doctor leaned forward and watched its slow and circuitous descent.

There – that was it.

The Doctor snapped his fingers in satisfaction and grinned. Then his expression became more serious as he ran through the implications. On the screen the speck of dust was falling again. And once more, as it had almost reached the bottom of the picture, its pixelated form jumped mid-frame back to the top of the image and started descending again, following exactly the same path.

'Victoria!' the Doctor exclaimed, as if it were a mild expletive. As the perfect digital recording of the empty Banqueting Hall was fed back into the surveillance system yet again, the Doctor ran for the door.

'It's confirmed,' Warden Mithrael reported back to Trayx and Captain Logall. 'The ship is a Haddron cruiser.'

'Very well.' Trayx nodded. He was not surprised. In fact he had already briefed Logall on the assumption that this was the case. 'I imagine you did not expect to see action again for a while, Captain.'

Logall dipped his head slightly. 'That does not mean I shy away from it, sir.' He raised his head again as he spoke, looked directly at his commander in chief. Then he glanced first at Mithrael beside him, then at Prion standing silent and still at the back of the room.

Trayx smiled. 'I've seen your service record, Captain. In fact I chose you to command the garrison here. If you can call twenty men a garrison.'

Logall had stiffened visibly at this. He was frowning. 'Forty fighting personnel if we include Kesar's retinue, sir. And another dozen ancillaries and support staff.'

'I can see you're surprised.' Trayx was still on his

initial comment. 'This posting was a reward rather than a punishment, Captain Logall. I needed someone with impeccable credentials, with a record that I could trust absolutely. There is nobody I would rather have with me in the hours ahead.'

Logall relaxed slightly. 'Thank you, sir.'

'You have your orders, Captain. If you need anything more, Prion will do what he can for you.'

'Yes, sir.' Logall saluted and left.

'How long do we have?' Trayx asked Mithrael when Logall had left.

'Perhaps eight hours. If they don't increase speed. They must know we've spotted them by now.'

'They know nothing for sure,' Trayx said quietly. 'They may assume, they may even have information from their agent within Santespri if they are still in contact.' He turned to his aide-de-camp. 'What's your assessment, Prion?'

'We must assume their intentions are hostile,' Prion replied. His voice as ever was level and devoid of tangible emotion. He might as well have been discussing a chess problem. 'We stand little chance in an outright battle, assuming the ship carries a full complement.'

Mithrael shook his head. 'It could carry a whole legion.'

'Then we must assume it does,' Trayx said. 'Though that seems rather enthusiastic of Consul Mathesohn. If it is Mathesohn.'

'We have information that Mathesohn plans to remove Kesar,' Prion said. 'He has several options open to him. An outright attack would be difficult to conceal or to deny under normal circumstances. A single assassin would be more efficient and deniable.'

'So why the change?'

'Again,' Prion answered, 'several possibilities. First

a change in circumstances so that expedition and unquestioned success have become paramount. We have no information to support this theory.'

'And second?'

'Opportunity.'

'Meaning what, exactly?' Trayx asked. But he was beginning to see where Prion's logical train of thought was leading him.

'Mathesohn's motives are purely political and self-centred,' said Prion. 'Removal of Kesar is but the first step, logically, to his own accession to the position of Emperor. There are other obstacles, primarily his fellow Consuls, since he does not place much store by public opinion.'

Mithrael shook his head. 'Jank won't stand against him, any more than he would have opposed Kesar without considerable persuasion. So that just leaves –' He broke off, turning to Trayx.

'Yes, it leaves me. Are you suggesting,' he asked Prion, 'that Mathesohn sees an opportunity to dispose of Kesar in such a way that blame devolves to me?'

Prion nodded. 'Kesar's assassination while you were also here would be difficult enough. Were you to maintain that Mathesohn sent a whole legion merely to kill a single unarmed and disabled prisoner, he could plausibly shift the blame to you and claim your account is a fabrication in order to cover your own involvement in the assassination. Or, if you are also killed in the action, that too serves his purpose.'

Mithrael snorted. 'The word of that sewer rat against the General in Chief – who would believe him?'

But Trayx was not ready to dismiss the theory. 'Probably enough people to engender an atmosphere of serious uncertainty. It would create the sort of political landscape in which Mathesohn excels and where honest soldiers such as ourselves are like blind men in a dark dungeon.' He nodded seriously. 'Once again, I think you have made an accurate assessment of the situation, Prion.' He sighed. 'Once again you tell us what as honest soldiers we dare not think for ourselves.'

The monsters were everywhere in Jamie's dream. Daleks glided after him as he ran down smoke-filled corridors, and Cybermen lunged at him from both sides. Somewhere in the distance a Yeti roared, and the rasp of his tortured breathing was an Ice Warrior closing in for the kill. It grabbed him by the shoulders, shaking him fiercely and shouting in his ear.

But the voice was not the dry throaty hiss he expected. 'Wake up, Jamie,' the voice shouted. 'Oh dear, oh dear.' And he realised that it was the Doctor's voice.

'Wha-? What? What is it?' he mumbled as he slowly broke free of his dreams and regained the real world. The Doctor was leaning over him, shaking him by his shoulders. Jamie shook himself free and sat up.

'Oh, Jamie. Oh thank goodness you're awake.' The Doctor beamed at him.

'Aye, well now I am awake, what's going on?' Jamie demanded. 'Decided you do need our help after all, have you?' He looked round. The door to Victoria's room was ajar. 'Is Victoria awake as well?'

'But that's just it, Jamie.' The Doctor's expression was grave again. He was wringing his hands as he said, 'Victoria's gone. I think she may be in danger.'

Jamie was on his feet immediately. 'Why didn't you say? Where is she?'

'Well, I think she's in the Banqueting Hall, but –'

Jamie was already at the door. 'Then let's go and find her.

Come on, Doctor.' He turned left and headed off down the corridor.

Exasperated, the Doctor was following. 'Jamie!' he shouted. 'Jamie; come back. Oh dear, oh dear.'

'No, Doctor,' Jamie shouted back over his shoulder. 'If Victoria needs our help –'

'But Jamie, the Banqueting Hall's this way.'

'Oh,' said Jamie as he turned. 'Aye. Well, I thought this might be a short cut.'

But the Doctor did not seem to be listening. He was jumping from one foot to the other as if the floor was on fire under them, already edging back along the corridor. 'I really think we should hurry.'

Jamie caught the edge of panic in his voice. He started to run, aware of the sound of the Doctor's footsteps close on his heels as he hesitated at a junction.

'Left, Jamie,' the Doctor called from behind him.

Jamie nodded, as if he had known this and turned.

'Other left!' the Doctor shouted.

The lance was heavier than it looked. It had occurred to Victoria that she might use this as a weapon. But she could barely lift it.

'Keep away from me,' she said, her voice an octave higher than usual in fear. 'Who are you?'

But the man with the scar said nothing. He was stalking towards her in a most unpleasant way, his face contorted into what might be a malicious grin.

Victoria edged out of the alcove and backed away towards the door. 'If you come any closer, I shall scream.'

The man seemed unconcerned. But then, Victoria consoled herself, he had not heard her scream yet.

Suddenly he lunged at her, grabbed at her as she turned

to run. Victoria felt her hair yanked viciously as she turned, knew she was falling backwards. She screamed.

Jamie gritted his teeth at the sound of Victoria's terror and increased his speed. The Doctor was far behind him now. Jamie could feel the blood pounding in his ears, could hear his breath scraping against his throat as he ran.

The man's face was getting closer to Victoria's, the scar stretched white down his cheek. She had her hands round his neck as he reached for her, but he hardly seemed to notice. His own hands were on her shoulders, lifting her, turning her, breaking free of her grip and pinning her arms behind her back.

'That's the last time you'll scream,' he spat at her. 'Ever.' His breath was unpleasantly hot in Victoria's ear. She caught the smell of it at the back of her throat as she opened her mouth to scream again, as she realised that his hands were now around her throat and that she could not breathe. As her view of the room shimmered like a guttering candle. Then went out.

CHAPTER SEVEN
J'ADOUBE

The flickering of the light and the dancing of the shadows was the only movement in the room. Jamie skidded on the polished marble of the floor as he ran into the Banqueting Hall, saw Victoria's inert body and tried to change direction. He was already kneeling by her prone form when the Doctor arrived beside him.

'I haven't run like that in years,' the Doctor panted, mopping his flustered brow with a grimy handkerchief. He pulled his collar away from his neck as if hoping a cloud of steam would release itself into the atmosphere.

'Doctor –' Jamie's voice was uncharacteristically quiet – 'I don't think she's breathing.'

At once the Doctor was all concern. 'Oh, Victoria,' he murmured as his face crumpled. He elbowed Jamie out of the way as he shuffled forward on his knees and craned over the girl, putting his ear close to her mouth. After a moment, he straightened up, pulled a small mirror from his pocket and held it under Victoria's nose.

'Well, Doctor?'

'Give her a moment, Jamie, there's a good fellow.' The Doctor inspected the surface of the mirror, frowned, breathed on it himself as if checking it worked, then stuffed it back inside his coat.

'Well?' Jamie repeated anxiously.

'I think she's going to be all right,' the Doctor said, placing his forefinger carefully along the line of Victoria's jaw so that it pointed to the base of her ear. He was smiling faintly now, and patted Jamie reassuringly on the shoulder. 'Now, help me to sit her up, will you?'

Together they managed to move Victoria to a sitting position, the Doctor holding her legs down so she folded in the middle as Jamie struggled to lift her under the arms.

'Steady, Jamie,' the Doctor advised as he slowly raised her back from the floor. 'Gently does it. There we go. Yes. Good.' The Doctor clapped his hands together. 'Well done. Look, she's breathing quite normally now.'

Victoria coughed in answer, her eyelids flickering. Then she opened her eyes suddenly wide, grabbed the Doctor and pulled him forward into an awkward embrace. He struggled to maintain his balance while Jamie fought to keep Victoria from falling back again under the Doctor's weight.

'Oh, Doctor,' Victoria said through his coat between sobs. 'It was awful. There was this man. He had a dreadful scar. He attacked me. I don't know what happened.'

'There, there,' the Doctor mumbled soothingly. 'It's all right now. You'll soon catch your breath.'

'But the man…'

'Oh don't worry,' the Doctor said as he managed to disentangle himself from Victoria's grasp. 'Jamie sorted him out, didn't you Jamie?'

'Did I?' Jamie asked. 'Oh, aye,' he said quickly. 'He just ran off when he saw us coming.'

'You see,' the Doctor went on, 'there's nothing to worry about now.' He helped Victoria to her unsteady feet. 'Why don't you come back to our rooms and have a little sit down there? Then you can tell us all about it.'

'Thank you, Doctor.' She leaned on him for support as they headed for the door.

'You see,' the Doctor said, 'you've already got your colour back.'

Like the battlements, the loading bay was open directly to space. The osmotic shielding kept the atmosphere from bleeding away into space. When a ship needed to dock, the area was cleared and the shields lowered, reactivated once the forward section of the ship was within the bay. The shield then melded itself to the hull of the ship, whatever shape it might be, creating a perfect, airtight seal.

The beacon was a relatively small device, most of its bulk taken up with the propulsion and guidance systems. In its entirety, it stood only to Logall's shoulder as he tapped the course co-ordinates into the control panel. It was a gunmetal-grey, bullet-nosed projectile, smooth and functional. There was no thought for aesthetics or for extraneous capabilities. It was a small guided rocket with a subsonic pulse emitter built into its nose cone.

'Check those numbers for me,' Logall said to the engineer as he stepped back.

The engineer read off the co-ordinates and compared them with those on a notepad. 'Check,' he said when he was done. 'That should send it on an elliptical course away from the approaching ship and back towards Haddron.'

'Let's hope someone picks it up,' Logall said grimly as he closed the inspection hatch.

'What's it say?'

'Nothing much. We're in trouble, send help. It's just a preset signal.' Logall stepped away from the beacon. 'Right, let's get it into launch position.'

Around the top of the loading bay was an observation gallery. It was encased in heavy plastiglass shuttering, an airlock in effect. From the gallery, Logall and the engineer watched the stars shimmer slightly as the barrier was closed and the sudden rush of air from the bay misted the view as it dispersed into space. The beacon rocket was fitted into a tripod launcher, angled through the opening.

As they watched, a tiny jet of flame licked out of the base of the projectile. In a moment it was a splashing torrent of fire as the beacon lifted out of its moorings and rose slowly. It gathered speed quickly, hurling itself through the wide doorway of the loading bay. For a short while it was a shooting star, smearing its way across the firmament. Then it was just another point of light against the inky backdrop of space. Finally, it was lost to the naked eye.

'Do you think it will make it, sir?'

Logall did not turn. He continued to watch the blackness where the light had last glimmered and faded. 'Yes,' he lied. 'Of course it will.'

'My Lord.' Trayx inclined his head as he entered the room.

Kesar turned towards him. The blank holes that were his eyes seemed to focus on Trayx across the room. 'There is no need to be so formal when we are alone, my friend,' his voice grated.

Trayx sat down opposite Kesar. The chessboard was, as ever, between them. 'We are never alone,' he said. 'Someone always watches the watchers. But we need to talk.'

'You have time for a game?'

Trayx shook his head.

Kesar laughed, the filtered sound sending a vibrant echo around the stone-clad room. 'Good,' he said. 'You would probably win. I can understand why Cruger refuses to face you across the board.'

'Better that he had realised the odds on the field of battle,' Trayx retorted.

Kesar's mask caught the light as it angled slightly. Perhaps, behind the mask, he was smiling. 'Far better,' the electronic voice said quietly. 'But what is done is done. That game has been played and lost.'

'Perhaps not.' Trayx picked up a chess piece, felt the slightly rough surface of the black rook under his finger. It was shaped like a massive fortress jutting out from a base of craggy rock. He frowned, and looked back at the board. The other pieces too were oddly familiar. This was not the set that Kesar had been playing with earlier.

'You like it?' Kesar asked. 'Cruger has been working on making the set for me since we arrived here. It is almost complete now, just the white king remains unfinished.'

Trayx put down the rook and leaned forward to examine the other pieces. 'What is it made from?' The pawns on both sides, he could now see, were Haddron soldiers.

'A form of compacted carbonite, I believe. He had several pieces of the stone sent from the mines on Uvonola.'

'They're very good.' Trayx was surprised. 'He does this by hand?'

'Therapy perhaps.' Kesar picked up the black king and passed it to Trayx. 'He has put you on the black side, me on the white.' The scraping laugh echoed round the room again. 'An interesting conceit.'

'Very.' Trayx stared at the miniature figure of himself. He had expected a caricature, an ogre figure. But in fact it was not inaccurate. He returned the king to the board, noticing without surprise that Helana was his queen. A quick scan of the other figures satisfied his curiosity. Mathesohn and Frehlich were his bishops, the rooks on both sides as he had seen were modelled on Santespri. The other figures on each side were predictable, with the possible exception of the white queen, who seemed to be modelled on Kesar's dead mother. Only the white king was missing – presumably that would be Kesar.

'It remains to be seen whether his model of Kesar will depict the figure before or after this.' Kesar tapped the cheek of his mask with the tips of his fingers. 'I will let you know. It could change, perhaps, our interpretation of Cruger's game.'

Trayx nodded. Then a thought struck him. 'Where is Cruger?' He gestured to the board. 'I don't see a figure of him.'

'A good question. He says he would not deign to suggest he plays a major role in the game.'

'Does he?' Trayx shook his head. 'More likely he believes himself to be the main player in a different game.'

'And how is our game progressing?' Kesar asked quietly.

Trayx leaned back in the chair. 'I don't know. But there are developments that I need to apprise you of.'

'Oh?'

'We have detected a ship on a course to Santespri. Nothing is due, and certainly not a cruiser.'

'You are sure she is headed for us?'

'It looks that way. All external communications channels are jammed, we can't get anything out.'

Kesar was silent for a moment. 'Thus it begins,' he said at last, the words little more than an electronic buzz. 'So, no single assassin for me, but rather a whole host descending on our small encampment.'

'I've ordered a distress beacon be launched.'

'That won't get past a cruiser. Not if it is already close enough to be detectable.'

Trayx nodded. 'Probably not. But there is another reason for launching it.'

'Confirmation?' Kesar laughed again, but the sound was somehow flatter, less genuine this time. 'You are beginning to think like a politician, at last.'

130

'I don't take that as a compliment,' Trayx said. 'But yes, if the cruiser intercepts and destroys the beacon that will be proof enough. Until then I cannot justify a release of weapons to your men.'

'But with that proof, we can all stand together against the common foe,' Kesar said. 'And with that proof, we can ensure that all our differences are laid aside as we face the new threat together.'

'Perhaps not all of us.' Trayx stood up. 'There is one other thing. This Doctor.'

'What of him?'

'I trust him. I think he can help us.'

'I agree. And you were always a good judge of these things. Is that it?'

'Not quite. One of his companions, the girl, was attacked earlier. She is lucky to be alive, but she says she would recognise her assailant. Perhaps we can root out the rotten fruit from among your retinue?'

'Or yours, Trayx.' Kesar nodded slowly. 'Very well, bring her to lunch. And afterwards, I shall brief my men. When you have the confirmation we need, we can speak again.'

'Thank you.' Trayx crossed to the door, and rapped on it. A moment later it was opened from outside by the duty guard. Trayx turned back to Kesar before he left. He gave a short bow, then saluted. 'My Lord.'

As the door closed behind him, he could hear his friend's synthetic laughter. Perhaps it was indeed funny, but the proper protocols had to be seen to be observed.

Meals were a rare time when Kesar's staff met together. They all knew that the patrols had been increased, and even if they had not they could tell by the fact that there were fewer of them free from duties for the meal than was normal.

Lunch started quietly: they were all subdued, expecting Kesar to make some sort of announcement. But for the moment, he said nothing. He sat silently at the head of the long table in the Banqueting Hall. A tube inserted into a socket beside his mouth grille, carrying puréed food inside the mask.

Lieutenant Sponslor had been one of the last to arrive. He took his place halfway down the side of the table, his back to the fireplace. He was not hungry, but it was frowned on not to appear for a meal, even if you ate little. This was the main forum for discussion and the exchange of news among Kesar's retinue. From across the table, the new girl – Haden – smiled at him as he began a tentative attack on the food.

'Not hungry?' she asked.

He was not in a mood for talking, so he pretended he had not heard her. Over her shoulder he could see the shadowy form of one of the silent metal figures within its alcove. He imagined the huge armoured form striding towards him across the field of battle, and for a moment he could hear the clank of gears and hiss of servos through the imaginary smoke. And he shuddered.

As Sponslor's eyes focused again on reality, he realised that Haden was no longer looking at him. In fact, everyone was looking towards the main doorway. And the room was silent.

It was unusual for the meal to be interrupted. There was an unstated agreement that Kesar and his people would be left in peace during the meal. So the appearance of the two figures in the doorway was unusual to say the least. And while his fellows were merely surprised and disapproving in their silent observation, Sponslor was suddenly chilled to the bone as he saw that one of the figures was the dead woman.

*

The image on the monitor tracked along the length of the table. Expressions slid by as the Doctor and Trayx watched closely for any unusual reaction. Behind them, Jamie and Mithrael craned to see the screen.

'I still say we should have gone with her,' Jamie remarked.

The others ignored him, apart from the Doctor, who commented quietly, 'She'll be quite safe with Prion. And now I've sorted out the surveillance system, we can see everything that happens from here.' He leaned forward and tapped the screen, slowing and stopping the camera's movement with his other hand as he did so. 'There,' he said. 'That one.'

The focus adjusted slightly now that the camera's position was still. Two people were framed either side of the table, looking towards the camera – towards where Victoria and Prion would be standing. One was a young woman with short dark hair. Her expression was puzzled, curious. Opposite her sat a man. He was older, his face worn and lined. A scar ran down one of his cheeks, and he too seemed curious. But just for a moment, as the camera had closed on him, he had looked terrified.

Despite his surprise, Sponslor recovered quickly. His mind was racing as he worked through the possibilities. He must have been mistaken. She had not been dead, merely unconscious – probably fainted as much as asphyxiated. If he had not been interrupted by the other stranger, he could have finished the job. He *should* have finished the job. But he had been too intent on getting away unseen. Too satisfied with himself that he had finished his assignment, completed his mission.

The woman was walking slowly towards the table, looking along it, looking for a face. For his face. Sponslor knew that she could pick him out. He had a distinctive face. It was just a matter of time. He looked to the man with her, recognising Trayx's assistant Prion, and knowing he could expect no quarter there. He looked the other way, back along the table.

Everyone else was looking back towards him, seemed to be looking at him. Accusing. As if they already knew. Kesar's mask was impassive and inscrutable as ever. He had removed the feeding tube and closed the vent it slotted into. Now he was slowly rising to his feet. Beside him, Cruger too seemed to be staring at Sponslor as if demanding an explanation from him. As he glanced from Cruger to Kesar, Sponslor knew what his only course of action must be.

He pushed back his chair, stumbling to his feet. The chair overbalanced and crashed to the floor behind him as Sponslor turned.

In apparent slow motion, the girl was raising her hand to point at him. Prion was already striding towards him, his mouth open as he shouted, 'Stop him.'

From across the table, Haden lunged forward, grabbing at Sponslor's sleeve. But she was at full stretch and it was an easy matter to pull free as he turned to run.

Behind him, Sponslor could hear the heavy, fast footfalls of Prion in close pursuit. All along the table chairs were pushing back as people rose, turning to see what was happening. He kept running, heard the shouts from all around, saw Cruger's face close to his own as he pushed past the general.

Then he stopped dead.

In front of him stood Kesar. His mask leaned close to Sponslor as he skidded to a halt, reached out to steady himself. He grabbed at Kesar's shoulder to prevent himself from falling.

Kesar knocked his arm aside. 'Don't dare raise your hand to me.' There was a depth to the electronic voice that Sponslor had never heard before. A venom. He had served with Kesar since Bragadrok, knew him well enough to sense the anger behind the mask.

'My Lord,' Sponslor spluttered, out of breath and afraid, 'on my honour –'

Kesar's voice was quieter now, but the undercurrent of anger was still there. 'What do you know of honour?'

Sponslor sensed Prion close behind him. He knew he could never get past him, knew his only hope now was to push past Kesar and try to outrun Prion till he could find somewhere to hide. He drew a deep breath, and leapt forward, pushing Kesar aside.

But Kesar held on to him. Sponslor could hear the motors in the armour that encased Kesar's arm as they strained to hold him. He felt Kesar's grip tighten, and found himself flying backwards as his commander hurled him to the floor. The breath was knocked out of him as he landed, and he lay for a moment staring up at the ceiling of the Banqueting Hall.

Then Prion's emotionless face filled his field of vision and he felt himself hauled to his feet. Prion kept lifting him. He had Sponslor by the shoulders, lifted him clear of the floor. Sponslor could feel the incredible strength of Prion's grip even as that grip was broken and Prion hurled him across the room. He slid for several feet, his cheek scraping painfully along the cold floor. He struggled to gain control, to roll over on to his back, to stand up. He grabbed for support, pulled himself upright and tried to focus through his tears of exertion and pain.

And Sponslor found he was holding on to Cruger. The general's face was twisted in anger and disgust. 'Think very carefully how you will account for your actions,' Cruger said. 'We shall want to know every detail of what you have done and why. Understand?'

Sponslor understood. He knew that his interrogators would be unrelenting in their eagerness to find out the truth. Especially if Cruger was one of them. He felt Prion's iron grip on his shoulders again, and allowed himself to be turned and led from the room.

His only comfort was that the woman took a step backwards as he passed her. But from her expression, he guessed it was not from fear, but rather a combination of disgust and pity.

The Communications Room had a view of the landing area on the East Tower where Trayx's ship had settled. The room was in a lower area of the section of the fortress that joined the tower, so the view was little more than an ability to watch ships as they touched down or took off. Apart from the window and the door, the room was as stark as any other in the fortress. The communications and tracking equipment looked as if it had just been unpacked and pushed into a corner. Two of the garrison were on duty in the room, constantly checking and recalibrating the incoming information.

On the wall next to the window, a large flat-screen monitor showed a distant view of a starscape. A flashing annotation gave the agreed code name for the incoming ship and marked the tiny dot of light as it traversed the screen. They had designated it 'Rogue One', and the estimated time until it arrived was appended to the name on the screen. A thin dotted line projected its course to the edge of the screen – to the point of light labelled SANTESPRI.

Trayx could see the silhouette of his ship crouching over the battlements above them as the operator tracked the signal from the distress beacon. It was fed through a speaker set into the control panel so that the room was filled with the steady beep of the information packet. If the signal was received, that beep would be broken down into the wave forms that harmonised to produce it. Those waves contained the precoded substance of the distress message.

The door opened and Prion quietly stepped into the room. His face was impassive as he reported to Trayx, 'Lieutenant Sponslor is in confinement, sir. His quarters have been checked, but to no substantive result. The lock on his door had, however, been tampered with.'

'So he could have left his room after being confined for the night?'

'Yes. There is no direct evidence to support the supposition, but he could have left his room and killed Remas.' He lowered his voice to a whisper and drew Trayx aside, away from the operators. 'The surveillance recordings show him asleep in his room at the time of the murder. But we know from the incident with the Doctor's friend in the Banqueting Hall that such data is at best inconclusive.'

Trayx nodded. 'I agree. I think we have our murderer. But I should be happier with a proper confession. And a motive.'

'Sponslor is admitting nothing. He is saying nothing.'

'And we don't know what he was doing in the Banqueting Hall?'

Prion shook his head.

One of the operators was pointing to the main screen. 'Sir,' he called across, 'sorry to interrupt.'

'You have something.'

'Rogue One is altering course, sir. They're turning away.'

'What is their new heading?' Prion asked. As the operator read off the figures, he nodded slowly. 'They have detected the beacon,' he said quietly, 'and are moving to intercept.'

'You're sure?' Trayx snapped.

But before Prion could answer, the second operator called to them. 'That course correction takes them within range of the distress beacon, sir. The AI suggests they are moving to intercept.'

'Sorry,' Trayx said to Prion. 'Stupid question.'

On the screen the point of light labelled ROGUE ONE was now heading off at an angle to the line that projected its course to Santespri. After a moment, the line disappeared, and was immediately redrawn to show a sharp elbow bend in the course. The operator by the screen pointed to it. 'That's the projected launch point. The system assumes a distronic missile. They might try a wide dispersion beam from further out, but that would slow them down and they probably want to be sure they hit it.'

'And if they do take it out,' Trayx said, 'then it doesn't matter that they were delayed.'

'We're not going anywhere, and nobody else is coming here,' the operator agreed.

'We can't guarantee that Sponslor will talk,' Trayx said to Prion as they watched the screen. Rogue One was making slow progress along the dotted line, erasing it as it went. 'Find the girl, Victoria. She seems rather naive in these matters, but try to find out from her what Sponslor was doing in the Hall. We need to know why he was so worried about being caught that he tried to kill her.'

'Yes, sir.'

'Anything else?'

'Captain Logall and his team have mined the loading bay and the ancillary landing areas. They are now working in the main thoroughfares. He is producing maps for the garrison and Kesar's people are marking the routes that remain safe.'

Trayx sighed. 'It won't stop them getting in. But it might slow them down.' He slapped Prion on the shoulder. 'Make sure I get a map, won't you?'

'Of course, sir.'

Behind them the operators were intent on the screen. 'Projected missile launch in seven seconds,' one of them announced.

'Now we see,' Trayx said.

'Five seconds.'

'Rogue One is slowing to launch speed,' the second operator said.

'Three... two... one...'

'Missile away.' On the screen there was nothing to see except the slow movement of Rogue One along the next leg of the dotted line. 'And running true.'

The constant ping of the beacon was loud in their ears. Now it was joined by another tone, insistent, discordant, alien to the beacon's own harmony. The new tone was another rhythmic beat, but getting louder and faster all the while as the missile closed.

'Beacon has detected the inbound. Countermeasures released and active.'

'No change in missile course. Still running true.'

Prion stepped forward and pointed to the ship on the screen. 'Rogue One has changed course already. They are not waiting for visual confirmation of the kill.'

'Meaning?' Trayx asked.

'A human commander would want visual confirmation,' Prion said. 'He would not trust his instruments alone for a long-range missile kill of this importance.'

Trayx considered. Prion was right. For a moment there was silence in the room apart from the rising sound of the missile's targeting systems relayed through the beacon. The operators were both looking at Trayx. They too knew what that meant.

'All right. That's hardly a surprise. And it alters nothing.' Except their chances of survival.

One of the operators was checking the instruments again. 'Impact imminent.'

The beep of the beacon was drowned out now by the almost constant ping of the missile. The sound crashed to a volume that was unpleasant, that echoed round the room and made them all wince. All except Prion, who stared at the screen the whole time as if he could actually see the tiny, deadly projectile hurl itself at the beacon.

Then there was silence.

'The beacon is no longer transmitting,' one of the operators announced, breathless and unnecessary.

'Before you see the girl,' Trayx said to Prion, 'talk to Kesar. Tell him there is no longer any doubt. Tell him his retinue is now on active service under my command and may be officially considered part of the garrison. Then have Logall break out weapons for them.'

'Yes, sir.' Prion turned to leave.

'Oh.' Trayx's call paused him in the doorway. 'You'd better tell him what we're up against too. Tell him that all the evidence so far suggests that a large VETAC force with hostile intent will arrive at Santespri in just over four hours.'

Jamie was bored and frustrated. He did not take well to sitting around, though he understood the reasons for it. Captain Logall had asked that all three of them remain in their rooms while the garrison set up what he described as 'defensive measures'. Some pointed questions from the Doctor had resulted in an answer that convinced Jamie that he could not help, and that there was considerable danger in wandering around the fortress while Logall's men were in effect booby-trapping it against enemy incursion.

But he was still frustrated. And as he listened to Prion question Victoria again about what the man Sponslor had been doing when she saw him in the Banqueting Hall, his annoyance boiled over.

'Look, why do you keep going on at her about this?' he demanded. Jamie did not like Prion anyway. The man's lack of apparent emotion, his super-cool exterior, annoyed him. And Victoria's apparent attraction to him was enough to persuade Jamie that it was his duty to demonstrate to her just how shallow the man really was. Jamie had seen him throw Sponslor across the room, so he knew he was strong. Jamie had heard Prion talk about Haddron history, so he knew the man was articulate and learned. But there was something lacking, some depth of commitment or understanding which Jamie was sure he himself had.

Prion's level answer to his question did nothing to help Jamie understand or appreciate him. It did nothing to alleviate the feelings that Jamie would never realise were simple jealousy.

'We have yet to establish a motive for Sponslor's attack on Victoria,' Prion explained, apparently not having registered Jamie's aggressive tone. 'Nor do we have any indication of motive for the murder of Remas, for which we now believe Sponslor was responsible.'

'And you think Victoria knows why he went for her? She's a victim, not a criminal. She's told you everything she knows already.'

The Doctor coughed before Prion could answer. 'He does have a point, you know,' he told Prion. 'I think you might be better served by asking this Sponslor what he was doing rather than questioning us.'

'Perhaps,' Prion conceded. 'But we must explore every stratagem.'

Jamie snorted. 'This isn't one of your games of check.'

'Chess, Jamie,' Victoria corrected him quietly.

'Whatever it is. But it's not a simple game.'

'Now, Jamie,' the Doctor said quietly, 'chess is not actually that simple, you know.'

Jamie folded his arms. They all seemed to be against him now. 'Well it looked pretty simple to me,' he said sulkily. 'There can't be that many moves you can make with the bits.'

'Pieces,' Victoria said. 'They're called pieces.'

'Well, that's an interesting hypothesis, Jamie,' the Doctor said. Suddenly he seemed enthusiastic. 'Let's ask Mr Prion here if he can tell us just how many combinations of moves there actually are, shall we?'

'Why?' Jamie asked. He was not at all interested in the game, and couldn't understand the Doctor's sudden interest in his throwaway comment.

'Well, I think it's a very important consideration,' the Doctor said. He leaned towards Jamie slightly, and hissed, 'And it will stop him from questioning Victoria.'

'Oh. Aye.' Jamie considered this. 'You're right, Doctor. It might be important.'

'Splendid.' The Doctor clasped his hands together and turned back to Prion. 'So, can you help us explain the complexities of the game of kings to Jamie?'

As ever, Prion seemed unmoved by the change in direction of the conversation. He appeared able to switch topics easily, refocusing on the new subject without pause for thought. Perhaps this was why Trayx held him in such obvious esteem and looked to him for advice, Jamie thought. In the middle of a battle, he was forced to admit, such single-minded attention could be very useful.

'Consider a game of chess that lasts exactly *n* moves,' Prion said.

The Doctor cleared his throat. 'I think we should all be rather happier with some more empirical rather than theoretical data,' he said. 'Shall we assume, what, forty moves, Jamie?'

Jamie nodded. That sounded like a pretty short game from what little he knew, but if it kept Prion talking, so much the better.

Prion nodded. 'Very well. The number of possible games that last exactly forty moves is in the order of twenty-five times ten to the power of one hundred and fifteen.' This seemed to be the end of the conversation as far as Prion was concerned. Point made.

Jamie blinked. 'Big, then,' he said at last.

Prion nodded. 'Now, if you will excuse me, I have other duties I must attend to.'

'Is he right, Doctor?' Victoria asked as soon as the door had closed behind Prion.

'What? Oh yes.' The Doctor seemed to have his mind on other things. 'Yes, he's quite right, Victoria.'

'I bet he just said it that way because he couldn't work it out,' Jamie said.

'I doubt if we would have had time to listen to the answer, Jamie,' the Doctor replied. 'Now I wonder...' He tapped his chin with his index finger. 'What games are being played here? What combination of moves are we facing?'

Victoria frowned. 'What do you mean, Doctor?'

'Please, Victoria,' the Doctor waved her to silence. 'I'm wondering.'

The guard was a problem. Potentially. But if she kept her nerve, everything would probably be all right. Helana Trayx said nothing as she approached the door, just nodded to the duty soldier and waited for him to unlock it.

The guard made no comment. He unlocked the door, and stood back. The only sign of emotion, of disapproval, was when she pushed open the door without knocking and went inside. She closed the door behind her.

Kesar was sitting with his back to her. She wondered for a moment if he had heard the sound of the door. She had no idea how well his hearing sensors worked. But even as she considered this, Kesar said without turning, 'This one is a real problem. What do you think?'

She said nothing, realising his mistake. Instead she made an effort to keep her footsteps quiet, so that he might not yet discern the hard click of her high heels and distinguish it from the heavy boots of her husband.

Kesar continued speaking as she made her way over to join him at the chessboard. 'Cruger says that it is possible to achieve dominance in a single move.' The metal head remained bowed over the board, the lights flickering, reflected in the burnished surface of the cranium. 'I sometimes wonder how he dreams up these problems. Perhaps he has a digital predictor hidden away in his quarters. Anything is possible. He cannot bear to lose, you know.'

'Neither can you,' she said, and sat down beside him.

Kesar seemed frozen in position. Whether this was through surprise or concentration, she had no way of telling. She hoped it was surprise.

'You were expecting someone else?' she asked. 'My husband, perhaps?'

The metal face turned slowly towards her. 'I am always expecting someone else,' the voice croaked electronically. 'Perhaps it is you.'

'And since when,' she went on, 'have you had the concentration to consider problems without leaping immediately to possible solutions?'

He was silent for a moment, considering perhaps. Then he turned back to the board. 'Defeat makes thinkers of us all,' he said. The generated voice was quieter now, the rasp less harsh. 'There is nothing like it to mellow the soul and blunt the indiscreet edge of impulse.'

'You have indeed changed, my love.' She said it quietly, sadly. And she was surprised at the effect of her words.

Kesar's head snapped upwards and he turned quickly back to her. His expression, of course, was unreadable, but his whole body seemed to tense.

'I'm sorry,' she said quickly. 'I did not mean... That is,' she said, trying again to articulate the thought, 'I meant your character. Not your... body.'

His blank eyes were still on her. She could almost feel his stare, could imagine the disfigured remains of the real eyes behind the mask bubbled and misted by the heat of the explosion. She felt herself blush. She grasped at the straws of memory, sifting through them for something to say, to redeem the situation.

'Remember that night, just before the war, at Rutger's?' she said. 'You remember how my husband and Rutger spoke together while you came to me on the balcony? Remember the waves crashing into the rocks below us, showering us with their spray?'

Kesar said nothing.

'I really thought that our passion was as full as the sea that night,' she told him. She could hear the regret, the sadness in her voice as she spoke. 'But that was the start of it. That was when I had the first inklings of what I must do.' There was no response from him, no movement at all. 'Do you understand?'

Kesar's head inclined slightly. 'I think I do.' The words were drawn out, slow and grating. 'It was then that decisions were made. It was there, in the Seaview Room, that the die was cast.'

She exhaled loudly. 'You do remember. I knew you would.' She laughed – high and nervous. 'How could we forget?'

'How indeed?' He turned away sharply. His voice was quiet again, so quiet that she almost missed his words. 'The wine was good. Very good,' he said. 'It has been so long since I have actually tasted wine that has not been filtered, emasculated by this mask.'

His fingers clawed at his face. He seemed to be pulling the mask downward. But the glove could not hold its grip, and his fingertips skidded off the polished surface. There was a sound coming from behind the mask, an electronic gasp. A sob.

'It has been so long since I have experienced anything for myself. All is filtered now. Second-hand.' Another sob, and his body seemed to shake with the effort of it. 'Emasculated is indeed a good word.'

Helana reached out tentatively, uncertain whether to put her hand on his shoulder, whether to touch him. 'That is why I came,' she said. 'I cannot –' She broke off, trying to decide what to say, how to say it. 'Never again,' she said simply. 'My husband. I love my husband, Hans. I – I have always loved him. I always shall.'

Kesar was still facing away from her, though he was still now, the gasps and sobs having subsided.

'I'm sorry,' she said simply. 'But I felt I had to tell you. Once and for all.' She bit her lower lip as she tried to suppress her emotions. 'We shall never speak of it again,' she said quietly. 'Do you agree? Not to anyone.' Kesar turned now, as if understanding what she was asking of him. 'Please.' Could he tell how desperate she was? 'Please,' she said again. It was all she could say.

Kesar's voice was somehow even more flat, even more devoid of emotion than usual. 'Your husband,' he said, 'will never learn of your past indiscretions from Hans Kesar.'

And she laughed. A sudden gasp of pent-up emotion. Her hand flew to her mouth, as if in an attempt to keep the sound inside even after it had escaped her lips. 'Thank you.' she managed to say. 'Thank you.'

Then she ran to the door, and pulled it open. As the door closed behind her, Helana leaned back against it, her eyes closed and her breathing heavy.

'Are you all right?'

The guard's voice was close and sudden. Her eyes snapped open and she struggled to regain her composure.

'Yes, of course,' she said. 'Of course I'm all right.' She did not look at him as she started down the corridor. 'Everything is all right now.'

In his room, Kesar sat immobile. She was gone. He hardly dared to think through what she had said, what had been implied. He was just glad he was still alive. For a while, when she first came in, he had thought – had really thought – it might be her.

Slowly, Kesar got to his feet. He stared back at the chess problem, but he did not see it. His eyes – his real eyes – were brimming with tears. Instinctively, he made as if to wipe them away with the back of his gloved hand. And met the metal of the mask. The damned mask. So heavy. So uncomfortable. So inescapable.

He spared a single glance for the point in the wall where he knew the nearest camera was concealed, then turned and went to the *en suite* washroom. He closed and bolted the door. There were no cameras here. Here at least he was alone. Really alone.

He stood facing the mirror over the basin, watched his hand fumble with the small nuts at the side of the mask, heard the slight creak and complaint of the metal as he unscrewed them. Slowly, he pulled the faceplate away from the headpiece. And now he did wipe his damp eyes.

When the tears were gone, when he could see properly again, he ran his hands down his face, feeling the contours and the bone structure. He watched his reflected actions in the mirror, saw the fingers trace their paths. Then he ran cold water into the basin and splashed it on his face. It was good to feel the cool liquid, refreshing. Life. He pulled a towel towards him. And when he was done he spent a moment just staring at himself in the mirror.

He stared at his face, his real face, for several minutes. Then, reluctantly, he put the mask back on. The mask and all that went with it.

CHAPTER EIGHT
SACRIFICE

The mask was barely back in place when he heard the knock at the door. Although he knew that the visitor could not see his face – his real face – behind the metal facade, he took a moment to compose himself before answering.

It was Cruger. Kesar could tell at once that the general was pleased with himself.

'My Lord,' Cruger said. He bowed low.

'Good news?'

'Yes, my Lord. It is finished.'

'Finished?' He felt as if his heart had missed a beat.

'The chess set, my Lord. I have finished the final piece.'

And Kesar saw now that Cruger was holding the piece in his hand, was holding it out to him. Kesar took the figure, the white king, and lifted it up so that it filled his field of vision. The detail on the clothing, the robe, was perfect. The stance was noble, assured. Kesar held the figure close and looked at the face.

The face.

There was no face. Nor was there the blank metal mask that he had half expected. There was nothing. It was rounded smooth, unfinished.

'I could not decide, my Lord,' Cruger said, 'how to depict the would-be Emperor. You understand the problem, I am sure.'

Kesar nodded, said nothing. Was this what he had come

to – the culmination of his life – a blank?

'My Lord?'

Kesar was dimly aware that Cruger had been speaking to him again. 'I apologise, Cruger,' he said. 'My mind was elsewhere. This ship that is arriving…'

'Of course, my Lord. My apologies.' It was impossible to tell whether Cruger accepted the explanation. Probably not. 'I was inquiring whether you had solved the small problem I set you earlier?' He nodded towards the chessboard set up in the corner of the room. The chair was still pushed back from where Kesar had left it when Helana Trayx had departed.

Kesar could tell from Cruger's expression, from the hint of smugness in his voice, that he knew the answer. Cruger set problems for Kesar almost every day. And almost every day, Kesar allowed that he had not been able to find the solution. That of course was why Cruger continued to set them. He knew his commander was an impulsive and undisciplined thinker. Even though Cruger had seen Kesar's game of chess improve immeasurably since their incarceration, he still believed he set problems that Kesar could not solve.

But this time, this one time, perhaps because of the blank-faced king, Kesar let the pretence slip. 'Ah,' he breathed, his voice an electronic rasp, 'that small problem.' He took a step closer to Cruger, wanted to watch his expression closely, wanted to see deep into the man's eyes. 'Yes, I have solved it.'

Cruger covered his reaction well. But the astonishment and the anger were both there, commingled in his eyes. Just for a second. Then he was all praise for Kesar's skills.

'Show me, my Lord,' he said with apparent enthusiasm. 'I am delighted that this once I have been able to bring out your analytical prowess with my small conundrum.'

Kesar led the general to the board. The answer was straightforward, though it had eluded him for longer than usual. In fact, of the problems Cruger had set him, this was one of the most perplexing. Which made his confession that he had solved it all the more satisfying. For now at least.

Cruger was stroking his short grey beard, tugging at the end of it as he watched Kesar reach across the board. 'The problem was how white could achieve a position of dominance leading to probable victory in a single move, my Lord.'

'Thank you, Cruger. I remember.' The solution had come to him, as these things so often did, in an inspirational flash. It had been while he was examining his face in the mirror, moments before Cruger's arrival. Or, more importantly, moments after Helana's departure, for it was her visit that had triggered the insight. As he had thought back over what she had said, he had suddenly seen how Helana could so easily have become Queen Empress – could still, for that matter. She was the very image of a queen, after all.

Kesar picked up the white queen and moved it across the board. 'The queen exposes herself to three of black's pieces.'

Cruger nodded. His face was twisted into a smile, but his eyes were deep and dark with anger. 'Very good, my Lord. Exactly so.'

'Black can take the queen with any of three pieces. If he does not take the queen, then white will mate in the next move. But whichever piece black uses to capture the queen, he exposes another front that white can exploit with his remaining pieces. Mate in one, or in three. Not a happy choice.'

Cruger drew a deep breath. 'I am impressed, my Lord, I have to admit. It seems that your ability to process these problems may soon be a match for your improved game.'

'Perhaps. Though I confess I think you sometimes allow me to win our games. To massage my vanity perhaps.' He scratched gently at a metal cheek. 'What remains of it.'

'Of course not, my Lord.'

'Thank you for the piece, Cruger. For the king.'

'Thank you, my Lord. I am merely sad that my labours are now at an end.'

'But surely they are only now beginning?'

Cruger blinked. 'I'm sorry, my Lord?'

'Now that we are considered a part of the garrison of Santespri. Back in active service for the Republic. When this ship arrives, I think we shall have labours anew.'

'Indeed, my Lord.' Cruger nodded. 'Indeed.' He gestured back at the board. 'A game before this ship arrives, my Lord? We have time while Logall's men complete their preparations for our guests.'

'Hardly guests.'

'Visitors, then.'

'Visitors, if you insist. But I think we shall need to be well rested for their arrival, however we may describe them, Cruger.'

Cruger opened his hands, as if in polite disagreement. 'Then afterwards. Perhaps.'

Kesar nodded. 'Afterwards.'

'My Lord.' Cruger seemed genuinely disappointed at the thought of not playing. His step was sluggish, thoughtful as he made his way to the door.

'If you really want to play,' Kesar said, 'I think the Doctor might make an opponent worthy even of your game, Cruger.' Behind the mask, he smiled as he added, 'Or you could challenge the General in Chief if he can spare the time.'

Cruger bowed at the door. The irony of the suggestion was obviously not lost on him. 'The Doctor, perhaps,' he said as he left. 'I doubt Trayx would have the time.'

The door clicked shut, followed by the sound of the lock.

'I doubt, Trayx, that you would need much time,' Kesar said straight to the camera.

The bed was a stone slab draped with a single threadbare blanket. The sink was a hollow in the wall into which icy cold water dripped constantly. The only other sanitation was a small hole in the floor at the edge of the wall which vented directly through the osmotic shielding and into space. There were no windows, and the door was solid metal. There was no need for a grille in the door, for the surveillance camera fed images to a monitor outside the cell as well as to the guard room.

Sponslor was sitting on the bed. It was that or the floor. He was shivering from the cold, bracing himself to try to stop the shaking. Afraid that he would be thought afraid. He had been left for what seemed like forever. His whole life had come to this, had culminated in this tiny room on this barren rock. His dignity and honour had been stripped away with his boots and his under-armour. He was dressed in a thin coverall, his feet bare. His only hope, his only focused thought, was that he would have a visitor. He knew who he expected – who had to come, if only to discover whether he had completed his task. And when they came, he would be free. Or soon after. The plan – if it all *went* to plan – would see him set free.

There was no lock on the door. It was bolted with thick strips of steel. As they were pulled back, Sponslor heard the scrape of metal on metal. He did not stand. He knew who he was expecting, had rehearsed over and over what he would say. Had heard a hundred variations of the answer. There were no surprises left to him.

Or so he thought.

By instinct as much as training, he shot to his feet when he saw the figure framed in the doorway.

'As you were.' The voice was sombre, heavy, low.

Sponslor swore under his breath. He should have shown only contempt. It was too late to bluff, and he owed this man no allegiance.

'I wonder if you have had time to reflect on your situation yet.' Trayx did not move from the doorway. Sponslor said nothing. He picked at a nail, flicking the dirt he extracted across the room. 'I see you have not.'

Trayx was in the room now, standing in front of Sponslor, who could see his booted feet on the floor beside his own. Polished boots beside grubby skin.

'A shame,' Trayx went on. 'But hardly unexpected. We want – we need – to know what you were doing in the Banqueting Hall. Who you are working for, what is their agenda.'

Sponslor studied the boots, tried to rationalise the reflected light on the toecap of one. He said nothing.

Trayx exhaled heavily. His breath was a fine mist in the air beside Sponslor. 'I've brought you a visitor.'

Sponslor's head snapped up. Perhaps, after all…

'Allow me to make the introductions. Perhaps you did not realise who was in my entourage for this visit to Santespri.'

He looked back towards the open door. Sponslor followed his gaze, and saw that in the shadows beyond the threshold stood another figure. A shadow. Silent and dark.

'This is Sponslor,' Trayx was saying. 'He has no rank, no status. Not any more. I know you won't dignify him with one.' Trayx turned back to Sponslor. 'I don't think you have met before, have you? This is Tordoc. I'm sure you have heard of him.'

Sponslor tried to shake his head, but he was shivering more than ever now. A draught from the open door? No it was more than that. It was as if the newcomer had thrown a further chill into the room ahead of him.

Trayx smiled. It was not pleasant. 'Tordoc is, of course, the Lord High Interrogator of Haddron, Master of the Implements of Torture and Pain.'

Sponslor turned back to the door, his mouth hanging slack. He barely realised that he had stopped shivering. His whole body seemed frozen in position apart from his head. The shadowy figure stepped into the cell. He was wrapped in a black cloak, the hood hanging back over his shoulders so that his head emerged from it as if from a shell. And his face was dark and shadowed.

In the guardroom, a small group of people were clustered round the monitor showing the image from the cell. The voices emerged, tinny and distant, from a small speaker set in the base of the screen.

'Do you think he will get us the information we need?' Warden Mithrael asked.

It was Prion who answered. 'I believe it is possible. If anyone can, *he* can.'

On the screen Trayx left the cell, closing the door behind him.

'Can you not make it any louder?' Jamie asked.

'Oh Jamie,' Victoria was standing beside him, 'I'm not sure I want to hear.' Behind her, Trayx let himself quietly into the guardroom.

Two figures were alone now in the cell. One stood, looking down, his shadow falling across the man sitting terrified on the bed.

'What do you know about pain?'

Sponslor struggled to answer, but somehow his voice seemed to stick in his throat.

'It is caused by the stimulation of nerve endings,' the Interrogator continued. 'Pain, I mean.'

Sponslor tried not to listen. He tried to yawn, to look away, wanted to lie back casually on the bed. But instead he sat bolt upright, absolutely still, listening rapt to the Lord High Interrogator's words.

'Any stimulation can cause pain. Pressure. Heat. Cold, as you can tell in here. Tissue damage. The more extreme the stimulation, the more extreme the pain. A simple response mechanism. There are pain receptors all over the body, you know. And also at many internal points too. The stimulation initiates a response within the spinal cord, and relays the information to the brain. It is, as they say, all in the mind.'

The man's eyes were deep and dark as he leaned forward. 'But you knew that, I think. Or as much of it as you felt you needed to. Until now.'

Still Sponslor did not – could not – move or answer.

The Interrogator continued, as if he expected no reply. 'What is less obvious, less apparent, is that there are psychological factors governing the degree of pain an individual feels. It is not as straightforward as the strength of the stimulus determining the strength of the response. Oh no. We must also take into account the release in the brain and the spinal cord of endorphins and enkephalins.' He paused, smiled. 'Forgive me: they are peptides which mitigate the pain. Of course, their release – or not – may also be controlled or affected by the use of drugs. I expect you knew that too, if you thought about it.

'Another thing to take into account,' the Interrogator went on, 'is that stimulation of one body region may reduce pain felt in another. Or exacerbate it. A pain in one area can become a trigger zone – can cause pain to start in another.'

He reached out a hand from inside the cloak. Sponslor

watched, unable to move as it slowly closed on his face. He could see the lines on the tip of the index finger, the edge of the nail.

'In this case, even a light touch can be painful.' The man's finger dusted Sponslor's cheek. He was not aware, not really aware, if he actually felt the pain or not. But it was enough to break the spell of immobility. Sponslor pushed himself backward, his feet pressed hard against the cold stone floor, and he launched himself across the bed. In a moment he was huddled into a corner of the wall, the blanket pulled round him for comfort. He realised he was shivering again, could feel his teeth chattering, could hear the high-pitched whimper that escaped from between them.

The Interrogator had not moved, his finger was still extended into space. Now he used it to point at Sponslor, to stab the air as he spoke. 'It's fascinating, don't you think?' he said. 'Consider very carefully what I have just explained. And soon, very soon, we shall talk again.'

Sponslor was shaking now. Not just shivering, but shaking, as if he would fall apart. He drew the thin blanket closer round him, but it seemed to have no effect.

The Interrogator turned and walked slowly to the door. He knocked on it, once, and the bolts were drawn back. As he left, the man turned back. The light was behind him again, so that he seemed but a shadow. 'You seem cold,' he said, his voice freezing in the air as he spoke. 'I'll make sure that we turn up the heat.'

The Doctor, Victoria and Jamie stood at the back of the group. They watched on the screen for a while. Sponslor was still shaking, cowering behind the blanket.

'Oh Doctor, can we go now?' Victoria asked. 'There's nothing to see.'

157

'Couldn't hear much either,' Jamie complained.

'Yes, it was all a bit quiet, wasn't it,' the Doctor agreed. 'Though often that's the most effective way.'

'Do you think he'll tell us what's happening?'

'Now, Victoria, we'll just have to wait and see, won't we?' The Doctor coughed, and clapped his hands together. 'Now I think perhaps we should retire to our rooms for a while and let these gentlemen get on with preparing for our new arrivals.' He led them back to the door. 'Come along. We'll pop back a bit later to finish up here.'

'Letting him stew a bit, eh, Doctor?' Jamie asked.

'He looks terrified,' Victoria said, stealing a last glance back at the screen. 'Doctor, what did you say to him in there?'

They had been in their rooms for less than five minutes when Prion arrived.

'And what do *you* want?' Jamie asked, standing in the doorway so that Prion was forced to wait in the corridor.

'Two things,' Prion told him, not apparently distressed by Jamie's surly behaviour. 'The first is a message for the Doctor. The other concerns you all.'

'Then I think we should hear about it.' The Doctor popped up from behind Jamie and ushered Prion past him into the room. 'Now, what message have you for me?'

'General Cruger wonders if you would care for a chess match.'

'Does he now? That's very considerate of him, though we are going to be rather busy.'

'He is extremely eager,' Prion said, sounding anything but eager himself. 'He proposes a virtual match over the communications system.'

'And what does that mean?' Jamie asked.

Prion said nothing, but pointed to a corner of the room.

Jamie turned to look, knowing there was nothing to see. Yet even as he turned a low chess table swam into existence. It shimmered for a moment, as if in a heat haze, then solidified.

'That's amazing,' Victoria exclaimed.

Prion crossed to the virtual table. He stood behind it, looking back at the Doctor and his friends. They could just see his lower body through the projection of the table. He reached out and picked up a piece – the black king. 'You may play as if the pieces and the board were real,' he said, 'although, of course, they are not.' He opened his hand and let go of the king. It hovered in the air for a moment, then winked out of existence, reappearing a second later back on its square.

'I see.' The Doctor nodded. 'And General Cruger has an identical board in his room, I take it. So we can see the game, but not each other.'

Prion nodded. 'There is an audio link. If you accept his challenge.'

The Doctor tapped his chin thoughtfully. 'You mentioned two reasons for this visit,' he said at last. 'What's the other one?'

'I have asked the armourer to attend you shortly,' Prion replied. 'He will furnish you with battle armour for the imminent attack. You may take your choice of the available weapons once the garrison has been fully armed.'

The Doctor nodded slowly. 'You're very kind.'

'Weapons,' Jamie interrupted. 'Now that's more like it.'

'I shan't need any weapons,' Victoria said.

The Doctor agreed. 'Nor will I.'

'Och, Doctor –'

'Now, Jamie, please don't argue. I'm not sure we want armour either.'

Prion considered this. 'It is your decision, of course. I

would recommend armour for your own protection even if you do not intend to take an active role in the defence of Santespri.'

'Well I certainly do,' Jamie announced, drawing himself up to his full height.

The Doctor ignored his comment. 'Thank you, Prion. I shall not require armour myself, but I think some level of protection would be a sensible precaution for Jamie and Victoria.'

Victoria was not convinced. 'Oh, Doctor, I don't want to be stuck inside one of those heavy suits.'

'Perhaps under-armour?' Prion suggested. 'It offers a degree of protection in its own right, but remains lightweight and flexible.'

'Splendid.' The Doctor was beaming, his eyebrows raised and his face wide with his smile. 'And while you two sort yourselves out, I'll be happy to accept Cruger's challenge.' He paused for a moment, frowning. 'If I can remember the rules.'

The scrape of the bolts made Sponslor flinch. He stared at the cell door, willing it to stay shut. But it started to open. Slowly.

'All right.' His voice was high with nerves, loud with fear. 'What do you want to know?'

Then his eyes widened as he saw who it was. He exhaled, a long thin mist in the cold of the room.

The figure in the doorway held up a tiny electronic device, then put a finger to its lips. 'Shh.' The sound was barely audible.

Sponslor hardly needed to be told. He recognised the device. He had used it himself in the Banqueting Hall. He waited patiently until the process – the recording – was complete. He looked down at the blanket huddled round him, saw the pattern in sharp focus, and realised he had stopped shivering.

The figure stepped into the cell. Despite the fact that the device had done its job, the voice was kept low and quiet. 'I want to know if you completed your task.'

Sponslor smiled. Typical. Business first. 'Yes, of course I did.' He pushed himself off the bed. 'Now get me out of here.'

'Why?' The sound was a sharp hiss.

'Why? What do you mean –'

'You said you completed your task. Why do I need you now?'

'But –' Sponslor shook his head in disbelief, took a step forwards. 'You can't just leave me here.'

The chuckle was louder than the answer. 'Indeed I can't.'

After five minutes with the armourer, Jamie was reluctantly forced to agree that he should wear the under-armour only. The armour, he quickly discovered, was not just simple metal plating as he had assumed. There was a mass of electronic equipment built into the suits – targeting systems for the smart weapons, in-built communications links, tracking and positioning systems. While he reckoned he could get the hang of the heads-up display and control systems within the helmet, Jamie was also pretty sure that it would take him more than the couple of hours that now remained until the mysterious ship arrived.

What he was forced to accept instead was a set of tight-fitting trousers and tunic. The material was obviously strong and he could feel the heavy padding and reinforcement built into it. But it was light and flexible, as Prion had promised. It felt like soft leather and was about as bulky.

As he pulled on the tunic, Jamie could hear Victoria in the adjacent room thanking the armourer for his help. 'I can manage now, thank you,' she was saying. A moment later the armourer came back to see how Jamie was coping.

From the other side of the room, the Doctor's voice was audible as he played his game of chess.

'Oh, that's a cunning move. Yes, yes. But I think if I do this... it might present you with a problem... Aha! What do you think of that then?'

Cruger's responses were rather restrained, almost entirely limited to arcane phrases that Jamie assumed were something to do with the game. 'Knight to Queen's Bishop four,' he said this time.

'Hmm. That was quick,' the Doctor responded. 'And not very clever.'

The armourer checked Jamie had pulled the straps on the tunic tight, then nodded and excused himself. 'I have many other duties,' he explained.

'You don't talk much, do you?' the Doctor chided from the next room.

'Pawn to King five,' Cruger replied.

There was a movement from the far side of the room, and Jamie turned towards it. Victoria was standing in the doorway.

'Jamie,' she said, 'I'm not really sure...' Her voice tailed off and she looked down at the under-armour she wore.

Jamie looked too. And then looked closer. Victoria's trousers and tunic looked even tighter than his own, hugging her body and accentuating the curves she usually wrapped in looser garments. Her hair was tied back in a ponytail so that even her face seemed tighter and more streamlined than before.

'I'm going to ask the Doctor,' she said before Jamie had

162

recovered sufficiently to answer.

The Doctor looked up from the game as they entered the room. 'Ah, there you are. All ready?'

Victoria cleared her throat. 'Doctor…'

'Ah, Victoria.' He smiled. 'You look very, er, protected.' He turned quickly to Jamie. 'Doesn't she, Jamie? Wouldn't you say?'

'Protected,' Jamie repeated. 'Oh, yes. Very protected.' He nodded emphatically. 'You've got to stay safe, Victoria.'

'Well, I'm not sure –' she started.

'Now then,' the Doctor cut in, 'let's just finish this little game and then we can go and find out from Trayx what's happening and how we can help.' He turned back to the board. 'Now where were we? Oh yes.' He raised his voice. 'I'm afraid I have to leave you now, so it will have to be, let me see… Yes.' The Doctor reached out for a bishop, and moved it clear across the board. He set it down, stood back and surveyed his work. 'That should do it. Mate in two. Must dash.'

As the Doctor turned from the board, he somehow managed to link an arm each through Jamie's and Victoria's and lead them to the corridor. 'Come along then,' he said. 'No time to lose.'

As he left the work party laying mines along the access corridors, Darkling passed Haden and several of Kesar's troops arriving to help. It was a shock as well as a relief to see them in full battle armour and armed.

'Where are you off to?' Haden asked him as they passed. She kept her voice low, not wanting to attract attention from the others.

'Guardroom. I get to keep an eye on Sponslor – not that he's going anywhere. I think Logall's still mad at me.'

'Chance for a rest, at least.'

Darkling snorted. 'I imagine he'll keep an eye on me while I'm keeping an eye on the cell.'

They were being jostled in the corridor now. Men with heavy blocks of explosive were struggling past them, and Haden let herself be pushed along in their path.

Darkling took over from Gotall, and settled down in front of the screen. 'What's he up to?'

Gotall shrugged, pulling on his tunic. 'Nothing much. He just sits there. He looks at the blanket, looks at the door, looks away.' He paused in the doorway. 'He called out a while back, said he'd talk. Then silent again. Flipped if you ask me.'

'Great.' Darkling turned back to the screen. Had that been a noise from the cell, or just hiss from the microphone? He adjusted the volume. There was nothing. He leaned back in the chair, hands laced together behind his head. Then the noise came again, a short hiss of sound, lasting just a moment before it was gone. Typical, Darkling thought: an intermittent audio fault.

Sanjak's finger traced the point of light that represented Rogue One, the metal of his glove scraping against the glass of the screen. The ship was inching closer to Santespri, inexorably following the line of projected flight.

He pulled up the communications menu on the helmet's heads-up display with a focused alpha wave, and blinked at the call option. 'Rogue One has entered the exclusion zone, sir.'

Trayx's voice was close in his ear, echoing slightly within the helmet. 'Thank you. Go to phase-two alert. Let me know when they come within range of our countermeasures.'

*

Darkling swung his feet off the console and sat up straight as he heard the door opening behind him. 'No change, sir,' he said without looking round. 'All quiet.'

'Really?'

The voice was not one that Darkling was expecting, and he turned abruptly to see who was there. It was the strange Doctor and his friends. The Doctor was still dressed in the same eccentric attire as when he had first appeared. His two companions were in under-armour, which seemed to Darkling like a sensible move. The three of them seemed to be acting as if they owned the place, Darkling had heard. Mind you, for all he knew, maybe they did. So he was cautious when he answered. 'Yes, sir. He hasn't moved.'

The Doctor was frowning, heavy lines across his face as he joined Darkling at the console. 'Has he said anything?'

'No, sir. Well, not on my watch.'

'How very strange.' He observed the screen for a short while.

'He's just sitting there,' the boy said. He sounded bored. 'He won't tell us anything.'

'No, look, Jamie.' The Doctor pointed to the screen as he spoke, following Sponslor's slight movements with his finger, exaggerating them. 'He looks up at the door, then down at the blanket, then across the room. Then at the door again, back to the blanket, across the room.'

'He's flipped,' Darkling said.

'Oh, do you think so?' The Doctor continued to study the screen. 'You know,' he said after a pause, 'I don't think he's flipped at all. Can you get more sound on this?'

'There's just background hiss. He's not saying anything.' Darkling pointed to a wave form creeping across an adjacent screen. It was almost a flat line, except for the occasional flurry of activity that bubbled out from it. 'Just a fault on the microphone. Regular, intermittent. Hiss.'

'Turn it up.'

Darkling shrugged, and adjusted the volume. Silence, apart from the occasional hiss of interference.

'What is it, Doctor?' the girl asked.

The Doctor half turned, holding up both hands for silence, his face still fixed on the screen. 'Shh,' he hissed.

Then he froze. For a long moment he did not move. Sponslor looked at the door, and the hiss of static came again.

'That's no fault,' said the Doctor, suddenly all movement. He tapped the screen showing the wave form, then leaned close to the monitor so that his nose almost touched it. 'It's someone saying "Shh".' He stood upright again. 'Now why would they do that?'

'Why, Doctor? What is it?'

'Well, Victoria, it means that we are hearing someone saying "shh" to someone else regularly every few seconds.' He pointed to the wave form on the screen again. 'You see where the line peaks in exactly the same way each time.'

'So what does that mean?' Jamie asked.

'It means that the sound, and the pictures too, by the look of it, are following a loop. A recorded loop of about ten seconds. Like when you were in the Banqueting Hall, Victoria, and you seemed to disappear.'

'And that means we don't know what's really happening in that room.'

The Doctor nodded grimly. 'That's right. Unless I can work out the feed they've used to fool the camera and bypass it somehow.' He tapped the ends of his fingers together as he examined the controls.

'Oh Doctor, hurry.' The girl seemed more nervous than ever now.

166

'All right, Victoria, all right. I'm just trying to work it out.'

Darkling coughed. 'If it's not a stupid question,' he said, 'why don't you just go down there and look?'

The Doctor and Jamie exchanged glances, then left the room at a run. Victoria and Darkling watched the screen, waiting quietly for a report. Sure enough, after a couple of minutes, the image rolled and flickered. The Doctor seemed to appear suddenly in the cell, his face close to the camera so that it all but filled the screen. Over his shoulder they could see Jamie bending over something on the floor.

'Hello, can you hear me?' The Doctor's voice was loud and grave. 'I think you had better get Trayx down here,' he said. 'There's been another murder.'

CHAPTER NINE
FINE NETS AND STRATAGEMS

Trayx was annoyed but philosophical. 'He won't tell us anything now, but the fact that he's been killed is useful information in its own right.'

They were in the Banqueting Hall, which Trayx had made his centre of operations. The table was now covered with screens and control consoles. Cables snaked under the table and across the floor to concealed power and video outlets. The Observation Room was too near the main docking bays as well as being too small for comfort. It was from here that Trayx would command the defence of Santespri.

Prion was with Trayx, directing the setting up of the systems. 'We now know that we cannot trust everyone within the fortress,' he pointed out. 'Whether Sponslor killed Remas or not, there is still at least one traitor within these walls who is prepared to kill.'

'So what's your plan?' Jamie asked. 'Do we just sit here and wait for the ship to arrive?'

'Yes and no,' Trayx said. 'We'll set up the defences, assuming that the ship will dock. But at the same time, it will soon be within range of our countermeasures.'

'And what countermeasures are these, exactly?' the Doctor asked.

'Ah, I was forgetting the strange gaps in your knowledge.

The indications so far are that we are up against a force of VETACs. Perhaps a whole legion.'

'And these VETACs are soldiers?' Jamie asked.

'Indeed they are. The ultimate soldiers.' Trayx allowed Prion to explain.

'The Virtual Electro-Targeted Attack Computer is the most sophisticated armament in known space. The legionnaires are drone troops which have limited strategic and tactical reasoning capabilities. They are dependent on the instructions of a command unit relayed over a virtual network. The commander is usually backed up by a lieutenant with broadly similar capabilities to ensure a level of redundancy.'

Jamie nodded, as if this all made perfect sense to him.

'I still don't understand,' Victoria admitted.

'I think they're robots,' the Doctor explained. 'Robot troops.'

Victoria frowned. 'And how many of these robots are there in a legion?'

'A full legion of the Haddron Republic comprises a single VETAC command unit and as many troops as that unit can channel instructions to.' Prion seemed to think this answered the question.

'So how many is that?'

'Originally a VETAC commander could manipulate two hundred and fifty-six units. But that was soon enhanced to allow for five hundred and twelve.'

'Five hundred?' Victoria looked at the Doctor in horror.

Prion continued unperturbed. 'A modern legion would consist of one thousand and twenty-four units. Plus the commander and lieutenant.'

Jamie threw his hands up in disbelief. 'Now how on earth do we fight that?'

The Doctor seemed less worried, though his expression was grave. 'You mentioned some sort of countermeasures. Would I be right in thinking you have a software weapon of some sort?'

Trayx looked at Prion before he answered, but his ADC made no comment – his expression remained static. 'The arsenal does include two toxin projectiles. Soon, when the ship is within range, we will launch one of them into its immediate vicinity.' Trayx sighed, as if he were reluctant to take the offensive in this way. 'I'm sorry, Prion,' he said quietly. 'But there are few options left open to us.'

'It seems a strategically sound decision,' Prion said. 'There are, as you say, few options.' He turned to the Doctor. 'The projectile includes a subspace communications system. This will broadcast the toxin as a binary encoded pulse on a frequency the ship can detect and receive.'

The Doctor nodded. 'So if the ship receives the signal, it receives the virus – this toxin. The systems become infected.'

'Once in the VETAC command circuit, the toxin will replicate itself and infect the whole network. It will destroy the VETAC units' microcode and corrupt their software systems.'

Jamie was smirking now, looking round at the steady stream of soldiers busying themselves around the room. 'Och well, if that's the case, what's all the fuss and bother about?'

'There is no guarantee that the ship will receive the signal.' Trayx shook his head. 'We can't assume anything. The VETAC commander may not know we have countermeasures, but he will probably have taken precautions against them.'

'But you are going to try?' Victoria prompted.

'Oh yes. We shall try. Logall is bringing the projectiles here now so that I can enter the command codes to activate

171

the toxin. This is not something that is lightly done, you must realise. Only in extreme circumstances do we need to inflict contagion on our own VETAC forces.'

Prion's voice was quiet, and for the first time Jamie thought he could detect a hint of emotion – of anxiety – in it. 'If you will excuse me,' he said, 'I think it best that I check on the perimeter defences.'

'Indeed,' Trayx agreed. 'Report back to me later.'

'Wait,' Victoria called as Prion turned to leave. 'I'll come with you.'

'Victoria?' Jamie was aghast.

'Well it's better than waiting around here. Perhaps there's somewhere that I can help.' She stared at Jamie, as if daring him to disagree. 'Why don't you come too?' she asked.

They followed Prion through the flickering corridors, occasionally stepping carefully round mines and explosives, which he pointed out to them. They had not gone very far when Victoria said quietly to Jamie, 'Why do you dislike him so much?'

'I don't,' he protested, slightly too vehemently.

'Oh?'

Jamie shrugged. 'I just find him creepy. He's always so helpful and polite. He's – I don't know, he's too ready to please.'

'You don't like people being polite?' Victoria asked. There was more than a hint of accusation in her tone.

Jamie looked ahead to see if Prion had heard. He seemed not to have done, continuing along the corridor apparently unconcerned.

'He's always ready with the answer,' Jamie said. He was trying to work out quite what it was that unsettled him about Prion. 'He knows it all. He's never wrong, is he? How come he knows so much about what's going on? I just don't trust him.'

Prion paused, waited for them to catch up at the junction with another corridor. He waited before he set off along the next corridor. Then he said to Jamie, 'Trust is earned, or so it is said. I have to assume from your comments that I have not yet earned it from you.'

Jamie was amazed that Prion had overheard. He thought they had been far enough behind him to be well out of earshot. He covered his embarrassment by attacking: 'Well perhaps you'll tell us why you're so keen to be away from the main action with this toxin bomb thing? Are you not intending to take part in the battle?' He nodded to Victoria. That had told him.

Prion's answer was as calm and composed as ever. 'I see there is another gap in your knowledge that I should remedy. You know my name?'

'Yes of course.' Victoria gave a short laugh. 'It's Prion.'

'Actually it is Prion Seven.'

'What?'

'It is an abbreviation. I am the General in Chief's Primary Automaton.' As he spoke, Prion's head angled slightly, and Jamie could see again how symmetrical, how perfectly formed his features were. As the two friends watched, Prion reached across his chest and unclipped his tunic. It was heavier than the under-armour that Jamie and Victoria wore, though it seemed to fit him as tightly. 'I distance myself from the toxin because it could destroy me as surely as it could the VETAC commander that my construction is modelled upon.' While he spoke, Prion drew back the tunic. Jamie expected to see the pale skin beneath contrasting against the dark metal of the tunic. But there was no skin. Instead there was a metal framework with strange-looking boards slotted into place. Tiny lights winked on and off, and the faint humming of gears and motors was audible as Prion's hand and arm moved.

'Circuit boards,' said Prion, 'and other electronic paraphernalia that wouldn't interest you.'

'You're a robot,' Jamie breathed.

Prion nodded. 'If my social programming offends you,' he said, 'then I apologise on behalf of my programmers.' He refastened his tunic, pulling it tight as if it were a real garment rather than a shell. As if he were a real person. Then he turned and set off along the next corridor.

Jamie waited a moment before following. 'I'd never have guessed,' he said almost to himself. Then he became aware of Victoria standing beside him. 'Would you?' he asked.

'No.' Her voice was quiet as she started down the corridor after Prion. For some reason she was facing away from Jamie as she spoke. Her voice was quiet, so quiet he could barely hear her say, 'No, I wouldn't.'

The bullet-nosed projectile was silent in the darkness. It arced out over the battlements on an elliptical course towards Rogue One. It started broadcasting its message of destruction as soon as it was clear of the osmotic field, although none of the systems at Santespri risked monitoring it.

Beyond it, in the night-black sky, the tiny point of light that was Rogue One was growing ever larger, plainly visible now to the naked human eye.

'Projectile One away.' Sanjak traced the course of the projectile on the screen. A moment later the expert system plotted its course, agreeing with Sanjak's prediction. The line came close to the projected course of Rogue One.

Along the bottom of the screen, data scrolled across in a rolling strip of ever-updating information. Course and speed were calculated and recalculated. The estimated time to incursion – ETI – was now counting down into its final minutes.

There was a hush in the Banqueting Hall. Trayx and his immediate entourage, minus Prion, watched the screen. Warden Mithrael, Darkling and the Doctor all watched closely. With them was Helana Trayx. She was still wearing her long white gown, but visible through the slits at the side and at the low neck was the dark under-armour she now wore beneath it. Almost everyone else was down at the docking bays, manning the defences.

The relative calm was broken by the heavy booted footsteps of new arrivals. Kesar, Cruger and several of their soldiers, including Haden, crossed to join the group by the monitor.

'Status?' Kesar rasped.

'We've launched the first projectile, sir. The second has been primed and returned to the arsenal for possible use later.' Darkling pointed to the trace on the screen. 'It's approaching Rogue One. We have ETI in less than a minute.'

'Logall is setting up defensive positions in the docking bay and adjacent corridors,' Trayx said. 'Most of your men are with him.'

'Good.' Kesar leaned close to the screen. His metal face seemed to glow in the light from it. 'Will the countermeasures work?'

'I think we're about to find out,' the Doctor said. 'The ship is slowing.'

A moment later, the speed reading at the bottom of the screen started to decrease. The projectile edged closer to Rogue One.

'They must have detected it by now,' Mithrael said. 'Any moment – any moment now and they'll receive the signal.'

The flight deck was large and functional. The control consoles were fixed to the floor at the ergonomically most efficient points relative to the command station. There was no thought for or concession towards comfort.

The VETAC commander, designated VC5, was socketed into the main systems. An infrared link kept him in touch with every reading, every adjustment, every thought within the cruiser. Normally, it kept him in touch with everything monitored from outside as well. Normally.

But the cruiser was now within range of the fortress's countermeasures. There was no reason to suspect that countermeasures would be available or would be released if they were. But VC5 was programmed to be cautious. His artificial intelligence drew on the expert knowledge of the greatest commanders in Haddron history – their thoughts, words and deeds. Of the more recent commanders, he could also access the knowledge base compiled from brain scans, simulations and actual battlefield situations they had encountered. And VC5 counted it an advantage – an advantage in purely strategic rather than emotive terms – that one of those strategists, probably the greatest of them all, was now in command of Santespri. The entire experience and strategic thought processes of Milton Trayx were in effect wired into the VETAC battle network.

The use of a 'footbath' unit so close to the target was a natural precaution. The footbath was a single VETAC legionnaire connected to the ancillary external monitoring and communications. The main systems were shut down, and the VETAC trooper was not connected into the command network. In fact, it was not connected into anything within the ship other than the backup external monitors. An audio channel was used to relay information from the unit. It was inefficient, old-fashioned and safe.

'Projectile approaching on elliptical path.' The VETAC legionnaire's voice was flat and devoid of intonation, a scraping electronic verbalisation of its thought processes.

'Track it.' VC5's voice was slightly louder, slightly lower pitched. But it carried no more emotion than his subordinate's.

'Projectile is transmitting a signal. Signal now being received.' It took almost a million times as long for the voice to convey the information as it could have travelled to VC5 through the net. But it carried only the information intended: there was no bandwidth in speech for any extraneous material, for a 'piggyback program' or toxin.

'Analyse signal. Report contents.'

The VETAC trooper downloaded the signal from the monitoring systems. Its comtronic brain scanned through the digital contents looking for patterns within the ones and zeros. A separate function within the VETAC's computer-brain detected faults within the external monitors even as the patterns within the signal resolved themselves into the viral toxin that Trayx had authoriscd.

Lights started flashing discordantly on the console in front of the trooper. A klaxon sounded from deep within the electronic systems. The lights flashed faster, the klaxon became more insistent.

At the same time, warning lights flickered into life on the front panel of the VETAC itself. Its voice seemed strained, higher-pitched, as it struggled to make its report. 'Faults detected within – within – within external monitoring systems. Hypothesis: toxin received on carrier signal from projectile.'

The lights on the VETAC were on constantly now. The klaxon was a single continuous note that fought with its failing voice.

'Toxin detected within VETAC footbath unit.'

The klaxon cut out and the lights on the main control panel flickered and died. A moment later the console itself exploded, showering debris across the flight deck. A cloud of smoke erupted from the broken surface of the console. The VETAC trooper sank heavily to its knees as two other units stepped forward.

VC5's head turned slightly as he surveyed the scene. 'Extinguish fire,' he ordered the two units. 'Maintain strictest isolation for footbath unit.'

A stream of halon gas poured from nozzles built into the VETACs' wrists, killing the fire before it could take hold. Under normal circumstances, the fire would never have started, as the flight deck, like the rest of the ship, would have contained no atmosphere. But for the sound waves to carry the footbath unit's reports, there had to be an atmosphere, and air was carried for use when a human was on board.

The footbath unit was still struggling to complete its report. One heavy metal arm thrashed uncontrollably in front of its face. 'Analysis ind-ind-indic-indicates presence of of of –' Its voice was an electronic screech as it pitched forward on to its face. The final words were muffled and distorted as the pitch of the voice varied erratically before crashing to a low, drawn-out rumble. 'Joolyan toxinnn versssssionnn fiiiive poooiiint seeevvvvveeeennnnn.' After another moment, the VETAC lay completely still.

VC5 watched impassively as his soldier died. A pulsed message sped through the command net at the speed of light, directed to his second in command, VL9: 'An old version. Inefficient.'

The VETAC lieutenant's response was instant. 'Their other weapons systems and defensive munitions will be equally antiquated.'

'Agreed.' VC5's next signal, issued less than a hundredth of a second after his initial comment to VL9, was to the weapons officer. 'Destroy projectile.'

A single, smart, distronic missile lanced out from one of the tubes set into the cruiser's nose cone. Its targeting systems acquired the hostile projectile almost as soon as it left the tube. They locked on and determined the best approach. It assumed the projectile had defensive capabilities and was aware of its approach, although this was not in fact the case.

The missile arced round the projectile, scanning it and attempting to draw out any defences. Then it changed course abruptly and threw itself into the projectile's exhaust port. The distronic missile did not explode its warhead until it had used secondary charges to drill its way through to the centre of the projectile.

The explosion was silent in the vast vacuum of space, a brilliant burst of colour against the night blackness.

Trayx was the first to turn away from the monitor. 'Get Prion back here,' he told Darkling.

'Yes, sir.'

'And send a signal to Captain Logall.' Trayx was aware that he was breathing heavily. 'Tell him we can't stop them docking now.'

The whole of the main thoroughfare to the docking bay had been blocked off. Heavy duralinium blast shutters had been drawn across the corridor. They were a precaution against decompression, against a catastrophic failure of the osmotic field. But they also served as a defensive barrier.

It was not impossible to open them from the docking-bay side. Logall knew that an override program could be fed into the mechanism that would order the shutters to pull back. So he had ordered distronic charges placed within the opening mechanism itself. If the gears that controlled the heavy shutters began to move, the charges would blow apart the whole area behind them. It was crude as such traps go, Logall knew. But he hoped it would suffice. If nothing else, it should buy them time.

Logall was a veteran of Trophinamon. He had started his service during the civil war as a boy without a commission. That one final decisive battle had made him both a man and an officer. Most of his battle group had been cut down by one of Cruger's gunships, and he had assumed command of the few who survived. They had rallied, attacked a heavily fortified emplacement, and destroyed it. The moment had been decisive for Logall as well as for that part of the battle. In those moments he realised that he could never return to civilian life. Despite his reluctance at being called up for his military service, he now knew that it was a calling in more ways than one. And for the same reasons that he had found the thrill of the battle exhilarating as well as terrifying, he now relished the siege ahead almost as much as he was afraid of it.

'You're too valuable to fight with us,' Logall told Prion. He knew the automaton would not argue, just as he knew that what he said was true. Prion was a strategist, not a trooper. He would be of limited value at the barricades, but of immense help to his commander at the control centre. Logall turned from Prion to Jamie. 'But if you want to help, we need every man we can get. I take it you have combat experience?' There was a manner to the boy, a way in which he surveyed the preparations, in which he stood, that suggested he was not an onlooker by nature. He had certainly seen action. Perhaps more action than Logall had.

Jamie nodded. 'I've been in a fight or two,' he agreed.

'And what about you?' he asked the girl, Victoria.

'Oh, she'll go back with Prion,' Jamie said before she could answer.

Victoria looked at him. For a second it seemed as if she was going to argue. But then she bit her bottom lip, and nodded. 'All right,' she said quietly. 'Take care, Jamie. I'll tell the Doctor where you are.'

Logall waited as they said their goodbyes. Then Prion led Victoria away. Logall watched Jamie as he watched Victoria leave. Did he know, Logall wondered, that in all probability he would never see her again? He forced the thought from his mind. Start thinking that way and the logical progression might persuade him to give up now. 'All you need to know is that the objective is to stop them,' he said to Jamie. 'We can't let them pass. Above all, we keep them away from Kesar.' He grabbed a blast-bolter from a collection of weapons on the floor beside him and pushed it at Jamie.

Jamie took the heavy gun. 'And how will we tell them from us?'

Logall did not answer. He just stared.

'I mean,' Jamie went on, 'I've been in a few battles. There's smoke and confusion and rush. How will I know our people from theirs?'

'You'll know,' Logall told him. 'Believe me, you'll know.'

As he finished speaking, there was a low rumble of sound, and the floor shuddered under their feet.

'What was that?' Jamie asked.

'They've docked.' Logall pointed Jamie to his post. The

corridor was littered with makeshift barricades and areas of cover built out of packing cases, empty munitions boxes, benches and overturned tables – anything they could find. Logall's men – which now included Kesar's troops as well – were already in position ducked down behind the various pieces of cover.

Jamie settled himself into position behind a large metal crate. There was one other soldier there already. As Logall passed behind them to take up his own position, he heard Jamie introduce himself to her.

'And who are you?' he asked.

'Haden,' she told him. 'And I'd appreciate it if you keep your mouth shut and your attention focused on the shutters.'

Logall smiled to himself. It seemed that he need not worry about Jamie. He did not know Haden, but it looked like she would keep the boy in order.

'What happens now, sir?' Milles asked Logall as he settled into position. He had a clear view down the length of the corridor.

'Now we fight,' he said. All his attention was on the shutters. Any moment now they might start to open. And a second later the corridor behind them would be ablaze. The confusion and subsequent caution on the part of the VETAC commander could determine the course of the battle.

Except that it did not happen like that.

The shutters did not begin to slide open. The VETACs made no effort to operate the mechanism, and so the charges remained embedded in the systems, primed, ready, and waiting.

As Logall watched, there was a sudden, huge rush of flame from the metal shutters. Instinctively he ducked, covering his head, shouting for the others to get down as well. The sound of the blast came a split second later, drowning out his voice. The fireball followed that.

He risked a look over the barricade. The dark smoke was clearing slightly, and he could just make out the remains of the shutters. They had been blown to pieces: the whole middle section was missing and the metal at the sides was ragged and torn. Through the gap, the first VETACs were already appearing.

'Back,' Logall screamed. 'Fall back!' In a pitched battle like this they would stand no chance. They had to recapture the advantage. Energy bolts cut through the air close to him as he ran. Beside him Milles twisted and fell, the right side of his body ripped apart by a blast from a VETAC. He was vaguely aware of others rushing past him, turning, firing back into the smoke as they went. Haden was dragging Jamie as she raced for the next hold point. The heavy clang of metal feet on the stone floor echoed through the confusion.

Jamie's head was still ringing with the sound of the blast. He was dazed and confused as the woman dragged him away from the battle. He was shouting at her, telling her to stay and fight, although he could not hear his own voice. He caught sight of Logall as she pulled him back through the smoke. The captain was also running.

Then, as he twisted and finally managed to pull free, Jamie saw one of the attackers emerging from the smoke behind them. It strode towards him, light gleaming smokily off its armoured body. The figure was huge – tall and broad. It reminded Jamie of the suits of armour in the Banqueting Hall, though it seemed even larger as it approached. It was not slow and cumbersome as he would have expected from its bulk, but quick and lithe. The whole time, the metal head scanned to and fro for targets, its eyes glowing red from behind the heavy visor. The creature's right arm was pointing forward from the elbow, and he saw that at both sides of the gauntlet-like hand were nozzles. As he watched, the nozzles spat fire, sending energy bolts streaking through the mêlée.

The ground at Jamie's feet exploded into splinters of hot stone. He took one more quick look at the armoured robot, noted the grenades and weapons hanging from its belt and built into the very fabric of its structure. Then he turned and ran after Haden and Logall.

'You're just in time.' Logall's voice was hoarse, barely audible above the sound of explosions and energy weapons.

'Do it,' Haden hissed. 'Do it now.'

'What – what are you doing?' Jamie asked between rasping breaths. He could see now that Logall was crouched over a detonator, his hand poised over the firing button.

Then Logall smashed his hand down, and ducked. Beside him, Haden flung herself to the floor, hands over her head. Jamie followed, catching sight of several others pressed back against the walls as he went.

The sound was louder than anything so far. The initial report echoed through the fortress, followed by a low rumble of noise that built and built. The floor was shaking now, shaking much more than when the ship had docked. Jamie risked a look from between his arms as they shielded his face. At first he thought the whole corridor was full of thick choking smoke. But then it thinned and settled, and he realised that it was dust.

The explosion had brought down the ceiling and one wall of the corridor, filling it entirely with rubble, blocking off the VETAC advance.

Logall was on his feet already, dusting himself down. He coughed and sneezed as he surveyed the results of the detonation.

'What now?' Jamie asked between his own coughs.

'Back to the Banqueting Hall. We regroup and get fresh orders.'

Haden and the other survivors were already gathering themselves together. Several of them were limping. One needed help walking. A soldier carried a comrade over his shoulders, blood dripping to the floor in their wake.

'Well, that should stop them,' Jamie said as he caught up with Logall. As far as he could guess, the corridor must be blocked for about ten yards.

Logall looked at him. The captain's face was stained with smoke. Blood was smeared across his cheek. 'You saw them,' he said. 'You don't stop VETACs.'

CHAPTER TEN
KNIGHT MOVES

The net-slammer was inserted into a power cable, and followed it right to the main system control. It ignored life support and other essential systems, seeking out ancillary power usage and assimilating its capabilities and defences. Both were basic compared with the sorts of protected environments the program had been created to hack into and subvert.

The slammer's analysis together with its evaluation of what systems it could successfully attack and neutralise was fed directly back to VC5, using as a communications link the same power cable into which it had been injected. There was a typical symmetry and simplicity to the process. Elegant and efficient.

VC5 spent something under a third of a second evaluating the data from the slammer before passing back its orders. Immediately it received its instructions, the slammer started its assault on the power and communications network of Santespri. VC5 had already moved to his next priority.

Everyone was in the Banqueting Hall, yet the room still seemed relatively empty. People stood together in small groups, talking quietly. There was a constant, low babble of sound.

At one end of the room the walking wounded were being tended by two soldiers with training in first aid. Victoria was doing her best to help, bathing minor wounds and dressing them. Mithrael too was tending the wounded, showing a surprising degree of proficiency with bandages.

Jamie was with the Doctor watching as Trayx, Kesar and their command staff discussed tactics while watching the succession of images relayed to the screens set up on the table.

'You should have seen those things, Doctor,' Jamie whispered. 'They're vicious beasties.'

The Doctor replied in a low voice. 'Despite what we might think of Trayx and Kesar and the others, Jamie, you have to remember they're part of a huge republic – an empire in all but name. They rule thousands of worlds with a rod of iron. Those are their legionnaires, the main part of their army.'

'Aye, well, I can see how they keep those worlds in order.'

'Hmm.' The Doctor's attention seemed to be back on the screen, though it showed only an empty corridor. 'Perhaps it takes a civil war to bring home to them the problems with the way they treat others.'

'Meaning?'

'Meaning they've now been on the receiving end of their own military might.'

Jamie wiped his cheek with the back of his hand. There was a smear of blood across it when he pulled his hand away. 'Aye, only we're on the receiving end of it too.' He tried to wipe the blood off on his tunic, but it just smeared it more. 'I think it's time we got back to the TARDIS, Doctor,' he said quietly. 'There's no way these people can fight those things. We'd all be safe in there.'

The Doctor sucked in his cheeks, considering. 'What is the quickest way down to the lower levels?' he asked Logall suddenly. 'Down to where you first found us?'

Logall's face was grim. 'There is only one way. For

defensive reasons. Why do you want to know?'

'There's something down there that might help us.'

Logall snorted, and turned away. 'Forget it,' he said. 'The only way down is the other side of the collapsed section of corridor. With the VETACs.'

'So we're stuck here too,' Jamie hissed at the Doctor. 'What do we do now?'

'We wait, Jamie.' The Doctor saw the frustration on Jamie's face, and patted him on the shoulder. 'But not for long, I don't think. They'll make contact soon.'

'Who will?'

But Jamie's question was drowned out by Darkling's call. 'I'm getting a signal, sir.'

Trayx was nodding as if he had expected this. 'On the screen.'

Darkling threw a switch on the console in front of him, and the view on the main screen changed. The image of one of the staterooms was replaced with a close shot of the VETAC commander's head. The huge metal visor seemed almost to be leaning out of the monitor towards them. Lights flickered faintly behind the heavy blast screen.

The VETAC's voice erupted from the speakers in the monitor, a metallic scrape of near-expressionless sound. 'General in Chief Trayx, you will surrender Consul General Hans Kesar and his command staff to us immediately.'

'If you want him,' Trayx said levelly, 'then you come and get him.'

The VETAC commander showed no sign of frustration at Trayx's reply. 'We can kill you all at any time,' he said. A simple statement of fact.

The Doctor leaned forward, rubbing his chin as he watched the screen. 'Then why don't they? I wonder,' he muttered.

Before Trayx could respond, the lights went out. The whole room was plunged into sudden darkness. There was a shout, then another. Jamie heard Victoria scream. And then the monitors came back on. A moment later, a faint glow of red emergency lighting slightly alleviated the gloom.

'They cut the main power,' Darkling said.

'We can see that,' Cruger told him.

'Why are the screens working then?' Jamie asked. He was aware that practically everyone in the room was now crowded round the monitors, craning to see the VETAC commander, to hear what he was saying.

It was Kesar who answered Jamie's question. 'All the battlefield systems have backup power supplies built in.'

'But why do it?' the Doctor asked. 'What's the point?'

'What do you mean, Doctor?' Trayx asked.

'They must know you have backup systems. It demonstrates that they can shut all the main systems down – including, presumably, the life support. But you know that anyway.'

'To create confusion perhaps,' Prion suggested.

'You are now without power.' The VETAC's voice cut across any further discussion.

'Very observant of you,' the Doctor answered loudly. Then more quietly he added, 'Stupid machine.'

The VETAC continued as if it had not heard. 'You have five minutes to reach a decision. If at the end of that time you do not commit to surrender Kesar to us, we shall press home our attack.' The moment he finished speaking, the screen went blank.

'They've cut the link,' Darkling said.

Trayx was staring at the blank screen. Without turning he said, 'The reason they cut the ancillary power was to take out the lights. And the reason for that is simple. They can see in the dark, and we can't.' He tapped his chin with his forefinger. 'Prion, get whatever lighting you can set up in here. Candles will do if that's all we have.' Next he turned to Logall. 'We must assume they will eventually break through the main corridor, so start setting up defensive positions.'

The Doctor was shaking his head, as if in disagreement. 'No, no, no,' he muttered. Then louder, 'We're missing something here, you know.'

'Oh?'

'Why don't they just kill us?'

'They've got to get to us first,' Jamie said.

'No, Jamie, they haven't. That's the whole point. They can shut down the life support just as they can the lighting. Or they can destroy the osmotic shield which keeps the air in. I take it they don't need to breathe?' he asked Trayx.

'They want Kesar,' Trayx said slowly, working through it. 'But it seems they don't want him dead.' He shrugged. 'Maybe they have to be sure. Or maybe Mathesohn wants Kesar alive for some reason. I just don't know.'

Kesar asked quietly, 'Will you surrender me to them?'

'What?' Trayx was surprised.

'It seems the line of least resistance. The logical solution to the problem.'

'You know I can't do that. There are only two possibilities: they are here to kill you or, just possibly, to rescue you. Neither is acceptable. Whatever happens to us here now, you cannot become a martyr, nor can you be set free. We would have another civil war, and this time Haddron really would be torn apart.'

Jamie leaned close to the Doctor. 'Cruger's keeping very quiet.'

'Yes, Jamie. But they did say they wanted Kesar and his command staff. And I think that means Cruger, don't you?'

Darkling was watching a chronometer on the control

panel. 'We've had four minutes, sir.'

'Thank you.' Trayx turned to face them all now. 'We have an excellent defensive position here. And we will not let them have Kesar. We hold out until help arrives.'

VC5 reopened the communications link. He already knew the likely response to his ultimatum, but there was a three per cent chance that Trayx would surrender Kesar and Cruger to him.

'Have you reached a decision?'

Trayx's face was large on the monitor on the VETAC cruiser. Behind him, VC5 could see other people clustered round the communications equipment. The image was washed out by the infrared which tried to compensate for the lack of light. There seemed to be candles positioned around the room in the background. Expert systems linked into the monitor were already assessing the data, estimating the number of people in the room, pattern-matching their identities and their weaponry to gauge the strength and resolution of the defensive force.

'We have.' Trayx's voice had an edge of determination to it. The percentages were dropping.

'And what is your decision?'

Trayx's expression was unchanged. 'We do not surrender,' he said. 'Our defensive position is sound, and you cannot get in. I suggest you retreat before our reinforcements arrive.'

A predictable response. 'Our scanners show no reinforcements, and your distress beacon was destroyed before its signal was received.'

'That may be. But I repeat, you can't get in.'

VC5 sent a signal to his lieutenant as he closed the channel without reply. Phase Two would commence at once.

*

The image on the monitor faded to black. Silence. For a while nobody moved or spoke.

'Well, that's it, then,' Jamie whispered to the Doctor.

Victoria had joined them now, leaving Mithrael to finish doing what he could for the wounded soldiers at the other end of the Hall. 'Do you think they can get in?' she asked quietly as a general murmur started up. Everyone knew that this was a watershed moment. There would be no turning back now.

The Doctor was pensive. His brow was heavy with frown lines. The general level of noise was louder now, so it was all the more surprising that his voice cut through it all and stopped it dead. 'What was that?' he asked sharply.

Trayx and Kesar both turned to face the Doctor. Behind them Cruger, Darkling, Haden and Logall followed their example. Then everyone was looking at the Doctor.

'Didn't anyone else hear it?' he asked.

But before they could answer, a metallic scraping sound carried menacingly through the air to them. As one, everybody turned towards the noise.

With the main monitor now a grey blank and the emergency lights little more than a red glow, the predominant lighting in the room was from the candles that Logall and his team had set up. There was a smoky quality to the air, the smell of burning wax seeming to make the atmosphere even heavier. Dark trails of smoke meandered upward from the old candles as dust burned with the wax and the wick. Somehow the fact that less of the room was visible made it seem even larger. The alcoves were dark holes in the dimly lit walls, and the ceiling was a sky of blackness high above them.

The sound had come from one of the alcoves. But even as they stared into the unforgiving darkness, a similar sound came from further down the room.

Directly opposite the Doctor, Jamie and Victoria a single solitary candle illuminated the suit of armour standing on its low plinth within another of the alcoves. Victoria's eyes seemed drawn to the light of the candle, and she could almost sense the Doctor and Jamie also looking the same way. The tiny flame fluttered as if in a breeze. Multiple reflections of its pale light danced on the polished surfaces of the armour. The candlelight was liquid running over the shape, tracing its contours as it flickered and danced.

Except that the candle's flame moved less than the mirror images. The shape of the armour seemed to exaggerate the movement, seemed to suggest movement where there could be none.

The metallic scrapes were growing more frequent now, joined by other sounds. There was a chinking noise, like a chain blowing against a stone wall in the wind. Creaks like ancient joints working stiffly to absorb recent oil. The screeching and tearing of tortured metal as it grated against uneven surfaces and flexed in long-forgotten ways.

And as she listened to the sounds, Victoria realised that the illusion of movement from the armoured suit was not illusory at all. 'It's moving.' she breathed. Then louder, 'Doctor, it's moving!'

In the pallid half-light a huge metal hand flexed. Segmented fingers of metal creaked as the plates slid over each other. An arm reached out, slowly, emerging from the gloom into the light of several candles. A heavy steel boot slammed down on the marble floor as the figure lurched forward and down off its plinth. All along both sides of the Banqueting Hall, the armoured figures were stepping uncertainly into the flickering light. Expressionless, visored faces turned slowly back and forth as if seeking out something. Or someone.

Rivets and bolts gleamed as they caught the light. Small lights winked into existence on the breastplates of the figures, so that in the gloom they seemed to glow with inner life.

Victoria realised she was clutching the Doctor tightly to her. Jamie seemed to have both of them wrapped in his arms as they backed away, towards the main door. The trio circled slowly, a bizarre dance across the candlelit floor as they twisted and watched and tracked a path through the slowly advancing creatures.

All around them, the soldiers were making for the door with similar wariness. Logall and several of his men were backing cautiously away, herding the others ahead of them as they faced back at the suited figures, weapons levelled.

'What are they?' Victoria asked, her voice breaking in the effort to avoid sobbing.

'VETACs.' Kesar's brittle voice was close to them as everyone clustered in the doorway. 'They have waited dormant here for years. Relics of bygone battles and distant ages.'

'Not the latest models,' Prion said. 'But efficient and deadly enough.'

'At least now we know what Sponslor was doing,' Trayx added.

Prion nodded. 'He reset the command frequency to the same network as the attackers.'

Logall and his men were dangerously close to the VETACs now. 'What do we do, sir?' he shouted back over his shoulder.

'Any suggestions, Doctor?'

'As it happens, yes,' the Doctor said. 'Run!'

The movement of the VETACs was getting less jerky, as if they were growing used to their renewed mobility. Rather than lurching slowly, raggedly forward, they were now marching. The figures formed a V-shaped formation, the point of the V towards the people now turning to run from the room. Behind them, more of the massive creatures were turning towards the wounded at the far end of the hall.

Several of the unwounded soldiers had also been at the far end of the room, together with Mithrael. Now they were cut off from the main party, caught behind the VETACs. They tried to push their way through, but three of the huge metal figures were facing them. Fire erupted from their outstretched arms and engulfed the screaming soldiers, wounded and able-bodied alike.

Logall hesitated long enough to loose a volley of energy bolts at the leading VETAC. The shots splashed across the VETAC's chest. It seemed to glow for a moment, rocking back on its feet. But then the colour drained away and the metal beneath was unmarked. In response, a bolt of lighting ripped out from the raised hand of the metal figure. It stabbed across the room, lancing into the soldier beside Logall and knocking the man off his feet. He crashed to the floor and lay still.

At the far end of the room, Warden Mithrael stood defiant, arms folded as the soldiers around him screamed and died. He said nothing, did nothing. Waiting for death. Beside him, a woman was caught full in the blast of a VETAC's fire, was hurled backwards to land in a broken, smoking mess against the wall. Mithrael's jaw tightened, his cheek quivered slightly, but otherwise he remained firm and still. He was still standing unmoved when the next burst of liquid flame engulfed him. The flames licked round his upright form, taking hold and bursting through his armour, but still he did not move or fall. At last he crumpled, first to his knees, then forward on to his blackened face.

*

Victoria was running, running faster than ever before, or so it seemed. Her hair was breaking free of its ponytail and stinging in her eyes. In front of her Helana Trayx's white gown blew back, away from her body as she ran. It occurred to Victoria that she should have thought to put her own clothes back on over the under-armour as Helana had done. And almost immediately she was glad she had not. She felt weighed down and sluggish as it was. Jamie was dragging her by the wrist as her feet seemed to be getting heavier and slower.

Behind her Logall, Darkling, Haden and a few others were running backwards, firing all the time. At the far end of the corridor, as she looked back over her shoulder and tried to shake the hair from her face, Victoria saw the VETACs framed in the doorway. They were moving fast now – faster than such heavy creatures had any right to move. They were almost running.

A bolt of lighting cut into the wall above Victoria, blowing chunks of plaster and stone across the corridor. A soldier close beside her collapsed in a smoking ruin as his legs were blown from under him. There was a smell of burning in the air. The only light came from the occasional red emergency bulbs and the destructive fire that shot from the VETACs' arms and from the soldiers' weapons.

Another soldier was caught in a blast, knocked sideways into the wall and bouncing back into the corridor. Victoria screamed as she jumped over the body, as she saw the sightless eyes staring back up at her. She could not even hear her scream above the sound of the battle.

Ahead of them the corridor stretched seemingly for ever in a straight line. No cover. No escape.

Then a door.

'In here, quick,' the Doctor shouted. Again his voice

seemed to carry where other sound was lost.

'No, Doctor, keep running.' Trayx was shouting, barely audible.

The Doctor dragged him into the room, Trayx's face a mask of surprise at the Doctor's sudden strength. 'We'll all be dead before we reach the next doorway.'

They tumbled into the room after the Doctor and Trayx. Logall was last in, his right shoulder sagging and smoking through the armour. His face was contorted with pain as he pushed the door shut and collapsed against it, slipping slowly down until he was sitting on the floor. Haden reached over him and slammed bolts home. Then she stooped down to help Logall. Darkling joined her, helping to loosen the captain's armour. The room was stained blood red by the emergency lighting.

'The door is duralinium-lined.' Prion's voice was as calm as ever. Apart from Kesar, he was the only one whose forehead wasn't running with perspiration. Helana was retching in the corner of the room, trying to get her breath back. 'It will hold them for a short while.'

'So what's your plan, Doctor?' Trayx asked between gasps.

'Plan? Well, we escape. Get as far away as possible before they get through the door.'

Trayx nodded. 'Good plan,' he muttered.

'Doctor,' Jamie was looking round. 'Doctor –'

'It's all right, Jamie.' The Doctor was mopping his brow with his handkerchief. 'We'll get our breath back first, then be on our way.'

'There is one small flaw in your plan, however.' Trayx was leaning forward, hands on knees and breathing deeply.

'Oh?'

'This room has only one door.'

'What?'

'Aye, Doctor,' Jamie said. 'I was trying to tell you.'

The noise echoed round the small room like an explosion. It was a heavy metallic thud, as if something had slammed into the other side of the door. Everyone turned to look as the sound was repeated. Splinters of wood flew from the door, revealing the dented metal beneath.

'Oh my word,' the Doctor said. His finger was looped into the corner of his mouth. 'I think I might have been a bit of a silly billy.'

The VETACs from the Banqueting Hall had split into two groups. One was smashing its way into the room where their ultimate objective – Kesar – was cornered. The other group had made its way to the point where the main access corridor was blocked.

With VETACs now working from both sides to clear the rubble, it would not be long before the way was passable.

VC5 knew all of this: through the VETAC units he experienced it all as if he were there. It seemed as if the objective was almost achieved, though the corridor would still need to be cleared for the return to the cruiser. But VC5 knew enough about Milton Trayx, had enough of Trayx's expertise programmed into his own expert systems, to know that nothing was yet certain.

Jamie was once more at a loose end. Together with the surviving soldiers he stood facing the door as the wooden shell splintered and the metal beneath dented and bulged under the impact of the blows from outside. It could not be long before the door collapsed inward. And then...

Behind Jamie, Victoria sat with Helana. Trayx had spent a few moments reassuring his wife before huddling into a muted conference with Prion, Kesar, Cruger and the Doctor.

Helana sat quietly, clasping one hand tightly in the other for a short while, then swapping them round. She seemed to be staring into space – her only reaction had been when Victoria put her arm gently round Helana's shoulders. Then she had smiled. It was a thin nervous smile, but a show of appreciation nonetheless.

At the back of the room, the Doctor had finished his abject apologies and was now explaining how he intended to redeem the situation.

'The sonic signal,' the Doctor was saying, 'should resonate at a frequency which is in harmony with the individual molecules in the mortar between these stones.' He pointed to the heavy stone blocks from which the back wall of the room was built.

'And what does that mean?' Cruger asked.

'It means you should stand clear,' the Doctor replied, holding up his sonic screwdriver. With his free hand, he shielded his eyes. 'Could be some dust,' he warned, and promptly sneezed.

It took only a few seconds before the sonic screwdriver began to have a visible effect. Distressed mortar was trickling like sand from between the stones in the wall, falling to the floor and making little heaps in line with the edges of the stone blocks.

The Doctor lowered the sonic screwdriver at last, slipping it into his coat pocket. 'Now where's Jamie got to?' he asked, flicking his hanky in front of his face in a fruitless attempt to disperse some of the fine dust that clogged the air by the wall. 'Jamie,' he called as he coughed. 'Jamie, come over here and lend a hand, will you?'

'That door's not going to hold much longer,' Jamie told them when he arrived. 'What is it you want, Doctor?'

'I'd like a few of those stone blocks removed, if you can

manage that. Just enough to make room for us all to squeeze through.'

Jamie looked dubiously at the wall – the blocks were large and obviously heavy.

'Don't worry, Prion will lend a hand, won't you, Prion? Good, I thought you would.' The Doctor smiled. 'I imagine he's quite strong under that unassuming exterior.'

'Doctor,' Jamie hissed, 'he's a –'

'I know, Jamie. It's all right. And we need his strength. Unless you can manage it on your own.' He raised an eyebrow, as if the question was genuine.

It took Jamie, Prion, Trayx and Darkling to shift the first stone block. There was little room to manoeuvre it even with the mortar gone. But once that first block was gone, the others were easier to push through to the far side of the wall. Before long, there was a gap almost big enough for a man in battle armour to squeeze through.

Almost.

Then the door sagged inward, twisting around on the surviving lower hinge, wrenching free and pivoting downward to the floor. Through the opening, half a dozen VETACs were visible. Already they were stepping forward, pushing the door away from them even as it fell, crossing the threshold into the small room. Bolts of blaster fire scythed across the room, cutting down two of the soldiers where they stood.

Darkling and Haden fired almost simultaneously. The leading VETAC was held in place, framed in the doorway by the power of the blast. It seemed to be struggling to proceed, as if caught in a fierce wind, battling its way forwards.

'Come on!' At the back of the small room, Trayx pushed Victoria after his wife through the hole they had made in the wall. Cruger was close behind her. The Doctor was practically jumping up and down beside the gap in the stonework. 'Hurry up, quickly.' He waved to Jamie. 'You next.'

'I'm not –' Jamie started.

'Yes you are,' Trayx said before he could finish. He put his hand behind Jamie's head and forced it down as he propelled him through the gap. Jamie coughed as the dust caught in his throat. He forced his way between the stones, felt them scrape at his shoulders through the padded under-armour. Then he was free and falling forward into the corridor beyond. Victoria helped him to his feet, and Jamie turned in time to help drag the Doctor through after him.

Logall saw it all through a blur. The pain in his wounded shoulder was like a knife thrust deep into him. He was slumped at the base of the wall beside the door, looking up at the VETAC that was held back by Darkling and Haden's combined fire. The few other troops who had survived the attack in the Banqueting Hall and the subsequent chase down the corridor were already making their way through the gap in the wall. Soon only Haden and Darkling would be left. And Logall.

He struggled to pull himself upright. He had no idea where his weapon was, could not see it in the dim light. The output from Darkling's blaster was already fading – it needed a chance to recharge itself. 'Go!' Logall shouted hoarsely at the two soldiers. 'Get out now.'

They were backing away, but they would have to stop firing to turn and force their way through the narrow hole in the wall. And as soon as one of them stopped firing, or as soon as Darkling's weapon expended its main power, the VETACs would be on them.

Logall staggered forward, pushing himself away from the wall, hoping that one of the two would see him. He smiled grimly through the pain as he heard Haden shout to Darkling to cease fire. And he stumbled into the now advancing VETAC.

'Get out,' Logall shouted again. He did not look back to see if they were obeying him. 'That's an order.'

The VETAC was swinging round, the weapon pod built into the right arm coming up to cover him. To kill him. Logall hurled himself forward with the last of his energy. He saw the flames erupting from the VETAC's forearm as he dived towards it. He felt the icy fire eating through his armour and into his body as he reached out with clawed hand. His fingers scrabbled across the VETAC's control unit, felt for the recess he knew was located between the unit and the armpit, felt his fingertips brush against the small ring set into the recess.

He grasped the ring tight, held on with the last of his strength, felt the force of the blast hurling him backwards. And felt the pressure of his fingers round the ring. Knew that he was still holding it.

The warning bleep was louder than the blood in his ears as Logall fell back. The red light flashing in time to the bleep was all he could see. The light of the VETAC's control unit flashed faster, the bleep was quickening, gaining volume as it rose in pitch. As it reached a crescendo, Logall closed his eyes. Or, perhaps, it just went dark.

Haden pulled Darkling through the gap. She could hear the destruct warning from the VETAC behind them and knew what Logall had done. As soon as Darkling was clear, she pushed him ahead of her down the corridor after the others. Then she dived out of the way.

A second later, a huge ball of smoke and fire exploded through the hole in the wall, showering debris across the corridor. In among the stone and dust were the small fragments of the VETAC. Shards of stone rained down on them as they ran. The heat of the blast overtook them, while the blast wave carried them forward like a tail wind. She grabbed at Darkling, and felt his arm round her as he dragged her along.

There were few of them left now, thought Trayx: himself and Helana, the Doctor and his companions, Kesar, Prion and Cruger and eight troopers, including Darkling and Haden. They hardly spoke as they traversed the dimly lit passageways. Trayx led the way, his face set in a determined expression as he marched swiftly along the corridors of Santespri.

Before long they reached a set of heavy doors. They were made of thick, dark metal, studded with large rivets and braced with bands of duralinium. Trayx stood aside to let Kesar through first.

As he passed, Kesar paused, and turned to Trayx. 'So,' he said, 'we are all prisoners now, it seems.' Then he stepped through the doorway.

'Where are we?' Victoria asked.

'This is the entrance to the Secure Area,' Trayx said. 'The prison, in effect. It was built to keep Kesar and his fellows in. But it can equally well keep the VETACs out.'

'Aye, but will it?' Jamie wondered.

'For a while,' Prion answered. 'Even their weaponry and resources will take time to penetrate the security.'

'So we just wait in here until they do get through? Is that it?'

'Not entirely.' Trayx held his hand up to stop his wife as she approached the doorway. Then he beckoned two of the soldiers to join her. 'Sanjak, Howper. You three will head back for my ship. We're lucky that the VETACs did not destroy it on their final approach, and we can't afford to ignore the opportunity it presents.'

'I'm not leaving you,' Helana said quietly. 'Not ever.'

'You are leaving us.' Trayx's voice was firm. 'I want you away from here. I can't afford to have you here with me when I need a clear mind. And I do need you to go for help.'

'Someone else can go.'

'No. You must go. Get a message to Consul Jank. If anyone can persuade him to take a stand, to finally make a decision for himself, it is you.'

She considered. Finally she nodded, her face pale and drawn. 'I'll get help,' she said. Then she leaned forward, put her arm round Trayx's neck and pulled him close to her. She kissed him long and hard.

'Doctor,' Trayx said when he was done. 'There is room on the ship for one other person.'

The Doctor nodded. 'Thank you,' he said. 'I would appreciate that.'

Jamie's mouth dropped open. 'Doctor, you're not leaving us —'

But the Doctor was waving him to silence. 'No, Jamie, no,' he said quietly. 'He didn't mean me.'

Jamie's eyes widened slightly as he realised what Trayx had meant.

'Victoria,' the Doctor was calling.

'Yes, Doctor?'

'I want you to do something for me, if you would.'

'Yes?'

'Go with Helana, will you? Look after her, and make sure she's all right.'

Victoria looked from the Doctor to Jamie, then back again.

'Please, Victoria.' The Doctor's voice was deathly quiet. 'It is important. We'll see you again soon.'

She was still looking into the Doctor's face when Helana Trayx took Victoria's arm. 'Thank you,' she said. 'We'd better be on our way.'

Trayx and the Doctor stood together, Jamie beside them, as they watched Victoria, Helana and the two soldiers start off down the corridor. They watched until the figures were out of sight. Then they turned and crossed into the Secure Area. Trayx closed and sealed the huge blast doors behind them.

CHAPTER ELEVEN

POISONED PAWN

The dust was thick and heavy, huge opaque clouds of it rolling along the floor of the corridor. Every detonation that the sappers set off added to the grey fog of pulverised stone. But the VETACs' optical systems were able to pick out each discrete mote of material and eliminate it from the picture fed into their processing systems. The area behind the speck of dust was filled in by an expert system that analysed the space around it, and then filled in the blank.

The resultant picture was slightly grainy, slightly uneven, since there was so much alien material to be eliminated and replaced, but once computer-enhanced and sharpened it was more than adequate to show VC5 the progress his units were making in digging through the obstruction in the main corridor. A similarly enhanced picture from the less sophisticated units on the far side of the barrier showed him that they were making equally encouraging progress.

Soon, very soon, the main force of VETACs would breach the fortress.

Their journey seemed unnervingly slow to Victoria. The area they were in was better furnished than where they had left the Doctor, Jamie and the others. The walls were panelled with dark wood that looked like oak, and there was a thin faded carpet running down the middle of the corridor.

Every so often, the corridor widened into a formal room.

If colour had once been a theme separating the rooms, the paintwork and fabrics were so faded and worn now that it was impossible to tell. The result was that while they were undoubtedly making progress, each room seemed much like the last. To Victoria it was as if they were going in endless circles, chasing their own shadows and waiting to be found.

The two soldiers were taking it in turns to scout ahead or bring up the rear. Howper was the more serious, and Victoria guessed he was older. Sanjak seemed happy to be doing something. He had more energy than his colleague, led them forward more quickly when he was out in front. Perhaps he was simply reckless.

'How much further?' Helana asked Howper as he passed her, swapping places with Sanjak at an intersection. It was the third time she had asked in as many minutes.

'This is the old residential area,' Howper explained patiently. His visor was up so that they could see his face. Victoria could almost sense him biting his lip, trying to keep his voice calm and sound helpful. 'After this we cut through to the communications suite, and then on up the East Tower to the landing area.'

'How long?'

Sanjak answered as he passed. 'Depends who we meet on the way.'

Helana blinked, did not reply. She watched Sanjak as he checked the next section of corridor. Victoria could sense her anxiety. Her fear. She wasn't used to this sort of thing, whereas the soldiers took it almost for granted, were almost grateful for the opportunity to reuse old skills. The situation was nothing new for Victoria either, but she could not say she welcomed it. She put an arm round Helana's shoulder, held her a moment. The woman did not resist.

'This reminds me of my father's house,' Victoria said.

Helana looked at her, and Victoria could sense her making an effort to calm herself. 'Your father is a lord?' she asked at last.

'No. He was a gentleman.'

'My father is a lord,' Helana said after a moment. Victoria could tell she had noticed the past tense in her comment. Could see she had decided not to ask. And Victoria was grateful for that. 'Fear,' Helana went on, 'war, all this. It was something others did. My brothers in the Ninth. My husband. Kesar.'

'You know Kesar well?'

Helana turned sharply at Victoria's question. She opened her mouth to answer, but then seemed to change her mind, and closed it again.

Ahead of them, Sanjak was now beckoning for them to follow.

'Kesar and my husband have been friends since they were boys,' Helana said as they crept forward to the next room. But Victoria knew that this was not the answer she had been about to give. 'They're like family. They were like family.'

Victoria took her hand, led her forward. 'I know what you mean,' she said. 'The Doctor and Jamie are like my family.' She paused, considered. Somehow that wasn't quite what she had meant to say. 'They are my only family,' she said.

'Do you think we'll make it?' Helana's voice was strained. This was what was behind every question she had already asked, though unspoken for fear of the answer.

So Victoria told her the truth. She deserved that, would know if she heard anything else. 'I don't know,' Victoria said. 'I truly don't.'

'I thought you were a general.' The Doctor's voice was low, as if he did not want to embarrass Kesar with the question.

Trayx had set up his makeshift command centre in Kesar's quarters. Now Trayx, Prion and Cruger were seated round the chess table talking through their options. Jamie was close by, listening and occasionally offering comments. The half-dozen surviving soldiers were posted around the immediate area, keeping in touch via the communicators built into their armour. Howper and Sanjak occasionally called in progress reports.

Kesar was standing in the corner of the room. In his hand he held the faceless white king from the chess set that Cruger had fashioned for him. He turned in answer to the Doctor's words, his bronzed featureless face offering no hint of his real reaction. His voice was quiet, a metallic scrape that echoed slightly off the nearby stonework. 'I am a politician,' he said. 'My aspirations to military leadership were laid to rest with my cause.'

The Doctor nodded. 'A diplomat's answer,' he replied. He reached out for the chess piece. 'May I?' The Doctor took the king, feeling its weight, its smooth surface as he held it. 'You made this?'

'Cruger.'

'Really? Perhaps I underestimated his artistic and aesthetic leanings.' The Doctor handed the king back to Kesar. 'Be good when it's finished,' he said.

Kesar's laugh was a dry rasp. 'I still do not know where you come from, Doctor. But it seems they have chess there.'

The Doctor nodded again. 'They have chess everywhere. And nowhere does anyone how it originated. Fascinating, don't you think?'

'There is a story,' Kesar said, 'that the game was invented by a servant for his king.'

'I may have heard that legend.'

'For reward, he asked only that he be given an amount

of laish.' Kesar's head tilted slightly. 'Is this the same story?'

'If laish is like grain or corn, then probably. There are many variations of it.' The Doctor looked round. Jamie had grown bored with Trayx's deliberations and was coming over to join him and Kesar. 'The legend on Jamie's world says that the servant asked for the amount of rice that would result from placing a single grain on the first square of the board.'

'That single grain would be doubled on the second square,' Kesar continued the story. 'And repeatedly doubled. One grain, then two, then four, then eight, and so on.'

Jamie was listening now as the Doctor agreed. 'That doesn't sound much,' he said. 'What are we talking about?'

Kesar's face swung slowly round until he faced Jamie. 'I do not know anything about your world,' he said. 'But the entire Haddron Republic would take over a thousand years to produce the laish the king promised to his servant.'

'A nineteen-digit number of grains,' the Doctor said. He smiled suddenly, his face seeming to grow sideways to accommodate the expression. 'How was it Dante described the hierarchy of angels? Oh yes, "myriads more than the entire progressive doubling of the chess squares".'

Jamie did not seem to be impressed. 'About the same as the number of these VETACs we're facing then, Doctor.'

'Oh that's hardly fair, Jamie.'

'We should be doing something.' He was bouncing on the balls of his feet, impatient and anxious. His voice rose in volume and pitch. 'Victoria's in goodness knows what danger, Trayx and the others are trying to think of a way to keep the VETACs out, and you just stand here talking about a game.'

'Calmly, Jamie.' The Doctor patted him on the shoulder. 'We'll have something to do soon enough. But for the moment, why not get to know our comrades and their ways?' He cleared his throat, his face growing more serious. 'Now then, you've heard of Tolstoy?'

'No. What's that?'

'*He*, Jamie, he was a great Russian writer. Anyway, when he was a soldier in the Caucasus –'

'The what?'

'The Caucasus, Jamie. Anyway, he was a young officer there, and one night he abandoned his post so that he could go and play chess with another soldier. He got caught, and was arrested.'

'Serves him right.'

'The point is, Jamie, that the game of chess meant a lot to him. By his actions, he forfeited the St George Cross he was to have been awarded the next day as well, you know.'

'Doctor.' Jamie's voice was lower now. 'I don't care.'

'Oh?' The Doctor's face fell. 'Oh. Well. Never mind.' He patted Jamie on the shoulder again, as if in sympathy. 'Let's go and see how they've been managing without me, shall we?' He tugged at his lapels, tripped slightly on the stone-flagged floor, and waved impatiently to Jamie and Kesar. 'Come along.'

As they neared the chess table, Trayx stood up. 'No,' he was saying loudly. 'No, I cannot allow that. If anyone goes it should be me.'

'On the contrary.' Cruger was calm by comparison. 'It should be anyone *but* you.'

Prion's voice was as level and emotionless as ever. 'He is right, my Lord. You cannot be spared, although your leadership would imbue the venture with its best chance of success.'

'Then I should go.'

'Oh dear.' The Doctor's overly sympathetic tones cut the

conversation dead. He stood beside the table, rubbing his hands slowly. 'Having a bit of a tiff, are we? Perhaps I can help.' He sat down abruptly on a spare chair. 'Now what seems to be the problem?'

'No problem, Doctor,' Trayx reassured him, his former cool already restored. 'A slight disagreement over who should lead a small expeditionary force.'

'Hmm, so I hear.'

'An expedition?' Jamie was enthusiastic. 'I'll go.'

'What expedition?' Kesar asked.

'To the armoury,' Trayx said. 'We still have a copy of the toxin. It may be possible to release it manually into the VETAC command network.'

Kesar nodded. 'A good plan. And now you are arguing over who will get the toxin?'

'Logall was the obvious choice,' Cruger said. 'An experienced field commander, but he is dead. Prion cannot go for obvious reasons.'

'Oh?' Jamie asked. 'And what are they?'

'The toxin would destroy me,' Prion said simply.

'Oh, aye...' Jamie said quietly.

'That leaves the three of us.' Cruger gestured to himself, Trayx and Kesar. 'I assume that the Doctor's forte is not in military matters, and the boy lacks local knowledge.'

'What?'

'You don't know the way, Jamie,' the Doctor said quietly.

'I agree,' Kesar's voice grated over the table as he sat between the Doctor and Cruger. 'Trayx cannot be spared – he is our chief strategist. Without him, we are lost, whatever happens. Therefore I shall lead the effort.'

'No.' Trayx's voice was firm. 'No, if I am not to lead it, then you are certainly not to leave the Secure Area. That would be to present the VETACs with their prize on a salver.' He drew a deep breath. 'Cruger is right. I am forced to admit that he is the only experienced field commander who can be spared.'

'But I thought the VETACs were after him too,' Jamie pointed out.

Cruger shrugged. 'Whether they kill me here, skulking in the shadows, or out there fighting matters not a whit to them. But I know which I should prefer.'

Trayx stood up. 'We can spare three of the troopers.' He smiled thinly. 'Half our garrison.'

Cruger stood too. 'Very well,' he said. 'Of my soldiers, I shall take Haden and Gunson. I suggest one other from your garrison.' He smiled, his beard parting to reveal thin, sharp teeth. 'Just a fair balance of our forces.'

'And to get you into the armoury,' Trayx said. 'Take Darkling. He has seen action before, and his conduct this day has been of the highest order.'

'I'll come too,' Jamie said.

Cruger turned to him. 'I think not,' he said. 'No disrespect, but I need a force I can rely on completely. I cannot take a risk, however small, with an unknown. These soldiers, I know. And they know me.'

VC5 and VL9 stood side by side watching the VETACs dig through the last of the rubble. Heavy weapons were of no use as they might bring down the whole section of corridor roof. Tunnelling up through the ceiling or down through the floor had been discounted as possibly dangerous – either floor or ceiling could be mined. But they were in no hurry. Their primary target, their quarry, was Kesar. And he was going nowhere.

There were only three possible physical escape routes. There was the VETACs' own cruiser, and there was the long-range shuttle that stood on the main landing pad.

The third possibility was another beacon stored within the fortress. VC5 was confident that he had covered all of these eventualities.

Cruger led the way, proud and confident. Darkling reckoned there was a renewed confidence in the man. He seemed more upright, his voice more assertive as he led them through the dimly lit passageways towards the armoury.

While Cruger strode through the fortress, the three soldiers circled round him, weapons held ready as they peered round every corner and covered every alcove and shadow. But so far there was nothing.

As Gunson rounded the next corner and Cruger marched after him, Darkling paused. He held his hand out as Haden made to follow. She waited while he pulled her close, just for a moment. Then she slipped from his grasp and darted after the others.

Darkling smiled beneath his visor. He flipped open the communications channel back to Trayx and reported where they were. Not far now. Just a couple more minutes and they would be there.

'How does the virtual chess game work?'

Kesar looked up from the chess table. He had been arranging Cruger's hand-carved pieces in position. 'It is controlled from Cruger's quarters,' he told the Doctor. 'He initiates the game, and then the system responds in his quarters and one other location as chosen by Cruger himself. Why do you ask?'

'Curiosity. I had a thought.' The Doctor shrugged. 'Half a thought. It's gone now.' He tapped his chin with his index finger. 'I think I'll go and see how it works. Where is Cruger's room?'

Kesar told him. 'Hurry back if you hear anything, Doctor. It would be a shame to be parted from such august company.'

The Doctor smiled. 'It certainly would. Coming, Jamie?'

'Aye, Doctor.' Jamie looked round the room. Prion and Trayx were conferring in hushed voices by the door. Kesar was sitting impassive by the chess table. 'At least it'll be something to do.'

'Any more news from Victoria?' the Doctor asked Prion as they reached the door.

'They are proceeding cautiously through the residential areas, Doctor. If all goes well, they should reach the ship before long.'

'Good. Keep us posted, will you?'

'Of course.'

The entrance to the armoury was blocked by thick vertical bars of solid duralinium. Their shadows cut across the uneven floor, backed by the red glow of the emergency lighting. The tips of the bars were sharpened points that bit into the floor. Cruger's face was alternate streaks of red and black as he approached the portcullis. He was actually reaching out for the entry coder set into the wall beside the portcullis before he remembered that it would do no good.

'Darkling,' he called. 'You know the entry codes.'

Darkling paused beside the box. For a brief moment he reflected on the wisdom of opening the prison armoury at the request of one of the inmates. But he dispelled the thought, and tapped in the access codes. The biometric scanner built into the coder read the contours of his finger, the electrical field of his body. From this it determined who he was and checked his security clearances and the code he had keyed in. With a sound like a huge sword being drawn from a tight scabbard, the portcullis lifted smoothly clear of the floor and disappeared into a dark cavity in the ceiling. The bars were barely raised before Cruger was ducking underneath. He paused the other side of the gateway.

'Where is it?' he asked, his voice at once both hushed and strained. 'Where is the beacon?'

Darkling motioned to Gunson to stand guard in the corridor. 'Any trouble, just press a few buttons,' he said, pointing at the entry coder. 'The security system will know you're not authorised and drop the gate.'

'Just make sure you're not standing under it,' Haden added.

'This way, sir.' Darkling set off along the red-stained passageway. Cruger was close on his heel.

The dust had not begun to settle as VC5 strode through it. The antistatic coating on his outer frame kept his armour shining bright as he clambered over the piles of rubble. It was not entirely clear yet, but it was passable. VL9 was close behind him. Ahead of them, several of the reactivated VETACs from the Banqueting Hall were dragging aside the last of the huge roof blocks that had closed the wide passage. The other VETACs from the hall had a separate objective. Through their vision circuits, VC5 could see that they were close to that objective now. From his estimations of the time taken by humans to make decisions and the speed of their locomotion, VC5 knew that the objective would be achieved in ample time. The priority now for the VETAC units from the cruiser was the Secure Area at the heart of the fortress.

It would have been just as efficient for VC5 to have monitored and controlled operations from the cruiser. But the artificial intelligence that motivated him had been programmed with the knowledge and thought processes of the best Haddron commanders. And without exception they had led their men from the front. The fact that this had been for reasons based on morale, courage, and their less efficient access to communications and battlefront data did nothing to lessen the impulse in VC5 to follow their example.

Once they were through the mist of dust, VL9 stood to one side, standing motionless in an alcove. He would wait there for the moment, until a secure command post was established. His primary purpose was to act as a backup, ready to take over from VC5 should there be a problem with the command net. But for now he was a redundant element, a simple relay in the chain of command. A switch.

The first battalion of VETACs marched through the dust after their commander. Their metal feet rang loudly on the stone floor, kicking up yet more dust to add to the thickening fog. Each unit collected data as it went – visual, aural, environmental. VC5 absorbed, catalogued and processed all of it. The computations and observations of a hundred VETAC units occupied a small part of his comtronic processor's parallax capacity. But a single battalion, a hundred units, together with the dozen antiquated VETACs from the hall, would be sufficient to secure the primary and secondary objectives.

The armoury was a vast area in the lower level of the fortress. But for the most part it was empty. The military needs of a strategically placed frontier post had been far in excess of those of a small prison.

Darkling led Cruger and Haden past a multitude of rooms. Each opened on to the main corridor. Each was barred with a heavy portcullis not unlike the one that had closed off the main entrance. The first few rooms had been stacked with spare weapons – handguns, small field weaponry, crates of ammunition and explosives. But soon the rooms were empty, hung heavy with cobwebs.

At the end of the long corridor the way was blocked by a single metal door. Beside it was another entry coder, and Darkling tapped in the opening sequence.

The door swung slowly open. Beyond it was a small room, blood red in the dim light. In the centre of the room stood the bullet-nosed spider-legged projectile. On the readout two-thirds of the way up the device a single word flashed repeatedly: 'Primed.'

'Well, there it is,' Darkling said. 'Now what do we do with it?'

'It's too heavy to carry,' Haden pointed out. 'Could we broadcast from here? Hope they pick up the signal?'

Darkling shook his head. 'It would never get through their firewalls.'

Cruger was at the device, examining the panel set into its side. He tapped in a sequence, and a moment later a small drawer emerged from the side of the device. On it was a shining optical disc, its surface glowing red as it caught the light.

Cruger took the disc, and carefully pushed it into a pocket built into the sleeve of his armour. 'Let's go,' he said and strode from the room.

'Simple as that?' Haden murmured as she followed.

'Looked good to me,' Darkling replied, equally quietly.

The VETACs were fanning out, spreading through the sections of Santespri as they went, securing each area. Somewhere within VC5's brain, or perhaps out on the network – since it came to the same thing – a map of the fortress shaded slowly green as the VETACs took control.

VC5 was positioned at the junction of three of the major thoroughfares, a strategic position given the layout of the fortress. From here he watched through his troops' eyes as they worked their way through the staterooms, checking each in turn and securing it.

A small force made its way directly to the Secure Area where the prisoners had been held. Logically, this would be Trayx's command centre. It was designated 'Objective One'.

The next section was clear, and Sanjak beckoned for Victoria and Helana to come forward. They tiptoed quickly across the room, Howper close behind them.

'Right, we're getting close to the landing area now,' Sanjak said.

'Good.' The relief was evident in Victoria's voice.

'Yes and no. We're also close now to the docking and loading bays. Where the VETAC cruiser is.'

'But we haven't seen any VETACs,' Helana pointed out.

'Logall's men mined the corridors,' Howper explained. 'That has kept them out. But they'll be through before long. And when they are...' He looked round nervously, pulling his visor down over his face.

'They'll be looking for us?' Helana asked.

'Perhaps. They'll be searching the whole fortress.'

'Then we had better hurry,' Victoria said. 'Which is the quickest way?'

'Ah, there we are.' The Doctor stepped back from a cupboard, and almost at once a chessboard appeared beside him, hovering impossibly in the air.

'How did you do that?' Jamie asked.

'Oh it's a fairly simple system, Jamie.' The Doctor suddenly dived back into the cupboard, wires and circuitry emerging around him as if displaced by his presence. 'Now I wonder what this is for.'

Jamie shook his head. He looked round for somewhere to sit down and found a chair in a corner of Cruger's room. He slumped down and watched as more wires and pieces of equipment spilled out of the cupboard.

After a while the Doctor's smiling face appeared in the middle of the confusion. 'I think he cheats, you know.'

But before Jamie could comment, Prion's voice cut him short. It seemed to come from the very air, echoing round the room. 'Doctor, Jamie, I think you should return to Kesar's quarters,' Prion said. 'We have company.'

'Thank you. We're on our way,' the Doctor called out. He was already shambling across the room, shaking one foot between steps in a fruitless effort to dislodge several wires that were wrapped around his ankle.

As soon as he stepped out into the corridor, Jamie could hear the noise. There was a heavy thumping, regular, insistent. It was coming from the direction of the main doorway.

Gunson was standing with his back to them. 'There are noises,' he said quietly without looking round. 'Sounds like patrols, back towards the staterooms, but spreading out.'

Darkling nodded. 'They'll be checking and securing as they go. Standard procedure.' He turned to Cruger. 'Since we're here, sir, I'd feel happier with some heavier weaponry.'

'Very well.' Cruger considered. 'Two minutes, we can't delay any longer.'

It took less than that. Darkling and Haden grabbed heavy blasters. Darkling stuffed extra power packs into his pockets, and took another heavy blaster for Gunson. Haden took a handgun for Cruger.

Their journey back to the Secure Area was much slower than their journey out. They were far more cautious,

221

checking every section before making their way through it. At one point Gunson stopped them, waved them back, as three VETACs marched past. The huge metal figures seemed oblivious to their presence, the soldiers' heat and DNA signatures masked by the suppressing field of their battle armour. The VETACs continued on their way without a pause.

'We're lucky that we seem to be moving ahead of the main patrols,' Haden pointed out. 'They're taking it section by section.'

'So far,' Darkling said.

'This way.' Cruger gestured down the corridor, in the direction from which the VETACs had come.

Darkling frowned. 'The direct route is straight on, sir. That way will take us towards the main body of VETACs.'

'Exactly.'

'Sir?'

Cruger was smiling, thin bloodless lips barely visible between the grey of his beard and the white of his teeth. He held up the small optical disc, reflecting a rainbow of colours from its surface. 'They will already have laid siege to the Secure Area. But with this we can go on the offensive.'

Darkling looked from Cruger to Gunson and Haden. 'With respect, sir,' he said quietly, 'we need more than just the disc. We need to decide how to deploy it. We need a strategy, not a single all-or-nothing attack.'

'Are you disobeying my orders?' Cruger snapped. He was no longer smiling.

'I think the suggestion is ill-considered, sir. I ask you to think again.'

'Or what?'

Darkling swallowed. He was still getting no help from the others, but neither were they siding with Cruger. 'You may be a general, sir,' he said slowly, 'but given your status here, I outrank you.'

Cruger cocked his head slightly to one side. 'An interesting suggestion,' he said quietly. 'And what would your orders be? To return to the Secure Area, discover it is already compromised, and then continue with my plan? Having wasted time, lost the element of surprise, squandered our advantage?'

It was Haden who answered. 'We don't know that the Secure Area has yet been compromised, sir. It might be prudent to contact –'

But Cruger cut her off. He turned suddenly, his face dark in the red light, his voice sharp. 'Whatever the relative status of myself and this officer, you, Haden, are under my direct command.'

Haden held his gaze for a moment. Then she glanced at Darkling. 'Yes, sir,' she said quietly.

'I think the question may be academic,' Gunson said, pointing back along the corridor. His voice was quiet, almost a whisper. But a moment later the passageway exploded with sound.

The two VETACs that had appeared round the corner at the far end of the corridor both fired at once. The floor at Darkling's feet seemed to lift towards him as flagstones were thrown up by the force of the blast. He loosed a single shot in return, saw it glance off one of the VETACs, then he turned.

They were running through a forest of explosions, along the corridor in the direction Cruger had wanted to go. Towards the main body of VETACs. Chips of stone ripped into Darkling's face as he ran and he struggled to pull down his visor. Cruger was in front of him. Beside him Haden kept pace, her own visor already down. Behind them Gunson loosed several shots before he turned to follow.

The world was red and orange as they rounded a corner. Darkling turned, dropping to his knees as he brought the heavy blaster up, adjusted the setting. Haden was standing behind him, bracing her blaster across his shoulder for stability. In front of them Gunson twisted and loosed off another wild shot.

'Go for the one on the left,' Haden shouted. Her voice was loud in his ear.

Both weapons bleeped as they acquired the target.

Gunson hurled himself past them and swung round again to face the advancing VETACs.

Darkling opened the communications channel, tried to keep his voice calm as he reported back to Trayx. The wall next to him exploded, a chunk of stone catching him across the side of the helmet. His communicator let out a burst of static, then it went dead.

'Now.' He heard Haden's voice through the air, through his helmet rather than over the link. And he fired.

The combined blast caught the VETAC full in the chest, rocking it back on its feet. For a few seconds it pushed back into the wave of energy, as if struggling uphill. The second VETAC was already retargeting its weapons, raking the ground in front of Gunson, Haden and Darkling with a blaze of fire.

Then, suddenly, the first VETAC's chest exploded. The blast was colossal, the sound funnelled along the corridor towards the soldiers. The VETAC's head seemed to lift off its shoulders as the whole of its torso was consumed in a fireball of orange and yellow. Beside it, the other VETAC was knocked into the wall of the passageway by the blast. Its shots went awry, hammering into the ceiling and bringing down chunks of masonry.

'Back!' Darkling shouted over the noise. They would need a few moments to prepare for another concerted shot like that. He felt the weight of Haden's gun lifted from his shoulder, was aware of how sore it felt after taking the brunt of the recoil. Then he pulled himself to his feet and backed round the corner.

In front of them, the surviving VETAC was staggering forwards again. Its left leg dragged slightly, but it was still operational. It fired a long burst of energy down the corridor, and Darkling felt the heat of it through his armour as he dived out of the way.

Gunson was slower, and he had further to go to make the cover of the corner. The blast caught him in mid air as he leapt after Darkling. It turned him, lifted him, consumed him. His screams echoed off the walls, mixing with the sound of the shot, amplifying it, giving it a dying cadence.

Darkling watched as the charred body slammed into the floor. A single hand grasped at a flagstone. The metal of the gauntlet was slippery on the floor, was running molten across the knuckles. A tiny droplet of silver ran down the side of the hand, like a tear, and splashed to the floor. It solidified into a starburst as it hit the cold stone. Then the hand was still.

Darkling stopped dead. Haden was rooted to the spot in front of him. Ahead of them, along the corridor, stood three more VETACs. They levelled their blasters. Darkling could see right into the black nozzles, braced himself for the inevitable yellow blossom of energy.

Between Darkling and the VETACs, Cruger was pulling off his helmet. He dropped it to the floor, let it roll to one side, rocking slowly as he stepped forward to face the VETACs.

'I am General Cruger.' His voice was strong, confident. 'Check your command circuit.'

The VETACs hesitated for only a moment. Then they lowered their weapon-arms. 'General Cruger,' the leading VETAC intoned. 'Identity confirmed.'

Darkling watched the exchange, uncertain what was going on. The pit of his stomach seemed to have dropped away. Behind him he could hear the scrape of metal on stone as the damaged VETAC lurched forward over Gunson's body. 'What's going on?' he asked, his throat dry.

Cruger turned slowly towards him. He was smiling again, his teeth like a white gash across his face. 'Reinforcements have arrived. *My* reinforcements.' He walked slowly back towards Darkling and Haden. 'Did you really think this pathetic prison could hold us?' Closer still. 'You dare to suggest that you outrank me? A general of the Haddron Empire?'

'Republic.' Darkling's voice was husky as it caught in his throat. He pushed the visor away from his face, up and over his helmet. 'The Haddron Republic,' he managed to say through dry lips.

'No.' Cruger was standing right in front of him now. He reached out and took Darkling's blaster, flung it across the floor. The VETACs were a wall of silver behind him. 'No,' he said again. 'I think not.' Then he stepped back, jerking his head sharply as a gesture to Haden. 'Kill him,' Cruger told her.

'Sir?'

Her visor was still down. Darkling could not see her eyes, could not read her expression. 'You heard me. He is the enemy. Do it for me. For Haddron.' Cruger's smile twisted further. 'For your brother.'

She stared at him, her expression hidden beneath the visor.

'This is one of them,' Cruger went on. 'One of those who

would have destroyed our dreams of empire. One of those who killed your brother.'

She hesitated just a moment longer. Then Haden nodded. 'Yes, sir.' She pushed the visor up now, as she turned to face Darkling, as she brought the blaster up to cover him, as the VETACs turned to follow Cruger.

Darkling shook his head slowly, in both disbelief and horror. He tried to speak, but he had nothing to say and no voice to say it with. Her eyes were deep and dark, her face was inscrutable, set, grim. She tensed. He could imagine the curves of her body hardening, could feel the press of her former embrace, could smell her close to him, her lips on his. Memories.

The gun was close, aimed at the weak point in his armour between helmet and chest plate. He heard the slight creak of her armoured glove as she applied first pressure. Her mouth curled up slightly, a parody of the smiles they had exchanged. Over her shoulder he saw Cruger turn back to watch.

Her voice was quiet. But it had an edge to it. Aggressive, hard. 'Make it look good,' she said, just loud enough for him to hear.

Then she fired.

Immediately he felt the blast hit him, he was slamming backward, the sound of the report ricocheting round the inside of his helmet, his head. The world was a red mist, closing in as he felt the wall suddenly hard against his back – harder than he had expected or intended. Then he was falling forward again, the floor rushing up to meet him.

END GAME

CHAPTER TWELVE
LOST PIECES

Cruger addressed the nearest VETAC. 'Where is VC5?'

'You may speak to me,' the VETAC replied. 'I am VC5. We all are.'

'Not good enough. I want your commander here.' He pointed to the ground at his feet. 'Now.'

'It is inefficient and slow for me to join you. Nothing would be gained,' VC5 replied through the VETAC unit.

'Then I shall meet you halfway,' Cruger said. 'But old-fashioned as I am, I prefer to speak in person rather than through proxies.' He rapped the VETAC on the chest with the back of his hand. 'However efficient they may be.'

'Very well.'

Cruger smiled. 'Good.' Then he turned and pointed to his helmet lying where it had rolled after he dropped it. 'The communications unit in there is switched off,' he said. 'But it will give you the command frequency that Trayx and his cronies are using.' He smiled at Haden. 'That should short-cut some of the proceedings.'

She had lowered the visor on her helmet again, and he could not see her face. 'Yes, sir,' she said.

'You did well, Haden.' Cruger glanced back at Darkling's inert body further down the passage. 'You made the right decision.' He felt elated. It was working, everything was coming together exactly as he had planned. 'The Empire starts here,' he breathed.

*

The sound of hammering on the main doors seemed if anything to be getting louder.

'How long will those doors hold them?' Jamie asked.

'Who knows?' Trayx said with a shrug. 'There are shutters we can drop behind the doors, and we have two fallback positions from here. But none of those will last very long.'

The Doctor coughed quietly. 'And how are Victoria and your wife getting along?'

'They have just passed through the Baygent Suite,' Prion said. 'So far they have encountered no problems, but they are close to the point where the VETACs penetrated the fortress. They are proceeding with caution.'

Jamie frowned. 'How do you know?'

As always, Prion's reply was level and devoid of appreciable emotion. 'Howper and Sanjak have their communicators open. They give constant status and progress reports. It is easy to follow their progress.'

'Unlike Cruger and his team,' Trayx added.

'Why, what's happened to them?'

'No data,' Prion said. 'Gunson is not registering an ident signal. Darkling's communicator also offlined a short while ago.'

'And Cruger?' Kesar asked. 'What of him?'

'No data. His communicator is not sending. Nor is trooper Haden's.'

'Then we are on our own,' Kesar observed.

The Doctor cleared his throat. 'Er, that may not be such a bad thing,' he said. 'Actually.'

As he made his way through the fortress to meet with General Cruger, VC5 patched into Trayx's communications system. It was a simple matter to set a virtual machine within his processing unit to monitor the channel and extract relevant data. Within seconds, a VETAC patrol was diverted to intercept the small group of humans making for Trayx's shuttle.

'We're into the last section now,' Howper told them. 'Five minutes more, and we'll be there. Safe.'

'Thank goodness,' Victoria said.

Behind her, Sanjak signalled their current position to Prion.

The blackness was complete. It was warm, snug, soft. But slowly it hardened, and in the back of his mind Darkling could see a tiny point of red light. It seemed to be growing, approaching, rushing headlong towards him.

Then abruptly he was awake. And he was staring at a flagstone, so close he could see the ridges in the surface. His head was throbbing as he struggled to sit upright. From somewhere he could hear muffled voices, and he remembered where he was. He froze, turned slowly to see what was happening.

Down the corridor, a group of VETACs were walking away from him. Cruger was with them.

And Haden.

Haden, who had shot him. Who had shot him with the blaster set to its lowest setting, just enough to jolt him. The rest – the stumbling backwards, the fall – had been up to him. It had been up to him to make it look convincing, or they would both now be dead. A headache from his misjudged collision with the wall was a small price by comparison.

He keyed the communicator. But there was nothing except static. As the VETACs disappeared round a corner, Darkling pulled his helmet off. He breathed deeply for a few seconds. Then he turned his helmet over and felt inside, tracing the connections from throat mike and earpieces. Sure enough, one of the connectors was loose. He wiggled it with his fingers, trying to force it back into place.

'Come in,' he hissed into the helmet as loudly as he dared. 'Can anyone hear me?'

Again, there was just static. He considered his situation. It might be possible to get back to the Secure Area, back to Trayx, and report in person. But Cruger was probably right: the VETACs would be there by now. His best option was to follow Cruger and try to find out what was happening. At the same time he could try to fix his communicator, or find another.

As he stood up, swaying unsteadily on feet that felt as if they belonged to someone else, Darkling noticed Gunson's body lying across the corridor. He stumbled over to it, rolled it over and reached for the battered helmet. He was almost relieved to see that the comms unit was obviously smashed beyond repair. Removing the helmet, seeing whatever was left inside, spilling it out on to the floor, had not been a pleasant prospect.

It was as sudden as it was unexpected. One moment Victoria was making her furtive way across a sparsely furnished room. Helana Trayx was close beside her as they negotiated a path between a faded tapestry hanging on one wall and a low table in the middle of the room. From the other side of the room, an old man watched from a dusty portrait, his painted eyes following their hesitant progress. Ahead of them Sanjak was in the doorway, peering out into the corridor beyond.

The next moment there was a shout from behind them. Howper was running, overtaking them, leaping the table, catching it with his foot and sending it flying as he grabbed

Victoria's hand and dragged her along. Victoria grasped for Helana's hand in turn, pulled her after them. Beside them the tapestry exploded in a fireball of dusty orange thread and Helana screamed.

A bolt of energy shot over Victoria's head – from in front of them. She thought for a second they were cornered, then saw Sanjak framed in the doorway. A curl of smoke was twisting its way out of the barrel of his gun as he shouted at them to hurry.

She risked one quick look over her shoulder as they reached the door. And wished she hadn't.

The leading VETAC had reached the low table, which was standing at an angle where Howper had knocked it with his foot. The VETAC seemed not to notice it in the rush forward. For all their bulk, the creatures were certainly fast. The robot's heavy metal boot crashed down on the table, shattering it to pieces as the VETAC raced after its quarry. The VETACs behind it compounded the destruction, the wood shattering and grinding to sawdust and splinters under their feet.

It was to Darkling's advantage that they were following the route of one of his regular patrols. At last the evenings of mind-numbing boredom were of some use, he reflected, as he ducked into an alcove. He was able to follow at a distance with little fear of being seen. At one point, Haden turned and looked back. It was impossible to tell if she knew he was there. She probably guessed that he was conscious again by now and following, but she could not have known when she reset her blaster to the minimal that his communicator was down. She might well assume he was calling in backup. Although where he could get it from was an interesting question.

They were close to the Banqueting Hall now. Perhaps that was their destination. Darkling slipped closer, as close as he dared. He was straining to hear what Cruger was saying. At the same time he was fiddling with the connections inside his helmet, desperate to make contact.

It was obvious as they got close that the VETACs had set up a command centre of some sort in the Banqueting Hall. As they approached, Darkling could see the ranks of silver figures standing motionless inside the room, waiting. The hall was still lit predominantly by the candles that Logall and his men had brought through. The flickering light reflected off the angular surfaces of the VETAC troopers, so that the whole room seemed alive with dancing firelight.

Cruger and his party were at the door now. 'A guard of honour?' Cruger was asking. 'You may tell your commander that the Fifth Legion has acquitted itself well this day.'

'You may tell me yourself,' a loud metallic voice said as the door was closed behind Cruger, Haden and their VETAC guards.

But Darkling hardly heard the response, hardly noticed that the door had cut them off from him. He was standing in an alcove, his mouth hanging open in surprise. The Fifth Legion? What the hell was going on here? He sat down heavily on the floor, ripping the lining from the inside of his helmet. Now he had to get the circuits working again. Had to.

The Doctor and Kesar were playing chess, much to Jamie's disgust. He could just about follow the game – the general flow rather than the intricacies and nuances. But he still felt that this was a diversion from more important matters. The pounding on the main doors was as regular and insistent as ever, and Prion was giving them intermittent updates on

Victoria's progress, which suggested that she was at the very least in some trouble.

'Is Cruger a good chess player?' the Doctor asked suddenly.

Kesar paused, caught in mid-move. He completed the move, placing one of his knights further up the board. 'He would like to think so.' The reply was considered, the tempo of the electronic voice as measured as the metronome thump of the VETAC assault.

'You mean no.' The Doctor seemed to play his own move without looking at the board, without considering Kesar's.

'He is impulsive, given to acts of temper and emotion rather than reason and logic.'

'I've heard that said about you as well.' Now the Doctor did look at the board. 'But your play seems to give the lie to those rumours.'

Kesar's mask-face tilted slightly so that it was angled directly at the Doctor. 'Defeat makes philosophers of us all,' he said.

'Except for Cruger, it seems.'

'Perhaps he has yet to admit his defeat.'

The Doctor pushed his queen across the board. Again, he barely seemed to consider the move, asking, 'The night that Remas was killed, you played chess then?'

'We did. I was in here. Cruger was in his own quarters.'

'I know.' The Doctor's face was stretched into a grin. 'I've seen the tapes. How did you think Cruger played that night? As impulsive as ever?'

'You tell me. I think you have seen the tapes.'

The Doctor leaned back, steepling his fingers. 'So I have,' he said. 'Check, by the way.' He waited while Kesar considered his next move. Then, as Kesar brought back a bishop to take the Doctor's rook, he went on: 'His play seemed fairly even and logical to me. A bit boring. Uninspired even. Safe.'

'It was not a typical game.'

'I thought you might say that.' The Doctor moved his queen again. 'But it was similar to the game he played against me. When Sponslor died.'

'What are you saying, Doctor?' Kesar was studying the board. His hand hesitated over a piece, then moved on to another. But still he did not play a move.

'Oh, I'm sorry. Checkmate.'

Kesar was laying down his king when Prion called across to them. Kesar's hand froze at his words.

'I'm getting a signal from Darkling,' Prion said. 'It's disjointed, broken up. But he says the VETACs are from the Fifth Legion.'

'Impossible.' Kesar's voice was a harsh scraping of rusty sound. 'That's impossible.'

'Oh? And why's that?' Jamie asked.

'Because there is no Fifth Legion.'

Trayx was beside them now. 'We don't know that,' he said quietly. 'We don't know anything for certain about the Fifth.'

'Oh?' the Doctor asked. His manner was apparently casual, but Jamie could see that his eyes were darting from Trayx to Kesar.

'The Fifth Legion disappeared, Doctor.' Trayx sat down between the Doctor and Kesar. 'Just before the beginning of the civil war, they were putting down a rebellion on one of the frontier worlds. A simple enough task.'

'So what happened?' Jamie asked.

'Nobody knows. They vanished. Disappeared from the face of the Republic.'

Kesar slowly got to his feet. 'Until now, it seems.' He seemed to be staring off into space, though the mask made it impossible to be sure.

'There is a high probability that their appearance here is connected to the war,' Prion said, and Jamie realised that even across the room the robot could hear perfectly every thing that was said.

'And why is that?' the Doctor asked.

'If it were not for the Fifth Legion,' Trayx replied, 'I might not have spoken out against Kesar. In which case, in all probability, he would now be Emperor of Haddron.'

Darkling pressed himself further back into the shadows of the alcove. He was pretty sure he had managed to get through to Prion before the comms unit packed up again. A few words only, but it should be enough. His problem now was what to do next. It was apparent that he would never make it back through the fortress to the Secure Area without being spotted by a VETAC patrol, so his options were somewhat limited.

Added to that, he was tired. Very tired. His head was still throbbing, and he was having trouble focusing. He tried to concentrate. He knew this fortress, knew this area in particular. Where would be the best, the safest place to take refuge?

All Victoria could hear was the sound of her own breath as she stumbled after Sanjak and Helana. Her whole world was the sight of their feet on the stone floor and the stertorous sound of her panting. Her lungs were sore and her throat was ragged with the effort.

Behind Victoria, Howper was shouting into his helmet microphone.

A VETAC appeared ahead of them, at the junction with the next corridor. The first of many. Helana was screaming, Sanjak shouting as he dragged the women back the other way and into an opening they had just passed. Howper let off a long blast from his weapon and dived after them. The doorway exploded behind him.

'How – how do they know where we are?' Helana stammered through her gasps as she tried to catch her breath.

'I don't know,' Sanjak said, dragging Helana and Victoria onward. 'But they know.'

They were reeling down another corridor now, Howper shouting at them from behind to hurry. Lumps of stone flew from the walls around them as fire raked along the passage, gaining on them as they raced for the far end.

The pain was sudden and intense, tearing at Victoria's shoulder. At first she thought she had been hit, then she realised that Helana had tripped, was falling, her weight pulling at Victoria. Sanjak was yanking her back to her feet, Howper skidding on the flagstones as he tried not to stumble into them, knock them flying.

Then, in the middle of it all, a burst of orange flame exploded in the heavy air. Helana screamed again, clutching her arm as she twisted and fell away from the fire. Howper turned, firing wildly back down the corridor. Sanjak was still holding on to both the women, dragging them onward, oblivious to their shouts and cries and screams, teeth gritted as he fought to pull them further.

It was only as they turned the corner, as Victoria heard the heavy sound of metal boots on the stone floor, that she realised Howper was no longer behind her. She shouted to Sanjak to stop, tried to make herself heard above the percussive detonations and Helana's sobs of pain.

But Sanjak was still dragging them on. 'Forget it,' he screamed back at her. 'It's too late to help him now.'

*

The room glittered in the flickering candlelight. It was difficult for Haden to pick out what was an ornament and what was a silent, standing VETAC. She had fought in the same battles as VETAC detachments, of course. Until the civil war, though, she had never had to fight *against* them. But whatever side they were on, they were as impressive and frightening as they were deadly and efficient.

For purely practical reasons, the VETAC commander and his lieutenant were even bulkier than the troops. For the leaders, mobility and speed was less important than defence. For the Fifth Legion, VC5 was a walking command centre with VL9 as backup and command staff rolled into one. As with any military unit, there was a degree of leeway in terms of delegation, but for the most part a VETAC legionnaire was not capable of command decisions. Its relatively basic processor, devoid of AI and expert system-support, was simply not up to the task.

Neither Haden nor Cruger was particularly tall, and standing between VC5 and VL9 they were dwarfed by the huge metal figures. But whereas Haden was diffident, uncertain what was happening or whose side the VETACs – and she – were really on, Cruger was assertive and confident.

'I have already provided you with the enemy's command frequency,' he said, his voice silky smooth. 'Permit me to offer one further gesture of goodwill.'

'Your profile is in the command chain,' VL9 said. 'No gesture is necessary.'

'Indulge me. In terms of the military strategy to defeat Trayx, I leave that to you. I don't pretend to be a match for him on the field of battle. I learned that, if nothing else, at Trophinamon.'

'What is this gesture?' VC5 demanded.

'An ally. Access to someone within Trayx's group who will work for you.'

'A traitor?'

Cruger smiled. 'In a way. And then again, it is the person Trayx trusts most.' He glanced at Haden. 'You see, anyone can be suborned, if you just have the right lever. Or frequency range.'

'So what happened to this Fifth Legion?' Jamie asked. 'Why is it so important?'

Trayx gestured for Prion to answer. 'They were on duty out on the rim, among the frontier worlds of the Republic. Their last mission was to put down a rebellion on Sertus Minor. They never reported back in.'

'Well perhaps these rebels wiped them out. That's possible, isn't it?'

Trayx shook his head. 'The relief team found that the rebellion had been crushed. Sertus Minor was completely subjugated. There had been a small disagreement over changes in the level of taxation being levied from Haddron. Not really a rebellion at all.'

'Wasn't sending a legion of VETACs a little extreme in that case?' the Doctor asked.

'Standard policy, Doctor. We cannot afford dissent, especially so far from Haddron. Allow one world to get away with it, and others would follow.'

'So who were these rebels?' Jamie asked. 'Just ordinary people who wouldn't pay their taxes?'

'In effect,' Trayx agreed.

'And you wiped them out?'

'As I said, it's standard policy. They knew that when they refused the taxes.'

'Yes, well maybe they just couldn't afford to pay,' Jamie

snapped back. 'Did you not think of that?'

'I don't think that is the issue here,' Trayx said heavily.

'Oh, isn't it?'

The Doctor caught Jamie by the hand. 'It's an issue, certainly, but there are more pressing matters just now.' He turned to Trayx. 'You must forgive my friend,' he said, 'but he has been on the receiving end of a greater power putting down a rebellion himself,' He continued quickly before either Trayx or Jamie could answer this. 'When we have a moment perhaps we could discuss some alternative ways in which you could maintain your reach without actually wiping out entire populations.'

'But Doctor –' Jamie started.

'Now, Jamie,' the Doctor cut in, 'we have to acknowledge, if not condone, that you don't get to run an empire – forgive me, a republic – across half a galaxy by being nice to people.' He turned back to Trayx and Prion. 'Now, you said something about the Fifth Legion being responsible for the civil war.'

Trayx looked at Prion, but he did not answer. Instead, it was Kesar who spoke: 'The Fifth Legion was loyal to Kesar, to me. When it vanished, this was seen as a final indication that I was unfit to rule. It was used as a lever by the anti-imperial forces.'

'It was the decisive moment,' Trayx agreed. 'When Mathesohn and Frehling told me Kesar had lost the Fifth, that was when I finally decided what I had to do.'

'And that was to oppose Kesar?' the Doctor asked. Trayx nodded. 'And now the Fifth Legion just turns up again, as suddenly and unexpectedly as it disappeared.'

'Which suggests,' Trayx said slowly, 'that its disappearance was engineered to have exactly the effect it did. Given their obvious mission here, I would surmise that the Legion was somehow commandeered by Mathesohn. What is your analysis, Prion?'

But still Prion said nothing. He was standing absolutely still, his eyes apparently focused on the far wall of the room.

'Prion?' Trayx took a step towards his ADC. 'Are you all right?'

Prion turned slowly, as if in answer, until he was staring straight into Trayx's face. Then, without changing his expression, without sound or comment, he launched himself at the General in Chief. Prion's hands were outstretched, closing round Trayx's neck, bearing him to the floor.

'Frequency open,' VL9 reported. 'Control is established.'

An image swam into existence in the air above the banqueting table, projected from a small unit built into VL9's upper torso. It was the view through Prion's eyes.

Haden stared at the image. It was tinged red, either from the way it was transmitted and displayed or from the emergency lighting in Kesar's quarters. Trayx's face was staring back at her, his eyes wide, bulging, his hands just visible at the bottom of the picture as he struggled desperately to break Prion's grip on his throat. The background was moving – there was a rush of people towards Trayx, and the walls were rushing past, the floor swinging into view as Prion pushed Trayx to the ground and stood over him.

She stared at the images, mouth open in a mixture of horror and disbelief. She barely realised that the faint sound coming from beside her was Cruger's quiet chuckle of satisfaction.

The Doctor was the first to reach them. He struggled in vain to prise Prion's hands away from Trayx's throat. Jamie was beside him in a moment, adding his strength to the Doctor's.

Lazro, the soldier standing guard at the door to Kesar's quarters was running to join them, pulling Prion backwards. Kesar himself helped Lazro, and eventually they managed to drag Prion back. At the same time, Jamie was finally able to get his fingers under Prion's and lift them away. Trayx hurled himself backwards, gasping and spluttering for breath as he collapsed on the floor.

Prion turned, struggling violently to shake off his attackers. Kesar was flung away across the room. The Doctor and Jamie were rushing to grab Prion's arms. But already he had a grip on Lazro. He had the man by the shoulders and was lifting him off the floor.

Jamie pulled at Prion's arm, trying to drag it back down, practically hanging from it. Lazro was shouting, struggling to break free. The Doctor was ripping open Prion's tunic, calling to Jamie to try to hold the automaton still for a moment.

Then suddenly, Lazro was flying through the air, pitched head first across the room. He crashed into the wall, his head connecting with a loud crack. Slowly, he slumped down to the ground. His feet ended up curled above the rest of his body. His head was against the floor, angled awkwardly and bearing most of his weight. A trickle of blood emerged from the corner of Lazro's open mouth, running down his cheek towards a sightless staring eye.

Prion was turning again now, his hands clamped round Jamie's shoulders as they had been moments before round Lazro's.

'He's got me, Doctor!' Jamie shouted. 'Hurry up!'

Kesar was helping Trayx to his feet, and they stumbled back towards the struggling figures.

Trayx pulled a hand blaster from a holster at his side. 'Stand clear,' he shouted, bringing the blaster up.

'No,' the Doctor shouted back. His hand was inside the tunic now, grasping at Prion's chest. 'I'm nearly there. Hold on, Jamie.'

'What?' Jamie shouted back. He was above Prion's head now, his arms flailing and legs kicking as he struggled without effect to get free. Prion was poised to hurl him after Lazro.

And stayed poised.

The Doctor stepped back, grinning. 'There,' he said in evident satisfaction. 'That should do it.'

'Doctor.' Jamie's voice was calmer now. He had stopped struggling when he realised Prion was frozen in position. But the robot's grip still held him tight. 'How do I get down?'

The Doctor's grin sagged into a deep frown. 'Oh,' he said. 'I have no idea.'

The image above the table had cut out suddenly. One moment it had shown Jamie's face, upside down, as Prion was about to fling him across the room. Then it was gone. Blank.

'Contact lost,' VL9 said. 'Primary Automaton unit deactivated.'

Cruger's quiet laughter turned to a grunt of annoyance.

Unseen, on the unlit gallery above him, a darker shape moved, flitted across between balustrades.

In the deepest of the shadows, Darkling settled back as comfortably as he could to watch the scene below. He stifled a yawn, shaking his head in a vain effort to clear it. A few moments later he was asleep.

'That's it.' The Doctor pushed Prion's tunic back into position and dusted it down with the back of his hand. 'You can put Jamie down now,' he said.

'Of course,' Prion replied, slowly swinging Jamie back down to the ground.

As soon as Prion let go of him, Jamie stepped back, away from the robot. 'You keep away from me, you metal monster.'

'What has happened?' Prion asked simply.

'Somebody tapped into your command frequency,' the Doctor told him. 'I'm afraid things got a little unpleasant there for a while.'

'Then it is possible they could do so again,' Prion observed without emotion. 'You will have to close down this unit.'

'Yes,' Jamie agreed, 'well, I'm all in favour of that.'

'It does seem prudent,' Trayx said.

'Oh, nonsense,' the Doctor huffed. 'I've set it up so that Prion here is operating on a frequency that changes randomly every few milliseconds. Even he doesn't know what frequency he's on at any given time now.'

'Is that possible?' Kesar asked.

'Evidently.'

'Then why is this not the normal operating procedure?'

'Well,' the Doctor admitted, 'it's probably a bit advanced for your engineers, but fortunately I've managed to adapt the systems a bit. So long as nobody has programmed any nasty behaviour directly into his processing core, everything should be all right now.'

As he spoke, Prion's head slowly fell forward until he was staring at the floor.

'I think,' the Doctor added, catching sight of this.

But Prion was already looking up again. 'Sanjak reports they have been ambushed,' he said. 'Howper is dead. Helana Trayx wounded.' He turned to Trayx. 'Not a serious wound.'

'Thank goodness.'

'What about Victoria?' Jamie asked.

'No data. Sanjak requests assistance, says the VETACs seem to be monitoring their progress.'

'Where are they?' Jamie snapped. 'I'll go and help.'

'Don't be silly, Jamie,' the Doctor said. 'You'd never find them, and you'll never get there in time.'

'Doctor, Victoria's in danger. They're asking for help.' Jamie did not wait for an answer, but ran from the room.

'Oh dear oh dear oh dear.' The Doctor was hopping from one foot to the other. 'I'd better go and get him.'

'No, Doctor,' Trayx said. 'You wait here. I'll get him. Where is Sanjak?'

'East Tower, level three.'

'Tell him we'll decide what help we can offer.' Trayx was already at the door, shouting for Jamie to come back.

'No, wait,' the Doctor told Prion. 'Don't tell him anything yet.'

'Why?'

'Is Sanjak telling you where he is?'

'Yes.'

'All the time?'

'His communicator is open, he reports progress and events as they occur.'

The Doctor nodded. 'Then that's it, don't you see?'

Kesar said quietly, 'The VETACs are monitoring the channel.'

The Doctor nodded vigorously. 'If they can cut into your command frequency, Prion, then listening to our communications is child's play. Just tell Sanjak to cut off all communications. That will be more help than more soldiers running about the place getting shot at.'

As he finished speaking, Trayx returned with Jamie, and had evidently caught the Doctor's last words. 'How will we know what's happening to them?' Trayx asked.

'We won't,' the Doctor conceded. 'But neither will anyone else.' He put his hand on Jamie's shoulder. 'That's more help to Victoria than anything else we can do for now, Jamie,' he said quietly.

Jamie did not answer. But he seemed slightly more content to wait.

'You'd better tell Cruger the same,' Kesar said. 'If you ever re-establish contact.'

'You won't re-establish contact with Cruger,' the Doctor said.

'Oh? How can you be so sure?' Trayx demanded.

For answer, the Doctor led them to the corner of the room. 'Let's have a game of chess, shall we?' He raised his voice. 'Now then, General Cruger, I'm ready.'

In answer, the virtual chess table materialised in front of them. The Doctor stepped forward and moved a pawn. 'Pawn to queen's bishop four.'

A moment later, a black pawn moved forwards. 'Pawn to king's knight four,' Cruger's voice said clearly.

Jamie was astounded. 'He's in his quarters.'

The Doctor played another move. 'No, he's not,' he said. 'But there were times when he wanted you to think he was.'

'Such as?'

'What was he doing when Remas was murdered?'

'He was –' Trayx broke off.

'He was playing chess with me,' Kesar said.

'Exactly. But he isn't visible on the surveillance tapes. You just hear his voice, and see his moves.'

'And when Sponslor was killed,' Jamie said slowly.

The Doctor nodded. 'He was playing chess against me. Or so we thought.' He moved a bishop across the board. 'In fact, it was just a machine.' He watched the countermove, then brought the white queen forward. 'And a very stupid machine too, I must say. Check.' The Doctor stood defiantly in front of the board, hands thrust into his coat pockets. 'Fool's mate, in fact.'

CHAPTER THIRTEEN
RESIGNATION

Cruger and Haden were standing at the side of the Banqueting Hall. All around them, the VETACs stood still and tall, a forest of metal. Only VC5 and VL9 were at all animated as they directed the VETAC legionnaires throughout the fortress. With the loss of the information from Sanjak's reports, VC5 was organising a search of the East Tower and surrounding areas.

'So close,' Cruger said softly. 'So nearly there.'

'Sir?'

He answered Haden without looking at her. 'The empire,' he murmured, 'so nearly within my grasp. Our grasp.'

'Yes, sir.' She waited, but he said nothing more. So she asked, 'The Fifth, sir? What happened to them?'

'We – I held them in reserve.'

'For the war?'

'Yes. The war.' Cruger was staring across the room, his gaze apparently focused on the huge painting above the far doorway. 'I knew there would be a war – it was inevitable.'

Haden frowned. There was something here that made no sense. Something that was worrying her. 'But the war began,' she said slowly, 'because the Fifth Legion disappeared.'

'An overreaction.' His voice was quiet, but there was a harshness to it. 'That is not how it was intended to be.'

'I don't understand, sir.'

'There was dissent in the army when the Fifth was lost.

Stirrings against Kesar within the ranks and the officers. They were in support of the ideal, but now the man, it seemed, had failed them.' He shook his head slowly. 'In their hour of need, at their opportune moment, he had let them down.' Cruger's upper lip curled, baring his teeth as he snarled, 'But then Mathesohn turned it to his own advantage. He used it to persuade Trayx finally to make up his mind which side he was on.' Now he was looking at her, his eyes bright with emotion. 'That was not meant. It led to war, and it brought our forces firmly back under Kesar's control.'

'You expected the imperial forces to break from Kesar?' He was making even less sense now. 'But without Kesar there would be no chance of an empire. Who else –' she began. Then she realised. In an instant, the absurd made perfect sense. She exhaled, the candle flames nearby dancing in the sudden breeze.

Cruger nodded. 'Be mindful what you say,' he breathed. 'I shall yet become your Emperor.'

Helana was bent double, almost retching. Beside her, Victoria was in a similar state, and Sanjak was doing his best to keep alert while also drawing long deep breaths. Helana's arm ached, but the pain had mainly subsided now. Victoria had bound it up with a length of material ripped from the skirt of Helana's dress.

They had managed to evade the VETACs for a while now, and Sanjak had told them that their communications had been monitored. With luck – considerable luck – they could make it through the last few corridors to the landing area.

'One minute more,' Sanjak said. 'Then we must move.'

'Is it far?'

'No. We've had to circle round a bit to lose them. But the staircase is just through the next section.'

Helana nodded. She was still too breathless to speak, but she now recognised where they were. Not far now. Not too far. With luck.

Now that Lazro was dead, there were only two soldiers left with Trayx's group – Felda and Lanphier. Both were from the garrison. Felda was standing in the doorway to Kesar's quarters. 'They've started using heavy weaponry on the main doors,' he reported. 'They're blastproof, but they won't stand much more at this rate.'

'How long do we have?' Kesar asked.

Felda shrugged. 'An hour,' he suggested. 'At the most.'

'Then it's time we went on the offensive,' the Doctor said.

'Really?' Trayx raised an eyebrow. 'How?'

'I do have an idea,' he admitted. 'But first, it seems to me that the situation has changed rather.'

'In what way, Doctor?'

'Well, Jamie, we assumed the VETACs were here to kill Kesar because he's a political embarrassment.'

'We know that Mathesohn has sent assassins,' Trayx agreed.

'Ah, but now we also know, or at any rate strongly suspect, that General Cruger is the murderer. And you were surprised at the scale of Mathesohn's action.' Trayx nodded. 'Isn't it more likely,' the Doctor went on, 'that the VETACs are here in response to a signal, a signal we detected earlier? A signal sent by Cruger.'

Trayx considered this, his face grave. 'The Fifth Legion was loyal to Kesar,' he said. 'Cruger would be programmed into their command chain.'

'That is true.' Kesar's metallic voice cut across the room as he stepped forward to stand in front of the Doctor. 'Cruger has command over the Legion. They will follow his orders unless and until countermanded by someone higher up the command chain.'

'In which case,' the Doctor said, 'it now seems more probable that they are here not to assassinate you, but rather to rescue you.' Kesar said nothing, and the Doctor leaned forward so that his nose was almost touching Kesar's mask. 'And you must know that. So why is it that you don't seem especially enthusiastic about it?'

The stairs seemed to go on for ever, twisting upward ahead of them. Sanjak led the way, then Helana. Victoria was at the back.

'Hurry,' she urged them. Had she heard something behind them on the stairway, or was it imagination?

'Nearly there,' Sanjak called back.

Victoria felt a draught on her face as the door at the top of the stairs was opened. She turned the last corner, to see Sanjak standing in the open doorway.

'Come on,' he said as he stepped through. Victoria quietly closed the door behind them. There was no point in advertising the fact that they had come this way.

There was renewed enthusiasm in their gait as they crossed the top of the tower towards the shuttle. Sanjak was turning the whole time, checking every angle, swinging his blaster in arcs that covered the roof, the door, the ship. Helana was almost running, and Victoria could feel the weight lifted from her own steps, despite the fact that she knew this was probably the most dangerous stretch of all. If the VETACs were waiting anywhere for them, it would be here.

It was quiet, eerily quiet. The sky above them was pierced velvet, the stars shining through pinpoint holes. Even the air seemed fresher, although Victoria knew it must be cycled through the same filters and systems as the air inside the fortress.

They were almost there, Sanjak was reaching out for the entry coder by the main hatch. Then the hatch was opening, swinging out and upward. And Sanjak's hand was still reaching.

Helana screamed, turning towards Victoria and burying her face in her shoulder. Sanjak stepped back, bringing up the blaster. Victoria could hear herself screaming too, detached, an observer as the VETAC stepped through the hatch.

It had to stoop slightly to fit through, gripping the side of the door with one hand as it emerged. With the other hand it lashed out, almost casually, at Sanjak. The blow caught the end of the blaster as he was still swinging it forward. The gun was torn from his hands and sent clattering across the roof. The VETAC reached out again. Behind the massive silver figure, another was stepping through the hatch. Then another. And another.

Helana stopped screaming, her breath exhausted, her sobs muffled by Victoria's shoulder. From behind them, Victoria heard the sound of the door to the stairs being thrown open. In front of her, all she could see was silver – moving, blurring through her tears.

The heavy metal doors were glowing blood red. The VETAC legionnaires clustered around them were holding thermic torches. Under their combined power the doors were at last groaning and sagging from the strain. It would still take a while to burn through, but the task was feasible and they were making definite progress.

There was nothing in the computer brains of the VETACs that would impel them to update their commander on the situation. Through the command net VC5 already knew as well as they did what was happening. What they saw, he saw; what they knew, he knew. The network *was* the Legion.

The Doctor had finally agreed to explain his plan. They were seated round the chess table – Trayx, Prion, Kesar, Jamie and the Doctor. Felda and Lanphier brought them periodic reports from the main doors. None of these was good.

'Now, I think they may have overplayed their hand with Prion here,' the Doctor was saying. 'The way they were able to tap into his command frequency has given me an idea.'

'Yes, so what is it?' Trayx asked impatiently.

The Doctor held up his index finger, his eyebrows midway between quizzical and smiling. 'Ah,' he said, 'I'm glad you asked.'

But before he could further elaborate, Prion said, 'I am receiving a signal.'

'On the standard frequency?' Trayx asked. 'Sanjak knows better than to call in.'

'Cruger, perhaps,' Kesar suggested. 'Or Darkling again.'

'It is the commander of the Haddron Fifth Legion,' Prion said. 'He has a message for General in Chief Milton Trayx.'

'Then let's hear it.'

Prion continued to speak. But his words were not his own. The low, grating metallic voice of VC5 emerged from his lips, echoing in the confines of the room. For Jamie, it was one more reason not to trust Prion any further than he had to.

'This is the VETAC commander. You will surrender Hans Kesar, Consul General, to us immediately.'

Kesar leaned forward, but Trayx held up a hand. 'Say nothing,' he told Kesar. Then, to Prion he said, 'And if we refuse?'

'Your comrades will be executed.'

'You mean General Cruger, I assume.'

The voice was lacking in appreciable emotion, but Jamie sensed an air of satisfaction as the VETAC commander replied, 'I mean Trooper Sanjak, Victoria Waterfield, and Lady Helana Trayx.'

The effect of the words hung silent and heavy over the table. A nerve ticked below Trayx's eye. Kesar was as unreadable as ever. The Doctor's face was stern, lined with concern. Jamie looked from one to the other, not daring to speak, hardly daring to breathe.

Through the silence, Victoria's voice emerged uncannily from Prion's lips. 'Doctor, Jamie.' A sob, then, 'Oh, Doctor, I'm sorry.'

Almost at once, Victoria's voice changed back to the harsh rasp of the VETAC. 'You have one hour to deliver Kesar to us.'

As the VETAC commander finished speaking, Prion blinked twice. When he spoke again, his voice was his own. 'Transmission ended. Connection severed.'

'That doesn't give us much time,' the Doctor said. 'Jamie, I shall need your help if we're to rescue Victoria and the others in less than an hour.'

Jamie felt a smile spreading over his face. The Doctor had a plan. He always had a plan. 'What do you want me to do?'

'Well first,' the Doctor said as everyone leaned forward to catch his words, 'we need to capture a VETAC.'

A space had been cleared at the far end of the table. Helana, Victoria and Sanjak were seated there now. Haden could see that Sanjak had a bruise coming to the surface on his cheek and Helana's arm was in a makeshift sling. All three looked exhausted, and the women were obviously frightened, though Victoria was also defiant.

VC5 had finished delivering his ultimatum, and now stood facing the prisoners. Cruger was close by, his lips twisted into the merest hint of a smile.

'You traitor.' Helana's accusation was directed not at Cruger but at the VETAC. 'Why are you doing this?'

VC5's answer was immediate. 'For the good of Haddron. For the empire.'

'Haddron is a republic,' Sanjak said. 'It always will be.'

'Watch your tongue,' Cruger snapped, 'or I shall have it cut out.'

VC5's response was less violent. 'The republic is weakening. It needs a central power to hold it together. An empire would have the stability the republic lacks. This is for the good of Haddron.'

'And for an empire, you need an emperor,' Victoria said. 'Is that it?'

'Correct.'

Haden could see Cruger's smile widen at this. A glint of teeth in the candlelight.

But VC5's words froze the smile on his face. 'Kesar will be emperor,' the VETAC intoned. 'A powerful, charismatic figurehead is key to an efficient and lasting centralised empire.' He paused. 'We need Kesar,' VC5 said at last. 'Haddron needs Kesar.'

Helana's voice was quieter, more controlled when she answered. 'Haddron needs peace. The civil war brought us to our knees. Another would be the *coup de grâce*.'

'Nonsense,' Cruger retorted quickly.

But Sanjak was already on his feet. 'You claim this is for the good of Haddron?' he said before Cruger could interrupt further. 'Yet for the good of Haddron we had the war; for the good of Haddron we fought and killed each other; for the good of Haddron we weakened the republic to the point of collapse.' He sat down again, as if exhausted by his outburst. 'And what started the war?' he asked quietly.

'Enough of this,' Cruger hissed through clenched teeth.

Sanjak ignored Cruger. His hand was a fist, thumping on the table in time to his own answer.' 'You did. The Fifth Legion.'

'Explain.' The VETAC's voice rolled like thunder round the Hall. For once, Cruger seemed at a loss for words.

Instead, Haden stepped forward. It was time, she decided, to get involved. 'The disappearance of the Fifth Legion,' she said, choosing her words with care, 'is seen by some as the flashpoint, the deciding moment when war became inevitable.' She watched Cruger closely as she listened to the VETAC's reply.

'We were ordered into reserve,' VC5 said. His massive frame was swinging slowly round until he faced Cruger. 'We were ordered back to a reserve point by General Cruger.'

Jamie was listening in astonishment and disbelief to the Doctor's instructions. 'Now, Jamie, when you've found a VETAC, it's very important you don't destroy it. What I need is its command circuit.'

'I don't think finding it will be the problem.'

'Oh, jolly good. You know what a VETAC command circuit looks like then, do you?'

'I meant finding a VETAC,' Jamie said through half-clenched teeth. As if to emphasise the point, there was a loud crash from the direction of the main doors.

'Oh,' the Doctor said, 'yes, I see.' He cleared his throat. 'Now then, as I say, it's the command circuit we need. Prion can go with you, and I dare say Trayx can spare someone else too.'

'Indeed, Doctor,' Trayx said. 'But I should like to know what you intend.'

'Well, the VETACs could monitor our signals through the virtual network, yes?'

'Yes.'

'So, if we knew the frequency, there's no reason why Prion here couldn't monitor their communications in the same way. Is there?'

'No,' said Trayx slowly. 'No, there isn't.' He turned to Prion. 'That is possible?'

'Given the correct frequency.'

'But that's hardly a weapon, Doctor,' Jamie pointed out. 'They'll still kill Victoria and the others.'

The Doctor looked crestfallen, hurt by the accusation. 'One thing at a time Jamie,' he said sulkily. 'One thing at a time.' Then, suddenly, he brightened. 'Now –' the Doctor clapped his hands together – 'I have a question for you.' He was looking pointedly at Trayx.

'Yes, Doctor?'

'Why didn't you allow Kesar to speak to the VETAC commander just now? In fact, if they're here to rescue him, why didn't you –' he pointed at Kesar – 'just tell them to surrender?'

There was a long pause. Eventually, Kesar spoke. 'My voiceprint would be in their command circuit. But this is not my voice.'

'They must have other means of identification, surely.'

'Retina scans, pattern-matching of facial features. Neither of these would work either. DNA analysis can only be performed in actual close proximity.'

'To have Kesar speak, and for the VETAC commander not to recognise him, might compromise our potential advantage before we can use it,' Trayx said.

260

'Oh,' the Doctor replied slowly. 'I see.'

But Jamie sensed that somehow he did not fully accept their reasoning.

Both Felda and Lanphier were as incredulous as Jamie had been when he explained to them what they had to do.

'You're mad,' Lanphier told him, looking to Prion for support but getting no reaction at all.

'We only need one,' Jamie pointed out, not unreasonably, he thought.

But Felda shook his head. 'Suicide,' he said. 'Even if we could isolate one VETAC, Lanphier's right – it's madness. And as it is we're stuck in here and they're out there.' He pointed to the heavy metal doors at the end of the passage. They were glowing brilliant red now under the VETAC onslaught.

Jamie frowned. 'Those won't hold for an hour,' he said.

'Too right,' Lanphier agreed.

'Prognosis is twelve minutes at current rate of energy absorption,' Prion said.

'The VETAC commander must know that.'

'Of course.'

'So why give us a whole hour? He'll be in long before then.'

'No he won't,' Felda said. 'When it looks like they're about through those, we'll drop the shutters.'

'Shutters?'

Prion pointed out slots in the ceiling along the corridor above their heads. 'There are three blast-resistant shutters. They are not as strong as the doors, but they will keep the VETACs out for a while longer.'

'They'll get in eventually,' Lanphier said with a shrug. 'He's just getting impatient.'

But Jamie was not listening. He was looking at the ceiling, thinking. 'If these shutters will keep the VETACs out,' he said, 'would they keep one in?'

The hardest thing was not persuading Lanphier and Felda to give his plan a try, but convincing them that they should hasten the process of destroying the main doors. To the two soldiers, twelve minutes more was very probably an extension to their lives that they were loath to give up. But to Jamie it was twelve minutes closer to Victoria's execution.

Eventually, they agreed. With Prion estimating that the doors might hold for another nine minutes or more, Lanphier and Felda took up positions down the corridor and aimed their blasters back at the doors. Prion stood by the controls for the shutters, since Jamie had to admit that the automaton's reactions and judgement were likely to be better than his own. He still did not trust or like Prion, but his personal animosity gave way to pragmatism.

The doors exploded inward almost as soon as the soldiers fired. Jamie ducked back into an alcove as a ball of smoke and flames rolled towards him ahead of the blast. When he looked back, the smoke was clearing slightly and he could see a large jagged hole in the centre of the doors. As he watched, the light from behind was blocked out by a huge shape. A moment later the first VETAC legionnaire was through the hole and heading down the corridor. Behind it, others were pouring through the gap.

At once Jamie was relieved he had let Prion stand at the controls. The VETACs were much faster than he had expected. Despite their size they seemed to sprint down the corridor towards Lanphier and Felda, who were putting up a largely ineffectual crossfire.

'Now!' Jamie shouted. Prion had already reacted, and the first of the shutters – the one closest to the main doors –

came slamming down. Three VETACs were already past it, and immediately it was down, the shutter shook violently. Judging by the sound that accompanied this, Jamie guessed that one of the VETACs had smashed into the shutter at full speed. Perhaps deliberately. But the shutter held.

And now the second shutter was dropping, slicing down at the three VETACs. It caught the second a glancing blow on the shoulder, knocking it backwards off its feet. There was just one VETAC left now, flame erupting from its built-in weapons as it tried to acquire a target, sighting back along the blast wave from Lanphier's gun. The soldier dived out of the way as the floor where he had been standing erupted into flame.

Now it was up to Prion to time things right. Jamie could feel his thumb pressing into the side of his index finger as he clenched his fist. Now – now was the moment.

Prion pressed the button.

The third shutter dropped.

To Jamie it seemed to happen in slow motion. The shutter was falling, its weight dragging it heavily towards the floor. The VETAC was charging forward, flames and smoke surrounding it as it fired again, this time at Felda. For a long, breath-held moment it seemed that the shutter would miss the VETAC, would fall too late and let it through. But then metal connected with metal.

'Direct hit!' Felda shouted, the elation evident in his voice.

The shutter was across the VETAC's shoulder, had stopped it dead, was bearing it slowly to the ground. The huge robot collapsed to one knee, then the other, as the shutter forced its way down. Now the creature was leaning backward under the enormous weight, pushing back at the lower edge of the shutter, trying to lift it clear, to pull itself through the ever-decreasing gap.

And the shutter stopped. Slowly it started to lift again. Jamie could see the VETAC struggling to brace its legs beneath the weight, to stand upright, to pull through.

Then Lanphier stepped forward, sighted carefully along his blaster, and fired. The bolt of energy connected with the VETAC's wrist, eating through the weak point where the joint was pulled to its limit as the VETAC lifted the shutter.

The wrist joint gave way with a crack. The VETAC's gauntleted hand was blown off its arm and clattered to the floor. Unable now to sustain its fight against the weight of the shutter, the VETAC fell backward. The shutter pinned it on its back to the floor, the lower half of its body on the far side while the head and shoulders were pointing towards Jamie and his team.

'Now comes the tricky bit,' Jamie said. He nodded to Prion, who approached the VETAC cautiously.

The creature was still struggling, its arms flailing and slapping against the shutter. Its head was twisting to and fro violently. Energy bolts whistled past Jamie's ear as the VETAC tried to blast its way through the shutter, sending ricochets whistling and whining down the corridor.

'The arms.' Jamie called to Lanphier and Felda, 'try to get the arms.'

They hammered away at the flailing arms with the butts of their blasters, but it seemed to have little effect. Meanwhile, Prion was on his knees by the VETAC's head. His fingers were working their way inside the helmet, in through the neck joint. Jamie crouched beside him, trying to get a grip on the head, to hold it still.

Prion's whole hand was inside the helmet now, dark viscous liquid pouring out over his wrist as the head thrashed from side to side. A low growling sound was coming from the VETAC, its movements becoming more violent.

One of its arms caught Lanphier on the side of the leg, knocking him off his feet. He collapsed heavily to the floor with a curse.

'Are you all right?' Felda shouted.

'I'll live.'

Then suddenly the VETAC was silent. The growling stopped, the arms sagged, then fell back to the floor. Prion withdrew his hand from the helmet. In his palm was an oily, gooey mess of the viscous liquid. And nestling in that was a small circuit.

'Is that it?' Jamie asked.

Prion nodded. 'That is it,' he said.

It took the Doctor only a minute to connect the greasy component into the electronics within Prion's chest. Prion was sitting by the chessboard, the Doctor reaching under his tunic.

'How's that?' he asked rubbing his oily hands on his handkerchief.

'Accessing the virtual network.' Prion looked up at the Doctor. 'I'm in.'

'Good. Now then, where are Victoria and the others being held?'

'The Banqueting Hall. Cruger and Haden are also there.'

'Right then.' The Doctor straightened up. 'Let's go.'

'Go?' Trayx asked. 'Go where?'

'To rescue Victoria,' Jamie told him.

'And how do you propose we do that, Doctor?' Kesar asked.

'With the help of our friend Prion, here. Now that he's tapped into the VETAC network, he can broadcast a signal that overloads their command network. Something to disorient and confuse them while we rescue Victoria and the others.'

Trayx's mouth dropped open. 'Is that possible?' he asked Prion. 'Can it be done?'

'It can –' Prion began to say.

'Of course it can,' the Doctor interrupted. 'Now we just need to get close enough to the Banqueting Hall, and then we'll send the signal. I wonder if your man Darkling is still around.' He grinned. 'Who's coming, then?'

'There is a problem.' Everyone turned to Prion. 'In theory the Doctor's plan is possible,' he said. 'But to broadcast such a signal across the whole command net would require considerable energy.'

'How much energy?' the Doctor asked, his voice suddenly quiet.

'To ensure the VETAC network is completely disabled for at least thirty seconds, forty-seven gigawatts.'

This meant nothing to Jamie, though it sounded like a lot. 'How much do you have at the moment?' he asked.

'Gigawatts?'

'Yes.'

'Less than one,' Prion admitted.

'And,' Kesar said, 'they've shut off the main power.'

'Well,' said Jamie throwing up his hands, 'that's that, then.'

'Yes,' the Doctor admitted quietly, his face glum. 'I'm very much afraid it is.' He looked round at the expectant faces of his friends. 'Sorry,' he said.

CHAPTER FOURTEEN
RISKS AND GAMBITS

A muttering at first, but growing in volume, as if coming closer. Voices in the blackness. Darkling shifted position, feeling the hard surface against his back. He was drifting, as if in a dreamland in which Haden was alternately embracing him and shooting him. Then, as if a switch was thrown, he was awake and alert.

He held his breath, a thousand worries and dangers crowding in on him. Had he made a noise moving? Had he been seen lurking in the shadows on the gallery from the Banqueting Hall below? Had he cried out in his sleep – or snored even? But after a short while, when there were no shouts or shots or signs of movement around him, Darkling relaxed a little and breathed again. He inched his way quietly closer to the edge of the gallery and peered carefully through the balustrades into the room below.

At the end of the long table he could see Sanjak together with Helana and the girl who had come with the Doctor. Nearby Haden was standing beside Cruger. He traced the outline of her body with his eyes, imagining it through the distorting shape of the heavy, angular battle armour. She was not wearing a helmet, and he could see her face, her eyes, her lips. She looked slightly nervous, shifting her weight from one foot to the other.

By contrast, Cruger was standing almost to attention, his chin jutting out as he spoke with the VETAC commander.

*

'Doctor, we have only half an hour,' Kesar said. 'Is there *any* chance that your plan can be made to work?'

'Not without the extra power,' the Doctor admitted. 'If only there were some way of enhancing Prion's capabilities, generating more power or channelling some energy from somewhere.'

'Could we adapt the blaster power packs?' Lanphier asked.

Prion shook his head. 'The process would take time, and we would need several hundred power packs.'

Felda gave a short laugh. 'We've got about three.'

'The shuttle has a power supply, as does the VETAC cruiser of course,' Trayx said thoughtfully. 'But I doubt we could get to either.'

'What about the VETAC we killed?' Jamie asked. 'Does it have a power supply?'

'Yes,' Prion said, 'but again, not powerful enough.'

'What's he going to do with all this power, anyway?' Jamie demanded.

'Oh, Jamie, we've been through all this,' the Doctor admonished. 'Prion will focus the energy into the VETAC command network. It will overload their communications and should give them something of a breakdown. At any rate, it will leave them very confused, hopefully for some considerable time.'

Jamie was still not sure he entirely understood, but he nodded anyway. 'What do you mean by "focus"?' he asked at last.

The Doctor sighed. 'Well, Jamie, you know when you have a – what would you call it? – a burning glass, which you use to direct the heat of the sun and set fire to something?'

Jamie nodded. 'Oh, that,' he said.

The Doctor was speaking slowly, patiently. 'Well, that

focuses the energy from the sun –' He stopped, hand raised in mid gesture. 'Jamie,' he exclaimed, 'that's brilliant.' He grabbed Jamie's hand in both his and shook it vigorously. 'You're a genius.'

'I am?'

'Oh yes. Well –' the Doctor considered – 'one of us is.' He turned to Trayx. 'Now then, I need to get myself and Prion to the Stardial Chamber you showed me earlier. We can focus the latent energy collected from the stars there and channel it into Prion.'

'Can we?'

'Of course I can. You and Jamie go to the Banqueting Hall, and be ready to grab Victoria and the others as soon as Prion sends the signal.' He beamed from ear to ear. 'All right?'

'Just one thing, Doctor.'

'What now?'

'The Stardial Chamber is not far – it's in the next tower – but we happen to be sealed in the Secure Area with VETACs cutting through the shutters.' Trayx paused before asking the obvious question. 'How do you propose we get out of here?'

The Doctor sighed. 'You mean there isn't another way out?'

'Doctor, this is a prison. It was designed to keep people in. *We* are in.'

'Couldn't Prion send a signal to the VETACs at the shutters?' Jamie asked. 'Just tell them to go away?'

Trayx shook his head. 'As soon as they realised what had happened, and they would, they'd change their command frequency. Then we'd need another VETAC circuit to find out the new frequency.'

Jamie grimaced. 'I don't fancy going through that again.'

The Doctor was frowning, his brow lined with

concentration. 'How,' he asked slowly at last, 'when he killed Remas and Sponslor, did Cruger get out?'

For the first time, Cruger was feeling vulnerable. He was in danger of losing control of the situation.

'Why did you order us into reserve?' VC5 demanded.

'The war,' Cruger started, 'in case –'

'There was no war.' VC5 took a step closer to Cruger, towering over him. 'From the information we now have, your action may have precipitated the war. Explain.'

Cruger swallowed. 'I can explain, of course I can.' He glanced at Haden, but her expression was neutral. 'I have information that you are not privy to,' Cruger went on. He had a contingency plan, had hoped not to have to play this move. But now he was talking for his life. If the VETAC determined that Cruger's actions had been contrary to the goal that it was programmed for, it would cut him out of the command chain. If it seemed that Cruger had been disloyal – or worse – to Kesar, then he was finished.

'What is this information?'

'Not here,' Cruger hissed. He pointed to the three prisoners. They were out of earshot, but he had to get VC5 alone. 'I will tell – show – you the proof. But just you. Just you and me.' He nodded to Haden – he might well need backup. 'And her.'

The VETAC's huge metal face was a blank mask as it considered Cruger's words.

The door sprang open with a quiet click. The Doctor stepped out of Cruger's quarters and joined the others in the corridor. 'So far, so good,' he said.

'But what would he have done then?' Trayx asked. 'How will we discover which route he took?'

'We follow the trail,' the Doctor said. 'Easy.'

'What trail?' Kesar asked.

'Well, we know he wasn't tracked by your observation cameras.'

'Yes,' Trayx agreed.

'And we know that some of those cameras don't work.'

'None of them work right now, not without power.'

'True. But if you can remember which cameras haven't worked for a while, we should be able to narrow down the possibilities. Perhaps even plot the single possible route to where Remas was killed. Ignoring doors and walls, or course. We're looking for a secret way through those.'

Prion stepped forward. 'That information is available,' he said. 'There are two possible routes. One of them passes through a single wall between this secure area and an adjacent corridor outside the security zone.'

The Doctor rubbed his hands in glee. 'That must be it then.' He turned to the others. 'Now, I'd like Prion to come with me to the Stardial Chamber so I can hook him up. Jamie, Trayx and...' hesitated. His finger wavered between Felda and Lanphier as he muttered, 'Eeny, meeny, miny, mo...' He finished on Felda. 'You. You three go to the Banqueting Hall.' He paused, a sudden horrified expression on his face. 'Er, if that's all right with you,' he said to Trayx. 'I seem to be forgetting my manners.'

'Oh, please, Doctor.' Trayx smiled thinly. 'If you have a plan, by all means put it into operation. I am a soldier – I'm very used to following orders.'

The Doctor laughed and clapped his hands together. 'Oh, thank you.'

'What about us, sir?' Lanphier asked Trayx, indicating himself and Kesar.

'Oh you stay here,' the Doctor said before Trayx could

answer. 'Kesar is much too important to us to risk leaving.
And he'll need you to keep him company and make sure
he doesn't get into any trouble.' His face broke into a smile.
'You could play a little chess or something.'

They were in a small drawing room just outside the
Banqueting Hall. The predominant colour was blue – the
walls and the carpet were complementary shades of blue,
and so were the backs of the upright chairs against the
walls. There was wooden panelling on the lower part of the
walls, painted white. The fire surround was also white, the
panelling continuing above the mantelpiece to encompass
a large portrait of a man in battle armour. Other, smaller
portraits were hung at intervals round the room. All of
them depicted soldiers in uniform or armour.

At the far end of the room, opposite the door, a bay
window gave out directly into space. In front of it stood a
low sofa, again upholstered in blue.

Haden watched Cruger quizzically as he led the VETAC
commander to the centre of the room.

'Shut the door.'

Haden pushed the door closed and stood with her back to
it. She did not know what Cruger was up to, and she did not
trust him an inch. But his focus seemed to be on the VETAC.

'Well?' VC5's voice seemed louder in the smaller space.
'We are alone. Provide this evidence you claim to possess.'

'Very well.' Cruger reached into a pocket in the sleeve of
his armour. He drew out a small optical disc.

VC5 made no move to take the disc. 'What is this?'

'Proof. Data. Information.' Cruger held the disc out. 'You
should read it,' he said quietly.

Still VC5 hesitated. Then he reached out and took the
disc. 'Very well.'

Haden took a step forward, unsure now what to do. Cruger turned sharply, staring fiercely at her. She stepped back again.

A narrow slot had opened in the VETAC's chest. He pushed the disc into it, end on. A small red light started to flash beside the slot as the VETAC's systems accessed the data on the disc.

Cruger was watching closely.

'This is not the data you described.' VC5 was turning back towards Cruger now, his arm swinging up, the gunport built into it opening as he turned.

'No,' Cruger replied quietly. 'You are correct.'

VC5 seemed to hesitate at this. His arm dropped slightly, then rose again. It dropped back a second time as if it had hit an invisible barrier. There was a low rumble of sound coming from the robot and its movements were becoming jerky.

'The disc actually contains an executable toxin.' Cruger was smiling, his eyes gleaming intently. 'And you have just read it into your main processor.'

VC5 lurched forward. He was speaking, but the sounds that emerged were not coherent words. The low rasp of his voice was rising in pitch, becoming an electronic screech as the robot staggered towards Cruger.

Cruger stepped aside, allowing VC5 to blunder past him. The huge metal figure swung round shakily, lurched forward again, one arm outstretched as he reached for Cruger. The other arm scrabbled at his own chest.

Cruger was laughing now, almost hysterical. Tears were running down his face, catching in his thin beard. But Haden could see what the VETAC was doing. She wrenched the door open, felt it bang into her leg as she rushed to escape.

The sound of the door startled Cruger. He turned, and saw Haden trying to get out. Then he looked back at the VETAC, the laughter dying in his throat as realisation dawned.

273

The huge metal hand gained a purchase on the chest, the fingers working their way into the small crevice and grasping the ring of metal set into the indented well. VC5 was staggering back towards the door now, towards Cruger, getting as close as possible.

Haden had the door open, was through it. She pulled it shut behind her. Part of her mind was telling her that trapping Cruger in the room was a good idea. But most of it was focused on getting as much protection as possible between herself and the VETAC.

The door stopped. It was not yet shut, but it stopped. Then it was wrenched from her hand as Cruger dragged it open again. Behind him, Haden could see the VETAC commander. He was close now, stumbling – almost falling – toward them. His hand was on the detonator set into his chest, pulling, ripping the firing pin out.

Then Cruger slammed the door shut and they both dived to the ground, hands wrapped behind their heads.

In the drawing room, VC5 lurched heavily into the door. He collapsed against it, one hand clawing at the woodwork, splintering, pulling, ripping through to the duralinium core beneath. The electronic screech that had been his voice was counterpointed now by the ping of the detonator. The lights on his chest were flashing in unison – in time to the racing heartbeat of the countdown.

The whole room shook under the impact. The fireball scorched across the ceiling, stripping paint from the panelling and igniting several of the paintings. The windows cracked, and the carpet burned. The shattered shell of the VETAC commander collapsed in on itself, falling back from the scarred remains of the door.

*

It had not taken the Doctor long to work out how to open the part of the wall that Prion pointed out. A simple pressure point activated a concealed mechanism and a whole section of the wall swung open.

'He had help setting this up,' Trayx said.

'Probably from the unfortunate Remas,' the Doctor suggested. 'He must have been bringing in the equipment and materials that Cruger needed.'

'And Cruger killed him for it.'

The Doctor shrugged. 'He was finished with the man. And maybe Remas was causing trouble. Making threats, asking for more payment, who knows?'

Once in the corridor beyond the wall, and outside the Secure Area, they split into two parties as arranged. Jamie, Trayx and Felda set off cautiously towards the Banqueting Hall. The Doctor and Prion headed for the Stardial Chamber.

'Why didn't Cruger lead the VETACs into the Secure Area using the route we just took?' Prion asked. 'They could have taken us by surprise.'

'I'm not sure,' the Doctor admitted. 'But perhaps he is keeping it as a trump card of some sort. It may be that he doesn't want to tell the VETACs too much. They answer to Kesar rather than him, after all.'

'And that could be a problem for him?'

The Doctor nodded. 'I think Cruger and Kesar may be operating on different agendas. Cruger summoned the VETACs here using the sonic beacon I detected earlier. And he called them here without telling Kesar, but in order to rescue him.'

'So it would seem.'

They were almost there now. Just one more section to negotiate. So far they had seen no VETAC patrols, and the Doctor was striding onward as if he owned the place.

'Well, Kesar does not seem to me to be acting like a man who wants to be rescued.'

From their concealed vantage point, Jamie, Trayx and Felda had a good view of the main door into the Banqueting Hall. It was shut, flanked on either side by VETAC sentries.

'Now what?' Jamie asked.

'Now we wait,' Trayx said.

Cruger was already standing as Haden pulled herself up. He grabbed her by the hair, wrenching her to her feet. His small hand blaster was levelled at her face.

'You tried to kill me. You tried to shut me in there with that thing.' He jerked his head towards the door to the drawing room, as if he thought she might not know where he meant.

'I tried to shut myself out,' she snapped back. 'There is a difference.'

Cruger was shaking his head. 'I don't know what game you're playing, Haden –'

'What game *I'm* playing?' she yelled back at him, ignoring the blaster. 'What do you think *you're* doing?'

'Winning.'

'Oh really? Seems to me like the VETACs aren't so convinced of that.'

Cruger laughed. 'That hardly matters now, does it? Through VC5 I have infected their whole command network.' He jammed the blaster close to her face. 'By now there isn't a VETAC of the Fifth Legion still standing.'

Now Haden smiled. 'Perhaps,' she said quietly, 'you should tell him that.'

She was looking over Cruger's shoulder, and he half turned to follow her line of sight. Then he caught himself, paused, unsure whether she was bluffing or if there really was something behind him. And as he hesitated, VL9's massive hand closed over the blaster and wrenched it from Cruger's grasp.

Somehow, when he was walking quickly, the Doctor's coat looked even bigger on him. It billowed out like a cloak as he marched into the Stardial Chamber, swung immediately through a hundred and eighty degrees and marched out again just as quickly. Prion was still in the corridor outside as the Doctor re-emerged.

'VETACs,' he explained quietly.

Prion stepped forward, to the threshold, and carefully looked into the large room. He stepped back smartly. 'They are leaving,' he said.

'Oh, good.'

'Coming this way.'

'Oh.' The Doctor considered. 'Not so good.' He looked round frantically, pointing to the side of the door. 'Quick, hide.'

Prion watched as the Doctor pressed himself into the corner by the door into the chamber, then positioned himself opposite. A moment later, the VETAC patrol – four VETACs in all – marched from the Stardial Chamber. They did not turn or look as they emerged, but strode massively along the corridor without pause.

The Doctor had been pressing himself back into the wall as if hoping it would give way behind him, swallow him up. Now he pushed away, stepping out into the corridor even before the VETACs were out of sight.

'Ha ha.' He clapped his hands together, feet shuffling rapidly in a parody of a jig. Then suddenly he turned back to Prion. 'Right, here we go.' He led the way cautiously into the chamber.

'Doctor,' Prion said as he followed, 'they did not detect us.'

'No. No they didn't, did they?' The Doctor was standing in the middle of the room, finger in his mouth, and looking around thoughtfully.

'They have the ability to detect human DNA signatures,' Prion continued. Although his expression had not altered, his head was tilted slightly to one side in a strangely quizzical manner. 'Battle armour suppresses the signature. If one is wearing it.'

'Ah well, you're not human, are you, Prion?' the Doctor pointed out. His voice was slightly muffled by the finger still in his mouth.

'It was not *my* DNA signature I was meaning.'

The Doctor looked at Prion, as if only now hearing him for the first time. 'Well, perhaps their sensors weren't working properly.' He set off for a point at the far side of the room.

After a moment, Prion followed. 'I also have similar capabilities,' he said.

'Good, good,' the Doctor said absently.

'Perhaps,' Prion said when it was clear the Doctor was not about to add anything to this, 'my own sensors are also not working properly. It would explain much. About you.'

'Yes, yes. Now then, logically it should be here.' The Doctor held out his hands in front of him, as if sizing up an imaginary box. 'Under the floor perhaps?' He looked up for a moment at the stars and latticework high above. 'Yes, wouldn't want to interfere with the mechanism, would we?'

'What are you looking for, Doctor?' Prion asked.

'Here, help me move this block, there's a good chap.' The Doctor pointed to the floor. The edges of a square cut into the marble floor were barely visible where they caught the dim light, where the pattern on the stone slightly mismatched. The Doctor dropped to his hands and knees and started crawling round the floor. 'There must be a pressure point or something to open it somewhere.'

'Open what?'

'Well, this section of floor.' The Doctor paused and looked up at Prion. 'This is where the energy is collected. Or I hope it is. Rather like a big battery.'

'And there will be enough energy for the command pulse I shall send.'

'Oh yes,' the Doctor said with a laugh. 'More than enough, I should think. Potential energy. Kinetic energy. Energy from the radiant heat, the light. Lots of it.' He turned his attention back to the floor, crawling round again slapping at the marble with the flat of his hand. 'If we can only get at it.'

They both spent the best part of a minute crawling round hammering at the floor, but with no discernible effect.

'Are you sure, Doctor?' Prion asked at last.

'Sure?' The Doctor was annoyed. 'Of course I'm sure.' To punctuate his point he leapt to his feet and stamped heavily.

With a low grating of stone on stone, the section of floor suddenly started to lift rapidly upward, taking the Doctor with it. With a yelp, he leapt clear, landing beside Prion and grabbing his arm for support.

'Yes,' the Doctor said as he regained his composure, 'well, there we are then.'

Cruger was startled for only a moment. Then his face was composed once more. 'Thank goodness,' he said, his voice low and breathless. 'This soldier is insane. She has destroyed your commander.'

VL9 said nothing for a while, looking from Cruger to Haden. Then the massive metal creature whirled round with surprisingly speed and strode back into the Banqueting Hall. 'Follow me,' his voice carried back to them.

'*I* destroyed –' Haden started angrily.

'Silence,' VL9 roared. He was standing in the doorway waiting for them. 'We are computing courses of action.'

'Then I suggest you do it quickly,' Cruger said. 'She's a dangerous woman.'

Haden was about to reply to this, but as she turned to face Cruger, a slight movement caught her eye. She froze, watching, hardly daring to turn back to see properly. On the gallery above them, Darkling was clearly visible looking down into the hall. Looking down at her. Just for a second, then he was gone, back into the shadows.

'VC5 was destroyed by a malign data toxin,' VL9 said. 'He isolated his systems before the toxin could escape into the network.'

Cruger nodded. 'A noble gesture.'

VL9 stepped forward, his hand snapping out so that it was an inch from Cruger's chin. 'You forget, General Cruger –' his voice was quieter now – 'the network is the Legion.'

Cruger blinked. And in that moment, Haden could see raw fear behind his eyes. For the first time he was afraid, really afraid.

'Until he detached, VC5 was the network controller. But I am the backup unit,' VL9 was saying. 'We were as one. The same. What he saw, I saw. What he felt, I felt.'

Cruger took a step backwards, but Haden was blocking his way.

VL9's huge fist closed on Cruger's throat. 'I saw you give VC5 the toxin – give *us* the toxin.' The hand squeezed around Cruger's neck. His eyes were bulging, he was coughing for breath. 'I felt his systems rupture as the infection spread.' The voice was uneven now, as if the robot was biting back its approximation of tears. 'We felt *pain*.' VL9 pulled Cruger closer towards him.

Then suddenly Cruger was flying across the room. He crashed into the table, rolled, fell to the floor. Victoria and Helana both screamed. Sanjak was on his feet. Haden watched, petrified, rooted to the floor, hand to mouth.

Cruger was lying on his back, gasping for breath and clutching his throat, staring up at the VETAC legionnaires who clustered round him, reaching down for him.

The section of floor had slid upward until it was above the Doctor's head. Beneath it there was a large cabinet full of wires and electronic equipment. The whole thing pulsed with energy, lights glowing from deep within.

'Is this what you wanted, Doctor?'

'Oh yes. Yes, this will do very nicely, thank you.' The Doctor was already pulling several long cables from inside his coat, squeezing the large crocodile clips that were attached to the ends. 'Now all we have to do is connect you up.' He handed one end of each of the cables to Prion. 'Now if you could just attach those to whatever it is you use to provide energy to your, er...' His voice trailed away as he concentrated on the cabinet. 'We can – you know.'

Even before Prion had undone his tunic and pulled it back from his internal circuitry, the Doctor was burrowing his way into the machinery in the cabinet, pulling at wires and tapping at components.

'What now?' Prion asked, the cables clipped to various points under his tunic.

'Well,' the Doctor began, mumbling through teeth that were clenched on several wires, 'we light the blue touch paper and –' He broke off. 'That is,' he continued slightly more slowly and coherently, 'we make sure we establish a good, safe connection to the power stored in here.' He pulled at a couple of wires. 'What do you think, then? Red or yellow to begin with?'

Prion's answer was drowned out by the sound of the blast as the floor at the base of the cabinet exploded. Long cracks laced out across the marble floor, cutting through the inlaid circles and markings. Across the room, the VETAC patrol was already running towards the Doctor and Prion, following through with their attack.

CHAPTER FIFTEEN
CHECKMATE

The Doctor's face emerged from within the spaghetti tangle of wires and cables for long enough for him to cry out, 'Oh my word!' Then it disappeared again, several components flying out in its place.

Prion had turned at the first hint of sound. He stood facing the running VETACs, feet apart, braced against the recoil as he raised his arm. A small nozzle clicked up from the top of his wrist, standing proud of his battle armour. A moment later a trail of fire lanced out from it, dripping flame as it spouted across the chamber at the advancing VETACs.

The first of the legionnaires was engulfed in the stream of fire. For a few seconds it continued running, battling through the flames that splashed across its chest and face. Then the head seemed to lift from the body as it exploded. Orange lightning blazed out from its joints, erupted from its neck as the VETAC was blown to bits.

The other three VETACs paused, then moved swiftly to positions of cover. They fired almost in unison. The first burst caught Prion across the chest, tearing his tunic away from the circuitry and components beneath, scarring and scorching the metal casing. The cables attached to his power source were dripping plastic from their casings, but they held steady.

Prion twisted slightly under the force of the attack, protecting the cables and their connections.

The fire from the other VETACs caught him across the side of the head. The synthetic flesh peeled away, shrivelled under the heat, exposing the dull metal skull beneath. One side of his hair was a frazzled, blackened mess. His cheek blistered and burned as he dropped to one knee, firing back.

'Hurry, Doctor.' Prion's words were slightly slurred, slightly broken. Almost mechanical.

Inside the cabinet the Doctor held three wires, the ends of each stripped back to the metal. One was red, one yellow, one blue. The yellow wire was sparking alarmingly, and he was hard put to hold it away from his body without touching any of the components within the cabinet.

'Oh dear, oh dear,' the Doctor said, shaking his head. 'Now, red to blue or red to yellow?' He looked closely at each wire in turn, blinking and coughing as the yellow wire sparked again, right under his nose.

'Hu-rr-y.'

The cabinet rocked slightly under the force of an explosion close by. The Doctor tried crossing his fingers, but dropped the blue wire. He scrabbled desperately for it, grabbed it, held it close to the yellow. 'Blue and yellow makes –' he muttered. Then his face twisted into a look of anguished horror. 'Green! No, no, no. That can't be right.' He dropped the blue wire again, closed his eyes so hard his face crumpled round them, and jammed the yellow and red wires together.

Cruger twisted and turned, trying to push himself away as the metallic fingers of several VETACs reached down at him. Behind them, through the fingers, he could see VL9 standing close by. Haden was beside him.

A hand closed on Cruger's throat. It gripped tight. Tighter. Then, abruptly, the pressure was released, the hand sagged. The VETACs themselves sagged, falling slightly forward from the waist, as if the life had suddenly deserted them. Through the forest of fingers stretching down for him, Cruger could see VL9 also standing lifeless and still.

Without pausing to wonder what had happened, Cruger scrambled out from under the VETACs.

Victoria watched in amazement as everything stopped. Froze.

For a split second time stood still. Then the main doors to the Banqueting Hall burst open. In a blur of motion she was aware of running figures. Trayx and another soldier were racing across the room, negotiating the VETACs, which stood like statues. And with them was Jamie.

'Jamie!' she called out. 'Oh, Jamie.'

'Victoria, thank goodness you're all right.' He was breathless. 'Come on.' Beside her, Trayx was embracing Helana. The other soldier was grinning at Sanjak.

Then they were running again. Jamie was dragging Victoria back across the room. 'They'll wake up again soon,' he was warning her.

Trayx was half dragging, half carrying his wife. Sanjak and the other soldier were close behind them.

Cruger scrambled after the others, on his feet and running. But then a hand grabbed at his shoulder, dragged him back. He cried out, turned, tried to break free.

'You!' he screamed in rage.

'Not so fast, sir.' Haden was facing him now, her expression dark, her eyes hard.

'Let me go.'

'No. You're staying here.'

Cruger shook his head. 'Have you forgotten your brother so soon?'

'It wasn't the Republicans who killed my brother.' Her jaw was set, her teeth all but clenched. 'It was the war itself. The *senseless* war.' Her grip on his shoulder tightened. 'The war which *you* started. If anyone killed him, you did.'

Cruger was still now, not fighting her. His voice was quiet. 'Your problem, Haden, is that you haven't worked out whose side you're really on.'

'It's not me who has the problem,' she said. Her stare was piercingly hard.

'Oh yes it is.' His movement was sudden, taking her by surprise. He smashed her arm away from his shoulder, and grabbed her round the neck. She was strong and determined, but he was stronger. Her eyes were less hard now, bulging in their sockets as he squeezed. And squeezed. She sank to her knees, her hands pulling at his wrists, but with increasingly less strength or effect.

He was standing over her now, holding her body up from the floor even as he throttled the life out of it. Still she stared up at him, the accusation and disgust deep in her eyes. Then they glazed over, her head sagged slightly, and he dropped her to the ground. He stood over her for a moment, breathing heavily.

The huge, inert form of VL9 stood close by, as if watching him. Cruger spared it a quick glance as he crossed to where the bodies of several soldiers lay against the end wall. Their weapons were close by, where they had fallen when the VETACs killed the soldiers. He picked up a small hand blaster, weighed it in his palm, and strode from the room. His confidence grew with every step.

Darkling had watched from the gallery. His elation at seeing the rescue of Sanjak and the others rapidly changed to horror as Cruger grabbed Haden. He considered leaping down at them from the gallery. But they were too far away. At best he would achieve nothing worse than two broken legs.

So instead he ran, racing for the stairs, leaping down them three – four – at a time.

The doors to the hall were still open. The VETACs still stood in silent vigil. But Cruger was gone.

And Haden was lying face down on the floor.

Darkling was at Haden's side in a moment, pushing his way through the mass of VETACs standing between them. He knelt beside the body. He reached down, feeling for a pulse in her neck as he slowly turned the body over.

He drew in his breath sharply as the pale, contorted face rolled into view. Darkling clasped the inert form to his chest, rocking backward and forward on his knees as he cradled his lover in his arms.

Then, without warning, there was movement. Slowly, as if moving through thick viscous liquid, the VETACs were reactivating, coming back to life. Arms swung slightly, heads moved fractionally. VL9 drew himself upright as a fail-safe timed out inside his parallax-comtronic brain and automatically rerouted the legion's command functions through the backup frequency.

Urgency and passion combined as Darkling pressed his lips to Haden's. 'I'm sorry,' he whispered. 'So sorry.' Then he ran from the room, barely noticing the waking metal hands that clutched at him as he passed.

Sanjak had joined Lanphier and Felda at the shutters. The sound of the VETACs trying to break through was back, louder than ever now. They were through the first two shutters, and now the final one was denting outward, buckling under the onslaught.

'We hold them as long as we can,' Lanphier said. 'Then we fall back to Kesar's quarters.'

'As long as we can?' Sanjak asked. 'How long do you think that will be?'

'A few seconds,' Felda said. 'If we're lucky.'

Lanphier shrugged. 'I'm only telling you what the Doctor said.'

'So he's in command now, is he?' Felda snorted.

Lanphier's reply was quiet, almost to himself. 'Perhaps he always was.'

At first Cruger thought the room was empty. The door from the living area through to Kesar's sleeping quarters was closed. The chess set – his chess set – was on the table in the corner, the pieces in position for the start of a game.

'I thought you might drop by.'

He whirled round at the voice, peering into the red gloom by the chess table. It took him a moment to make out the figure sitting behind the table.

'Doctor. What a pleasant surprise.' He crossed to the table.

'Yes, isn't it?' The Doctor picked up one of the pieces – a rook fashioned in the shape of the asteroid fortress. Santespri in miniature. 'These are very good, you know.'

'Thank you.'

'I wondered where you got the materials. But then I realised that Remas probably brought them in for you. No doubt Warden Mithrael knew about that, turned a blind eye.'

'What of it?' Cruger sat opposite the Doctor, facing him across the board.

'Oh nothing. I imagine he was providing all sorts of material. Am I right?' The Doctor set the piece down. 'So that you could signal your VETAC friends, for example.'

'Friends?' Cruger smiled, his teeth stained red by the emergency lighting. 'Oh no, Doctor. You have it all wrong. I merely smoked them out. Brought them into the open so that I could destroy them with the toxin.'

'Really? That's jolly good.' The Doctor leaned forward, across the board. 'As an excuse, I mean. As a plan, it leaves a lot to be desired, I must say. Pretty stupid, wouldn't you agree?' His eyes were glinting in the red light, acquiring a depth Cruger had not noticed before. 'And you're not stupid, are you, General Cruger? Anything but, I would say.'

'You say a lot of things, Doctor.'

The Doctor sat back, laughing suddenly. 'Do I?'

'But words are cheap.'

'Aren't they?' The red glint was back now. 'But then life is very cheap to you, isn't it? The life of Remas, once he was no further use to you. Sponslor's life, too. The lives of your VETAC troops, if life they have. It seems to me that you have no conception of the real value of these things. And that's a pity.' He lifted another piece from the board – the white king. 'What *does* matter to you? Not life, except your own. So how about power?'

'Power?'

'Yes. That's what all this is about, isn't it?' The Doctor held out the white king. 'The face left unfinished. That's not a philosophical point, now is it? You left it unfinished so that nobody else would know it's meant to be you. Axell Cruger, Emperor of Haddron. Has a certain ring to it, I suppose.'

Cruger was on his feet now, his voice a snarl of pent-up emotion. 'I shall yet be Emperor, Doctor.'

'Oh really?' The Doctor gave a disdainful snort, returning the king to its position on the board. 'You – Emperor? Running the whole of Haddron?' He was looking directly at

Cruger now, deep into his eyes. 'You can't even play a decent game of chess.'

Cruger took a deep breath. For a moment it seemed he was about to shout back at the Doctor. But then he relaxed slightly. The trace of a smile was on his face as he reached down and started moving the chess pieces.

'If you're such a grand master, Doctor,' he said quietly, 'try this.'

'Try what?'

'A simple chess problem. It should pose no great difficulty to a man of your undoubted talents.'

'Oh really?' The Doctor was suddenly enthusiastic, watching closely as Cruger positioned the last pieces. 'Got to make checkmate in a single move or something, have I?'

'That's right.' Cruger's smile was almost a grin now. 'You have the black pieces.' He was backing slowly away from the board, watching carefully as the Doctor reached out for the black knight. 'Just one move, Doctor. That's all you get.'

The Doctor's hand was on the knight. 'Well, it's simple, isn't it? Hardly in the league of Kasparov or Capablanca.'

'Then play the move, Doctor.' Cruger's voice was barely a whisper as he watched the Doctor lift the knight. He had him now.

He kept to the shadows out of instinct and habit as much as from thought and decision. He had no plan as such, had not thought through what he should do or how he would achieve it. For the moment, he headed for the Secure Area. That was where they would be taking refuge, all of them.

The tears were dried on Darkling's cheeks. His face was a mask of determination as he pulled back into an alcove and watched VL9 and several other VETACs march past him. It must be close to the end now, he thought. He quickened his pace as he followed them.

'Simple,' the Doctor repeated as he lifted the knight. Then his hand froze. Slowly, carefully he replaced the piece. 'Or is it?'

Cruger also paused. He had been backing slowly away from the board. 'What's wrong, Doctor? Lacking the courage to play your move?'

'No. No, I don't think so.' The Doctor leaned back, tapping his finger tips together in front of his chin as he thought. 'A little too simple, perhaps. And chess is such a dangerous game.'

'Oh?'

'Oh yes. Ask poor old Middleton about his game at chess. I had to help him write a short poem to get out of that one.' He pondered the pieces in front of him. 'Checkmate by discovery, perhaps?'

Cruger frowned. 'What's wrong, Doctor?' His tone was insistent. 'Play the move.'

'Yes,' the Doctor murmured, '"for a score of kingdoms you should wrangle and I would call it fair play".'

'What?'

'*The Tempest*.' The Doctor was smiling. 'Miranda accuses Ferdinand of cheating at chess. Remember?'

Cruger shook his head. 'I do not know the work.'

'I meant, do you remember cheating?' Before Cruger could reply, the Doctor went on: 'You know, I wondered about this chess set. Carving it, making things. Not really your bent, is it? So, why do it?' He raised his eyebrows as he asked the question. 'Something to while away the endless empty hours? No. Like your little problem here, there's more to it than that.'

'Is there?'

'Oh yes, I think so. You needed to construct a signalling device. You knew you were kept under observation, at least for some of the time. So what could you do that would conceal the fact that you were actually calling for help?' The Doctor's hand hovered over the board, pointing at one piece after another. 'Which one is the signal device concealed inside?'

'Play the move, Doctor.' Cruger's voice was loud, almost a shout. 'If you can, then play the move.'

'All right,' the Doctor snapped back. 'Don't rush me.' He picked up the black knight again. 'Now this piece feels a little unbalanced to me, a bit top heavy.' He tossed it into the air, watching as Cruger took an involuntary step backwards before he caught it again. Then he seemed to fumble the catch, and the knight slipped from hand to hand as he scrabbled to catch it again.

Cruger was backing away more quickly now.

'Oh, butterfingers,' the Doctor chided himself amiably as he regained his grip on the chess piece. 'Oh look. What have we here?' Somehow he had prised the base from the knight. He held out the two parts for Cruger to see. 'And you know, there's something inside here too,' he said as he peered into the body of the knight. He sniffed cautiously, grimaced, and pushed the figure back on to its base. 'Smells rather like Zenon to me.'

The Doctor looked up at Cruger, and, if he was surprised to see that the man was now holding a gun, he did not show it.

'Very volatile stuff, Zenon. Especially Zenon VII,' the Doctor rebuked Cruger. 'Align a critical mass of it along the lines of force and the whole lot could go up.'

'Exactly, Doctor.' Cruger's eyes narrowed as he

approached the Doctor. 'The correct configuration of pieces containing Zenon, the answer to a puzzle, and another problem disappears.'

'Goes up in smoke, no doubt.'

'Indeed.'

The Doctor was backing away round the board as Cruger approached. He still held the black knight as they circled the table. As Cruger was in the corner of the room, behind the table, the door opposite opened. From Kesar's sleeping quarters, Trayx and Kesar emerged. Jamie, Victoria and Helana were close behind them. Prion came out last, limping badly. One side of his face was burned away to the scorched metal beneath. His tunic was ripped and torn from the side of his tarnished chest.

'Checkmate, I think, Cruger.' Trayx was smiling grimly.

'I think not,' Cruger replied. 'I have the gun.' He levelled it at Trayx. 'Time to say your goodbyes, I suggest.'

'Oh, do you think so?' the Doctor said before Cruger could fire. He was holding his hand up, as if to wave. Then he seemed to notice that he was still holding the chess piece. 'Oh, I'm so sorry,' he said in apparent alarm. 'Here, catch.'

It seemed almost a reflex action as the Doctor threw his hands up, tossing the black knight towards Cruger. It arced through the air, apparently on a course directly to Cruger's reaching hand. But then the knight twisted oddly, the top dipping, spinning the piece about its offset centre of gravity. It fell short of Cruger's desperate reach, clattering instead on to the chessboard. The knight landed perfectly on its base, rocking slightly, then righting itself in the middle of a black square close to the faceless white king.

Cruger was already turning, trying to get away from the board as the knight came to rest. But he was against the wall, the board itself between him and escape.

The explosion seemed to start with the knight. It erupted into a smoky orange fireball. A split second later, the pieces closest to it detonated too. The explosion spread across the board, outward from the knight, like a wave of bright orange fire. The sound was like a gunshot rattling and ricocheting round the room.

Cruger was covering his face with blistering hands, screaming and shouting as the dark smoke drifted slowly across the room. He collapsed to his knees with a moan.

'That sound,' Kesar croaked. 'I shall never forget that sound.' His face was turned blankly towards Trayx.

Nor I,' Trayx agreed. 'The corridor at the Senate that day. That awful day.'

'And the colour,' Kesar went on. 'Fiery death.'

Cruger was still on his knees, staring at his damaged hands in disbelief. His beard was singed into black streaks, and his face was red and blotched by the intense heat. His blaster lay forgotten on the floor close by.

Victoria ran to the Doctor, Jamie close behind. 'Doctor,' she said, 'you're all right.'

'Oh yes, I'm fine, thank you. Quite well.'

But the smile was wiped from his face by the sound of a large explosion from the corridor outside. Like an after-echo of the detonation in the room, the sound reverberated through the Secure Area. A moment later there were shouts, gunfire, and running feet.

The whole shutter had exploded inward. The VETACs were through the gap almost before Sanjak and the others had realised what had happened. Lanphier got off two blasts before he turned and ran. Sanjak and Felda were close behind him.

The VETAC assault leader pounded down the corridor

after them, his legionnaires forcing their way through the remains of the shutter one after another.

And behind the assault force was VL9, marching along the battle-scarred corridor to join his troops at the front.

The room was crowded with the three soldiers joining the others. A moment later the first VETAC appeared in the doorway. Sanjak, Felda and Lanphier were already aiming, about to fire.

'Wait.' The Doctor's voice was loud, carrying easily above the sound of marching feet and the noise of the explosions still ringing in everyone's ears. 'I suggest that we surrender.' He looked across at Trayx.

For a moment Trayx said nothing. His face was expressionless, set. Then, slowly, he nodded. 'Lay down your weapons,' he ordered with a heavy sigh.

As soon as the soldiers put down their blasters and stood back, the VETAC in the doorway lowered its arm and stepped into the room. Another followed, and then another. They stood round the door, facing their captives without comment.

Darkling watched from behind a tapestry as VL9 strode through the shattered remains of the main doors to the Secure Area. How many times had he and Haden parted company at those doors? How many times had he locked her inside? But never again. Through the debris, Darkling could see VL9 pushing his way through the hole in the outer shutter.

He stepped out into the corridor, about to follow. And a hand clamped down on his shoulder, pushed him forwards towards what was left of the doors.

'You will join the other prisoners in the Secure Area,' the VETAC intoned.

Prisoners – then Trayx had surrendered. Against all the odds, and for whatever reason, the General in Chief had yielded. And in doing so, had unknowingly just saved Darkling's life.

VL9 made his way to the centre of the room and looked round at the assembled humans.

'Kesar.' His voice was firm, arrogant, assured. 'We have come for you.'

Slowly Kesar stepped forward, turning his blank metal mask to face the VETAC lieutenant's own.

'What is this?' the VETAC demanded as Kesar stood in front of him.

'It is Kesar.' Cruger's voice was a hoarse croak from the back of the room. He forced his way through to join them. 'He was injured. His face, his hands, his voice, all have been replaced. But a DNA scan will confirm his identity.' He turned to Kesar, bowing his head stiffly, painfully. 'Your safety is assured, your rescue at hand, my Lord.'

Kesar reached out, pushing Cruger's shoulder back slightly so that he was forced to look up, into Kesar's blank, bronzed face. The voice was the same metallic rasp as ever, but there was a depth to it now, a kind of resignation.

'Rescue, Cruger? I am afraid not,' Kesar said. Slowly he raised his hands to his face, reaching behind the mask for the tiny wing nuts that held it in place. They clattered to the floor as he twisted them off. Then he lifted the mask away, dropping that too. It impacted heavily on the stone floor, rolling on to its cheek with a scraping sound.

Cruger gasped, scorched hand to his mouth.

Beneath the mask, the man's face was perfectly intact. There was no trace of scarring or burn marks from the explosion. Just a sad, pale face, the pallor of the skin almost grey from lack of daylight.

'You!' Cruger was shaking his head in disbelief.

'Yes,' Gerhart Rutger replied. 'Me.'

Behind Rutger, Helana Trayx gave a small cry, and turned away.

Her husband said, 'Why so surprised, Cruger? It was a Zenon VII device that killed Kesar that day, under the Senate. The sound, the colour of the flames are unmistakable. Your bomb, I think.'

'What's happening, Doctor?' Jamie hissed. 'Who is that if the real Kesar is dead?'

'I don't know, Jamie. But they couldn't let Kesar become a martyr, remember. Not now, and certainly not then.'

VL9 had watched the events without comment, until now. 'The DNA scan confirms that this is not Kesar.' He turned slowly towards Cruger. 'The chain of command is altered.'

'Yes,' Cruger said. His face was cracked into a sudden smile. The skin round his mouth, over his beard, was peeling back under the tension. 'Yes, it was my bomb. With Kesar dead, a martyr, his followers would have rallied under a new leader. But the moment has merely been postponed. And it is all the sweeter for that.' He turned to VL9. 'Prepare to execute the prisoners,' he said. 'All of them.'

'Wait.' Trayx's voice cut through the air. 'You are in no position to give commands, especially after that confession.'

'On the contrary.' Cruger's voice was almost sickly. 'The Fifth Legion is loyal to Kesar, not to you, Trayx.'

'But Kesar is dead,' Rutger pointed out.

'Exactly. So these VETACs now take their orders from the next person in Kesar's chain of command.' Cruger nodded, savouring the moment. 'They take their orders from me.'

CHAPTER SIXTEEN
THE DEATH OF KINGS

'Whatever the chain of command,' Trayx said, 'your loyalty is to Haddron. To the Republic.'

'Oh no, Trayx.' Cruger was almost laughing. 'That won't work. You know it won't.'

'Kesar was defeated,' Rutger said. 'He surrendered. And with him, his forces also capitulated at Trophinamon.'

VL9 swung round so his massive body was facing Rutger. 'This legion did not surrender.'

It was at this moment that Darkling stumbled into the room, falling through the line of VETACs by the door. Sanjak ran to help him up, but a VETAC grabbed him, held him back.

Darkling pulled himself to his feet. His eyes were wide as he looked round the group, searching. Eventually he fixed on Cruger.

'You will join your comrades,' VL9 said.

But Darkling was not listening. 'There you are,' he snarled at Cruger as he pulled himself to his feet. 'You murdering bastard.' He launched himself forward, past VL9, his hands reaching for Cruger's face. 'I'll kill you!' he screamed.

Cruger's jaw dropped and he stepped backwards, shaking his head in disbelief and fear. He could see death in Darkling's eyes.

But before Darkling reached Cruger, VL9 had plucked the soldier out of the air and slapped him aside with a single massive blow. Darkling crashed to the ground, his head connecting with the stone floor with a loud crack. He convulsed, once, then lay still. A trickle of blood drew a line between the flagstones.

'The chain of command is paramount,' VL9 said slowly. 'What are your orders, General Cruger?'

Helana was crying, burying her head in Trayx's shoulder. He wrapped his arm around her. 'Don't worry, my darling,' he said, loud enough for Cruger to hear. 'What can he do? One man and a single Legion, against the Republic.'

'You underestimate my influence,' Cruger said. 'And your Republic is already cracking open at the edges. The very centre is flawed and will split asunder.'

'Yes, well,' the Doctor said, 'I have a few ideas about that, actually.'

'Shut up,' Cruger hissed.

'Of course, if you'd rather not hear them –'

'Be quiet!'

'So what are you going to do with us?' Jamie asked.

Victoria's face was drawn and pale. 'Are you going to kill us?'

'Eventually.'

With a scraping, scratching sound, Prion pulled himself forward. His left leg was trailing, dragging along the floor behind him. 'What in-flu-ence?' His words were disjointed and slurred. His shattered face turned towards Cruger.

Cruger stared back at him, his lip curling in disdain. 'What is that to you, a mere automaton?'

'What in-flu-ence?' Prion repeated, his voice gaining some strength.

Cruger turned away, but the Doctor's voice stayed him: 'Oh, I think the question deserves an answer,' he said. 'We're not all automatons, you know.' The Doctor's face was suddenly in shadow as he leaned towards Cruger. 'What influence?'

'I have been building a power base back on Haddron,' Cruger said dismissively. 'Canvassing support in the name of Kesar.'

As Cruger made to address VL9, Prion lurched forward, another halting step towards Cruger. 'Then my sec-ondary prog-ram relates to you.' He was raising his arm, slowly, painfully. There was an audible whirr of motors from within the forearm as the small blaster nozzle clicked up into position, pointing directly at Cruger.

Beside Prion, Trayx's mouth dropped open. 'You,' he whispered hoarsely. 'Mathesohn's agent.' But his words were obliterated by the roar of noise as Prion fired.

Cruger had realised the danger almost too late. 'Protect me!' he screamed to the VETACs as he dived for cover, rolling away from the blast towards the door.

Behind where Cruger had been a moment earlier a VETAC legionnaire exploded into smoke and flame. Its fellows returned fire, sending Trayx and Rutger scurrying for cover together with the other soldiers. Trayx dragged his wife with him as he hit the floor. The Doctor had his arms round Victoria and Jamie, was pulling them down behind a chair. A second later their heads emerged round the sides as they watched the battle.

Prion was blasted back against the wall, the remaining synthetic skin was burning on his face as he swung round, trying to acquire his target.

But Cruger was running for the door, lunging towards it as the VETACs closed ranks behind him.

Then he screamed. It was a sound that embraced fear and surprise and anger all at once. 'No – wait, stop!' were the only discernible words in the sound. It was enough to halt the VETACs. They stood silently to attention awaiting new orders. Prion also waited, the side of his face running down the metal skull in ragged tears.

Darkling staggered through the VETACs. One half of his head was caked in blood, and his teeth were clenched with effort and determination. He was dragging Cruger behind him, one hand clamped over the general's mouth, the other braced round his shoulders.

Cruger was kicking and struggling, trying to wrench himself free. His screams and shouts were inarticulate gasps and squeals that escaped through Darkling's fingers.

'Here he is,' Darkling shouted, pulling Cruger in front of him, holding him out towards Prion, arms tight round him. 'Now finish this.' Cruger twisted as he struggled to break free, turned back towards Darkling. His face was a mask of fear and anger.

Darkling's lips were drawn back over his teeth. 'Make it look good,' he spat.

The blast caught both Cruger and Darkling as one, eating through their armour and scorching away the flesh beneath. Darkling still held Cruger tight as the older man shrieked. Cruger's mouth was wrenched open with the pain as he screamed his life out. Darkling was screaming too, but with laughter. Then the fireball engulfed them both.

The room was quiet and still for a long while. Helana's sobs were the only sound. The VETACs stood impassive. Prion was leaning against the wall, his face and the front of his body a shattered wreck. Slowly the Doctor stood up from behind the chair. Jamie and Victoria emerged behind him.

Trayx sat his wife down on a chair and turned to VL9. 'What happens to the chain of command now?' he demanded.

VL9 turned slowly, as if considering his response. 'Command reverts,' he said at last. 'The Fifth Legion presents itself to General in Chief Trayx for orders.'

Trayx nodded with grim satisfaction. 'Very well,' he said. 'You may stand down.'

VL9 bowed slightly, then turned to leave. His legionnaires fell into line behind him. Their movements seemed slightly sluggish.

'Wait,' Trayx called out as VL9 reached the door.

The robot swung round to face him. 'Sir.'

'Tell your legionnaires that they acquitted themselves well this day.' Trayx nodded. 'Carry on, VETAC commander. You have earned your field commission.'

VC5, as he now was, turned again. And when he marched from the room, the sluggishness was gone. His legionnaires followed, proud and massive after the battle.

The Doctor was tending to Prion, peering into an eye socket with the aid of a pencil torch. 'I think he can be fixed up without too much trouble,' he said at last.

'Good.' Rutger joined the Doctor. 'If we can access his secondary program, that will give us enough evidence to move against Mathesohn at last.' He paused, thoughtful, then asked quietly, 'Why didn't he kill me, Doctor? He was programmed to kill Kesar, probably on first contact.'

It was Prion who answered. His voice was quiet, slurred, almost inaudible. 'I nev-er met Ke-s-ar,' he said haltingly. 'D-N-A scans all neg-at-ive.'

'I imagine his orders were to kill Kesar and whoever else was behind the build-up of support for him back on Haddron,' Trayx said. He broke into a smile. 'I look forward to seeing Mathesohn's face when he discovers that he saved our lives.'

'But not Kesar's life, I fancy.'

'What do you mean, Doctor?' Victoria asked.

The Doctor nodded to Rutger. 'I rather think our friend here has finished playing that particular role.'

'It was always the intention to let Kesar die eventually,' Rutger said. 'Once his memory had faded and popular support dwindled. Now we can pre-empt that.'

Trayx nodded. 'Kesar dies a hero, battling against the corrupt plans of General Cruger,' he said. 'To the last he was loyal to his own vision of Haddron. And we must build now on that vision. On his dreams of empire.'

'But without the imperialism, eh?'

'That's right, Doctor,' Trayx said. 'There may be some dissent, especially from Mathesohn, Frehlich and their colleagues. But Rutger has played his part for long enough. And if it comes to the choice between betraying the Republic or my friend, God give me the courage to betray the Republic.' He exhaled, long and slow. 'Now, Doctor, you said you had some ideas. I should like to hear them.'

The Doctor beamed. 'That's very magnanimous of you. There are several possible paths forward for you. Now, heard of the concept of a commonwealth, for instance?'

It was hard to believe that so much had happened since they last ate at the same table. The VETACs were back on their ship, and power had been restored so that the room was no longer bathed in red. The bodies and debris had been cleared away, and a semblance of a victory feast assembled from cold odds and ends found in the kitchens.

The Doctor, Jamie and Victoria sat together. Opposite them the soldiers, Sanjak, Lanphier and Felda, joked and talked of other battles and fallen comrades. Helana Trayx sat beside her husband as before, rarely letting go of his hand, rarely looking away from his face. Beside Trayx, Rutger seemed withdrawn and quiet. The other side of Rutger, Prion sat stiffly in his chair. Devoid of artificial skin and armour, his VETAC heritage was apparent. His movements were still hesitant stutterings, far removed from the finesse and precision when they had first sat at this same table together.

The Doctor pushed his plate away with an embarrassed belch of satisfaction. His hand flew to his mouth. 'Manners,' he quipped. 'Well, now,' he went on quickly, 'I think it's time we looked for our, er, our transport. Just to check everything is in order, you understand.'

'Oh Doctor,' Victoria said. 'Everything's so peaceful here now. Can't we –'

He held up a finger to stop her. 'I like to leave everything tidy, Victoria,' he said. 'Everything put away in its proper place. No mess.'

'Oh yes?' Jamie did not sound convinced.

'Come along.' The Doctor was already on his way towards the door. He turned on his heel. 'Well, goodbye, everyone. It's been such fun.'

Trayx frowned. 'Indeed, Doctor. But we shall see you again as soon as you have checked on your ship. You will need help with the repairs, and we have much to talk about.'

'Yes,' the Doctor said. There was still a trace of embarrassment in his voice. 'Yes, of course. Now come along you two.'

When they had gone, Rutger leaned close to Trayx. 'A word,' he said quietly. 'In private, if I may.'

'Soon,' Trayx promised.

'It is important.' Rutger was looking at Helana as he spoke. She was still watching the door, looking after the Doctor and his friends.

'I know,' Trayx told his friend. He turned to look at his wife, then back to Rutger. He was smiling slightly. 'I have always known,' he murmured, just loud enough for Rutger to hear.

'Then why?'

Trayx did not answer. He stood up, pulling his wife to her feet as well. They stood facing each other for a moment. Then he leaned forward and kissed her.

Rutger watched, frowning. He had his answer, and it was no real surprise. But it did prompt another question. Had it really been the loss of the Fifth Legion that had turned Trayx against his childhood friend, which had motivated him to bring the might and power of Haddron crashing down on Hans Kesar?

'Tidy?' Jamie said to Victoria. 'I'm surprised he knows what the word means.'

'Now, I heard that, Jamie.' The Doctor unlocked the TARDIS door and pushed it open. 'After you, my dear.' He stepped politely aside to let Victoria enter.

'Thank you.' She smiled at him as she went past.

The Doctor smiled back, stepping smartly between Victoria and Jamie as the boy made to follow. His smile became a glare as he turned back to Jamie. Then he grunted and followed Victoria inside.

'Yes,' the Doctor said as he operated the door control. 'Tidiness is very important in these matters.'

Jamie leapt away from the closing doors with a yelp. 'Steady, Doctor.'

'Always leave things as you would hope and expect to find them,' the Doctor went on as he adjusted and set the controls. 'Isn't that right, Victoria?'

'Yes, Doctor,' she said meekly.

He was making his way from panel to panel on a circuit round the central TARDIS console. The familiar scraping rasp of dematerialisation underpinned the Doctor's words: 'Never leave business unfinished or loose ends dangling. Always clear away properly and make good after –' The Doctor stopped in mid-sentence, staring in horror at the console in front of him. 'Now who left that half-eaten sandwich there?' he demanded.

Next in the Doctor Who *50th Anniversary Collection:*

LAST OF THE GADERENE

MARK GATISS

ISBN 978 1 849 90597 8

The Doctor Who 50th Anniversary Collection
Eleven classic adventures
Eleven brilliant writers
One incredible Doctor

The aerodrome in Culverton has new owners, and they promise an era of prosperity for the idyllic village. But former Spitfire pilot Alex Whistler is suspicious – when black-shirted troops appear on the streets, he contacts his old friend Brigadier Lethbridge-Stewart at UNIT. The Third Doctor is sent to investigate – and soon uncovers a sinister plot to colonise the Earth. The Gaderene are on their way…

An adventure featuring the Third Doctor, as played by Jon Pertwee, and his companion Jo Grant.

DOCTOR WHO
The Encyclopedia

Gary Russell

Available for iPad
An unforgettable tour of space and time!

The ultimate series companion and episode guide, covering seven thrilling years of *Doctor Who*. Download everything that has happened, un-happened and happened again in the worlds of the Ninth, Tenth and Eleventh Doctors.

◊

Explore and search over three thousand entries by episode, character, place or object and see the connections that link them together

◊

Open interactive 'portals' for the Doctor, Amy, Rory, River and other major characters

◊

Build an A-Z of your favourites, explore galleries of imagery, and preview and buy must-have episodes